HONEYMOON IN PARIS

A Paris Romance

Juliette Sobanet

Montlake Romance

The characters and events portrayed in this book are fictitious. Any similarity to real persons, living or dead, is coincidental and not intended by the author.

Printed in the United States of America.

Published by Montlake Romance, Seattle

www.apub.com

ISBN-13: 9781477809815
ISBN-10: 1477809813

Library of Congress Control Number: 2013939494

To Jessica,

for being there through it all.

PROLOGUE

"I can't believe I'm about to become Mrs. Luc Olivier." Gazing down at my shimmering white gown and sparkly silver heels, I wondered if, in the history of the world, a bride had *ever* been this excited to walk down the aisle.

Or this in love.

Inside the sleek black limo, which wound through the cobblestone streets of Annecy en route to my outdoor wedding ceremony, my four bridesmaids lifted their champagne glasses to me in a toast.

To my right were Katie and Hannah, my closest friends from my college days back in DC. And to my left sat Lexi and Fiona, the fabulous girlfriends I'd made during my past year in Paris.

Lexi—the sassiest of them all—took the liberty of speaking first. "I'd like to make a toast to *Sleeping with Paris,* Charlotte's *former* single-girl blog—which I adored almost as much as I adore Charlotte herself. Your bitter diatribes on men who cheat and on the inadequacies of marriage were brilliant. And just because they got you into loads of trouble, don't let anyone tell you otherwise. If your new married self is even half as fabulous as your single self, I think we're going to be friends for a very long time."

Lexi had barely finished speaking when the more reserved and very British Fiona nudged her in the side. "Lex, this may not be the *best* moment to bring up Charlotte's *former* feelings on the institution of marriage. Obviously she's changed her viewpoint. And we're quite happy she did, I might add," Fiona said as she winked at me.

The girls were referring to the fact that one year ago, after finding out that my ex-fiancé, Jeff, was cheating on me through an online dating site, I moved to Paris alone and began writing an anonymous, man-hating, anti-marriage blog entitled *Sleeping with Paris*. In this online literary masterpiece—*ahem*—I shared lessons and personal anecdotes of my efforts to "date like a man" and never again be the fool who falls in love. Of course, on my first day in Paris, I met Luc: the man who, as it turned out, would make it *quite* difficult for me to follow my own advice.

Last spring, my blog posts were rolled into a feature-length article in the popular *Bella Magazine*, and once that article hit newsstands with my byline prominently displayed, my bitter diatribes weren't so anonymous any longer.

Today, as I sat there in a gorgeous wedding gown on my way to marry the man I was hopelessly and forever in love with, it was clear just how miserably I failed in my mission *not* to fall in love. And thankfully so.

While the blog certainly provided a humorous, healthy release after the betrayal I'd suffered from my previous engagement, Lexi couldn't have phrased it more aptly: my strong opinions on why women should never enter into committed relationships with members of the male species, *and* the personal stories I provided as proof, had gotten me into loads of trouble with friends, family, and worst of all, with Luc. As it turned out, broadcasting a man's shortcomings online and in print before knowing the whole story wasn't my smartest move (e.g.: throughout our year in Paris together, Luc wasn't cheating on me as I suspected, but instead had an adorable three-year-old daughter).

I thought I'd lost him forever . . . *until* he caught wind (by a little bird named Lexi) of the redeeming follow-up article I wrote for *Bella Magazine*'s August issue, in which I professed *my own* shortcomings this time—and my love for the one man who is different from all the rest: Luc.

It had only been four weeks since Luc had read the article and swooped back into my life, and only three weeks since he proposed. For a girl who went from opposing marriage on all fronts to one who accepts a surprise marriage proposal and plans a three-week mad dash down the aisle, I honestly couldn't have been more certain of my decision.

Snapping back to the present, I smiled warmly at my friends and raised my sparkling glass of bubbly to the group. "I don't mind you bringing up the blog, Lexi. As messy as it was, it's all part of my story with Luc. And every mistake along the way led to this moment—where I'm about to start the family I've always wanted to have with the most incredible man I've ever known."

"Cheers to that," Katie said, wiping a tear from her eye.

In fact, as I looked around at my four best friends who'd been there for every moment of the roller coaster of a year I'd had, and who'd dropped everything on *extremely* short notice to be here for my big day, I realized that each one of them had tears in their eyes.

"Thank you all for being here for me today," I said. "You're the best friends a girl could ever ask for. And that isn't going to change when I get married. I promise."

"Okay, you're killing me here," Hannah said, pulling out a tissue.

"Seriously, Char. Can we just drink our champagne?" Lexi said, biting her bottom lip. "I really don't think you want your hot bridesmaids strutting down that aisle with black smudges all over our faces. And if we keep up all this mushy friendship talk, that's exactly what's going to happen."

Giggles erupted throughout the limo as we *finally* took a sip of our champagne.

Just then, the limo pulled up to the lush, beautiful lawn facing the crystalline Lake Annecy and the surrounding mountains.

"Oh my God, Char, we're here!" Hannah squealed in her characteristic high-pitched voice, squeezing my leg so hard I'd be surprised if she didn't leave marks. "Are you nervous?"

Katie rubbed her ear and shot Hannah a warning look. "She's going to be nervous if you keep squealing like that, lady."

"Sorry, it's just so *gorgeous* here! And I can't believe Charlotte's getting married!" Hannah shrieked once more, practically bouncing out of her seat.

The girls' excited chatter faded into the background as I peeked through the window and glimpsed rows of white chairs adorned with elegant pink-and-lavender bouquets—all leading up to the most handsome groom I'd ever set eyes upon.

Luc stood at the edge of the lake, grinning his charming dimpled grin, and not looking the least bit nervous.

I always thought I'd be nervous on my wedding day, but as I opened the limo door and locked eyes with the man I was head over sparkly heels in love with, I realized there wasn't a nervous fiber in this bride's body.

ONE

A warm glow of morning sunlight whispered *bonjour* as I batted my eyelids open and smiled at the ruffled pillow on Luc's side of the bed. I peeked over at the clock and grinned even wider when I realized that it was ten A.M. and I had nowhere else to be. It was the last day of our luxurious Paris honeymoon and the last week of my incredible *four-week* paid vacation. I'd spent a considerable portion of this particular week wrapped in these very sheets in pure, unadulterated, knock-my-socks-off bliss with a man who I was madly in love with, and who loved me more than I ever knew I could be loved.

Luc Olivier.

I rolled his name around on my tongue, reveling in its perfect syllables, in the way it made my stomach leap, my heart swell, my legs quiver. And as I closed my eyes once more, I realized that no matter how tumultuous the past year had been, Luc had *always* made me feel this way, since the very first time our paths had crossed almost one year ago.

The heavenly aromas of buttery croissants, melted chocolate, and strong French coffee swirled through the expansive suite, arousing my senses, making my stomach growl. In the next room, a light clattering of plates and silverware mixed with the soft beat of Keren Ann's "Jardin D'Hiver"—one of my favorite French songs.

It's a song I used to play for my students back when I was a high school French teacher in DC. But as I slipped one bare leg over the crisp white sheets in our Paris honeymoon suite and felt an early fall breeze flitter across my skin, I remembered that the romantic week I'd been enjoying in the City of Lights was a far cry from my frenzied days in the nation's capital.

I discovered my lacy violet nightie hiding in the sheets by my feet and slipped it over my head, but just as I was about to get out of bed, Luc's rugged face appeared at our bedside. A mischievous grin peppered his unshaven cheeks while his chestnut eyes glinted in the orange morning light.

"*Bonjour, ma belle,*" he said, presenting me with a tray of fresh *pâtisseries*, two small *tasses de café*, and the morning *journal,* the way he'd done every single morning of our dreamy honeymoon.

Is this really my life?

"Let us take our *petit déjeuner* in bed, no?"

I giggled at Luc's adorable accent and decided it was best not to argue. "Whatever you say."

Luc rested the tray over my lap, then removed his jeans and T-shirt before slipping his lean body underneath the sheets, his legs intertwining with mine. The minute his hands reached my waist, he pressed his moist lips into the crook of my neck and left a trail of soft kisses down my shoulder. Tingles rolled down my spine while butterflies twirled through my stomach.

"If this is what heaven is like, sign me up," I said. I was tempted to tell him that breakfast could wait, but as I'd learned from our recent mornings together, Luc liked to drink his delicious French *café* while it was still hot. I couldn't say I blamed him.

"I know we have tried new kinds of pastries each morning," Luc began. "But this morning, I made a special trip over to my favorite *pâtisserie* on rue de Passy to bring you the world's best *pain au chocolat*. I hope you will like it."

I raised a flirty eyebrow at him. "You don't have to sell me on chocolate croissants, Luc. Trust me, I could eat more of these every day than I would ever admit to you."

Luc's charming grin lit up the room. "Me too," he said before we both took our first bites into the flaky, buttery delights.

A sliver of warm, gooey dark chocolate hit my tongue. "Oh my God, you weren't kidding. These *are* the best chocolate croissants in the world. Why have you been holding out on me?" I nudged him as I took another scrumptious bite.

Luc winked at me, then took a sip of his *café*. "I wanted to save the best for our last day in Paris. There is more to come." A hint of mischief sparkled in his eyes, making me wonder what else he had up his sexy sleeve.

"Oh? What do you have planned for today?"

"You'll see."

I leaned in and gave Luc a *chocolat*-covered kiss on the lips. When we resurfaced for air, I rested my forehead on his and whispered, "You know, if you want to feed me a *pain au chocolat* in bed every day for the rest of our lives, I'd be more than okay with that."

Luc's lips found mine once more, and this time I plummeted a little further into the depths of his touch, his scent, his kiss. When he pulled away, I laughed at the dab of chocolate I'd smeared on his cheek.

"Here, let me," I said, lifting a napkin from the tray.

But as I picked up the napkin, today's paper spilled onto my lap, the bold headline catching my eye.

"Ooh, that new romantic comedy I've been wanting to see—*Le Problème avec l'Amour*—is premiering in Paris this weekend."

"*The Problem with Love,*" Luc repeated as he slipped his arm around my waist and peered over my shoulder at the paper. "Never heard of it."

"Don't worry, I won't ask you to suffer through a girly movie with me. Fiona is in love with the lead actor, Marcel Boucher, so I've promised her we'd see it together next week."

Luc nodded without responding, then flipped to the second page of the paper.

The headline staring back at us made me gasp. "Students arrested in massive drug ring bust at the Cité Universitaire," I translated aloud, not believing my eyes as I continued skimming the article. The Cité Universitaire is the large campus situated in the fourteenth *arrondissement* of Paris, where both Luc and I had been living only a few months ago.

"This is insane, Luc. The leader of the drug ring was Pascal Girard, the guy that lived at the end of our hall! Do you remember him?"

Luc nestled his face into my neck and traced my collarbone with his lips. "The only thing I like to remember about living in that dorm was the day I first bumped into you wearing a skimpy towel in the shower. Do you realize that was almost one year ago? And now you are my beautiful wife. I am the luckiest man in the world."

Luc's words made me forget about our dorm's drug scandal and instead brought back a vivid flash of my first day in Paris *and* my first encounter with Luc. It had only been two days since I'd broken off my engagement with Jeff, my ex-fiancé. Even though I was more than a little burned from his tryst with the red-headed beauty he'd met online, I'd decided that no self-respecting Francophile woman would wallow around in self-pity on her first night in the City of Lights. So that evening, in the communal shower of my Paris dorm, Luc's steamy, towel-wrapped body bumped straight into mine . . . and we lived happily ever after.

Well, obviously that's not *exactly* how it all played out. But honestly, what relationship didn't have a few hiccups? I figured now that we'd already gotten the hard stuff out of the way, things would be smooth sailing from here on out.

Although, no matter how bumpy our relationship had become over the course of my first year in Paris, the steam from that first meeting in the showers *never* evaporated. And on this lazy morning, only one month after Luc had swooped back into my life, and only five days after we'd vowed to love each other for the rest of our lives, my clothes strewn all over the hotel floor and the half-eaten Lindt milk chocolate bar by our bedside were solid proof of that never-evaporating steam billowing between us.

I kissed Luc's chocolate-covered cheek and giggled. "And I'm the luckiest *woman* in the world. Seriously Luc, you've really out-done yourself with this honeymoon." I glanced around our ritzy suite at the Château Frontenac Hotel just off the Champs-Élysées, realizing how aptly named the hotel was. With its tall ceilings, crystal chandeliers, vases of freshly cut lilies, and regal furnishings, our suite resembled the inside of a mini castle. Of course we'd modernized the castle with bags of sinful chocolate from La Maison du Chocolat just across the street, colorful *macarons* from Ladurée around the corner, and sexy lingerie from Chez Isabelle, the raciest lingerie shop in Lyon—a place I'd become *quite* fond of since Luc and I had gotten back together.

"You know in French, the word for honeymoon, *la lune de miel,* refers to the first twenty-nine days after the wedding, when the couple is totally in love and everything is perfect." Luc ran his hand up my thigh and kissed my shoulder. "I wanted to start off this time by giving you a week in Paris that you would never forget, especially since I did not show you *this* Paris the first time around. And the good news, *chérie,* is that this is only day five."

Luc's hand crept further up my thigh, and as much as I wanted to let that hand go wherever it pleased, there was something important I needed to ask him.

"This week has been incredible, Luc. Really, the most amazing, romantic week of my entire life. I just have one question, though—how on earth are you affording all of this? You just finished your master's degree, you have Adeline to take care of, and you're a professor. I just don't want you to go into debt—"

Luc placed a finger on my lips. "That is not for you to worry about, *mon amour.* I promise you, we are not in any debt." He snatched the *journal* from my hands and tossed it to the floor. "Now finish your *pain au chocolat* because we have a busy day ahead of us. Today, *ma princesse,* I'm taking you shopping on the Champs-Élysées."

Now if an American man had ever called me "his princess", I probably would've laughed in his face. But whenever Luc called me his *princesse,* his *belle,* his *amour,* his *cœur*, I practically melted in a puddle at his feet.

In my melted puddle state, I decided to table the finance discussion until we arrived home in Lyon. Our lightning-fast, three-week engagement period hadn't allowed us the time to properly discuss the merging of finances, but surely we'd get to it next week. And if Luc wanted to take me shopping on the Champs-Élysées on our last day in Paris, who was I to argue?

I traced the outline of Luc's handsome face with my finger. "Before we hit the Champs, care to join me in the shower?"

"Do you even need to ask?" The grin to end all sexy grins slid onto Luc's lips before he removed the breakfast tray from my lap, pummeled me with kisses, then carried me into the shower.

Yes, the finance talk could definitely wait.

An hour and a whole lot of steam later, Luc and I emerged from the hotel elevator, our cheeks on fire with that newlywed glow we'd been carrying around all week. Hand in hand, we floated over the marble floor of the chic lobby, but just as we stepped out into the crisp autumn day, a swarm of camera-ready paparazzi stopped us in our tracks. And while I would've loved to think they were all waiting for the moment when Luc and Charlotte Olivier would walk out of this fancy hotel, they couldn't have been less interested in us. It was the sleek, black limo that had just pulled up to the curbside that had all the cameras poised and ready for clicking.

Luc sidestepped around them, not seeming the least bit interested in finding out who was about to step out of that limo.

"Wait, Luc. This is so exciting. Who do you think it is?"

He kissed me on the forehead, then tugged at my hand. "You are my star, *chérie*. Come, let's go shopping."

"I've never seen anyone famous," I said, peering around the cameras. "Let's just see who it is and then we'll go, okay?"

He eyed the photographers warily before giving a slight nod. How could Luc not be the least bit excited to see a celebrity?

A small crowd of tourists had gathered around the paparazzi, so I led Luc around the edge of the group until we had a clear view. As the limo door opened, a tall, slender man dressed in a crisp gray suit jacket and dark jeans appeared. His black hair was peppered with just enough gray to give him that distinguished, experienced look that only an older man could get away with. A rail-thin blonde who, from her profile, looked young enough to be the man's daughter, took his outstretched hand and shot a sultry gaze at the cameras.

Just as her big green eyes turned toward us, I recognized her face. She was starring in *Le Problème avec l'Amour* alongside one of France's most eligible heartthrobs, and my friend Fiona's biggest celebrity crush, Marcel Boucher. As I was trying to remember the actress's name, Luc turned to me, the look in his eyes one of pure bewilderment.

"Come on, Charlotte. Let's go," he said firmly.

But before we could even turn around, the young actress linked arms with her much older date, fixed her gaze on Luc, and strutted right up to us.

"Luc, what a nice surprise," she said in French. "*Obviously* you remember Vincent."

Luc's face went stone cold as he stared at the two of them, cameras clicking furiously around us. The older man nodded at Luc, the severity in his hazel eyes overriding the politeness of his outstretched hand.

Luc didn't take Vincent's hand, though. Instead he squeezed my hand so tight I almost yelped, then cleared his throat.

What in the hell is going on?

"This must be your new girlfriend," the girl purred, not masking the undertones of jealousy laced in her sex-kitten voice.

"This is Charlotte, my *wife*," Luc responded without hesitation.

But as Luc's eyes met mine, I saw something in them I hadn't seen all week.

Dread.

"And Charlotte," Luc began. "This is Brigitte, Adeline's mother . . . and my ex-wife."

TWO

I opened my mouth to say hello, *bonjour*, why in the hell are you crashing our honeymoon, *anything*, but all words had escaped me.

This was Luc's ex-wife? This bombshell of an actress who looked like she couldn't be more than twenty years old was Adeline's *mother*? How on earth had Luc never told me that *the* Brigitte he'd referred to so often, *the* Brigitte who'd been such a horrible mother, *the* Brigitte who'd made his life a living hell of divorce and custody battles for a majority of the past year was a famous actress? A famous actress who was staying at our hotel no less.

Did he not think this was an important piece of information to share with his *wife*?

Brigitte's icy green eyes combed the length of my body, disapproval written all over her dainty features. "How lovely to meet you, Charlotte. Luc didn't tell me he was getting married. Always keeping secrets, isn't he, *our* Luc?"

This time I squeezed Luc's hand so hard I was surprised it didn't shatter into a million pieces at our feet.

"And Luc didn't tell me you were an actress," I said through a gritted-teeth smile.

"Well, he never was very supportive of my career. I'm back in Paris for the premiere of my new film. I'm starring alongside Vincent's son, Marcel Boucher." She tilted her chin and gave Vincent an overdramatic kiss on the lips, making the picture-hungry paparazzi swoon with excitement.

A devilish grin appeared on Vincent's rugged face. "Yes, I met Brigitte when I came to visit Marcel on set, and the minute I saw her, I knew I had to have her. I can't believe you let this one get away, Luc." He slipped his arm around her nonexistent waist and kissed her on the neck. "I'm so glad you did, though," he said.

"How's the publishing business, Vincent?" Luc cut in with an edge to his tone I'd never quite heard before.

"Couldn't be better. We're opening up a new magazine which will be headquartered in Lyon, actually. Is your family still down that way?"

Luc's jaw tightened as he wrapped his arm around my shoulder. "Charlotte and I have a busy day planned, so we have to get going. Best of luck with the film premiere."

"Please give your father my best, Luc. And your mother and sister too," Vincent said coolly.

Luc didn't respond, instead only gracing this Vincent character with a flare of his nostrils. How did Luc know this man? And how did Vincent know Luc's family? Luc hadn't even spoken to his own father in years.

Luc grabbed my hand to lead me away from the swarming cameras, from his ex-wife's dagger-filled glare, and from this suave older man with whom he clearly had bad blood. But before we could escape, Brigitte's hand landed on Luc's arm, her plump, scarlet lips hovering an inch from his ear.

"I'm back in France for good now, Luc. And I want visitation rights to see Adeline. Vincent is setting me up with one of his lawyers, so it will *not* be in your best interest to fight me on this. A young girl needs her mother." Then her cutting gaze landed on me. "Her *real* mother. Not some knockoff who'll probably only be around for a year or two tops." She traced her hand up Luc's arm, resting it on his shoulder. "Luc Olivier, you and all of your secrets were never cut out for marriage—as your little Charlotte will soon find out."

"What was that?" I said as we left Brigitte, Vincent, and their entourage of photographers back at the hotel.

Luc shook his head as fiery red patches splashed across his cheeks. "I am so sorry, Charlotte. I had no idea she would be in Paris this week and staying at the same hotel with that *connard.*"

Noting Luc's charged use of the French word for *asshole,* I continued my questioning. "Do you think she planned this?"

"*Mais bien sûr. Everything* with Brigitte is calculated."

Orange and yellow leaves crunched underneath our feet as we walked past La Maison du Chocolat. But after that debacle, even chocolate didn't sound good.

"This morning in bed, when I told you that the movie I've been wanting to see was premiering in Paris this weekend, you knew it was Brigitte's film, didn't you? Why didn't you say something?" I said.

Luc just barely missed a pile of dog poo littering the sidewalk as he shook his head in frustration. "It's the last day of our honeymoon. It clearly wasn't the right time to mention her."

"When *was* going to be the right time, Luc? How could you have conveniently forgotten to tell me that your ex-wife is a famous actress? Is this how you're able to afford such a lavish honeymoon? And you insisted on paying for most of our wedding too. Are you getting alimony from her?"

"No, Brigitte is not giving me any money. It is only with her latest film that she has reached this status of fame. Before this, she'd only had minor roles in a few TV shows and movies. Then she started sleeping with that Australian film director, left me, took Adeline, and moved to Australia with him, thinking he would make her famous. I imagine that she left him the minute it worked."

"Clearly. She's a real piece of work, that ex-wife of yours."

"A piece of work?" Luc asked in his thickening accent—his English always deteriorated whenever he was angry.

"To put it nicely, it means she's difficult." I reached over and took Luc's hand, giving it a squeeze. As upset as I was that he hadn't told me the entire truth about Brigitte, I could only imagine how livid he felt that she'd stormed our hotel on the last day of this amazing honeymoon he'd planned for me.

Luc nodded. "*Oui,* Brigitte is a definitely piece of work."

"What about this Vincent Boucher guy? How do you know him?"

Luc picked up his pace as we rounded the corner onto the tree-lined Champs-Élysées, the crowds of tourists herding past us making me feel claustrophobic.

"Vincent Boucher knew my family a long time ago," Luc said. "And there is nothing else to tell."

"So you know his sons, the famous actors, Marcel and Nicolas Boucher?"

Luc's nostrils flared again, his eyes set firmly on the sidewalk ahead. "Yes, I grew up with them."

"Okay, so let me get this straight. You grew up with the Boucher brothers, and their *dad* is now dating your ex-wife? Your ex-wife who looks like she's about twenty years old?"

"Twenty-five."

"Could've fooled me," I said, searching Luc's distressed face. "Is there something you're not telling me, Luc? Something that happened between Vincent and your family?"

Luc stayed silent for a few moments as he squeezed my hand and proceeded to walk even faster. We passed by my favorite pizzeria on the Champs—Café di Roma. An older French couple lounged at one of the restaurant's outdoor tables, smoking their cigarettes and sipping on wine as if they hadn't a care in the world. The gray-haired woman eyed us curiously as we jetted past—surely wondering where we were going in such a hurry on this lazy fall afternoon when most of the country was still finishing up vacation.

Finally, Luc broke the silence. "It is a long story that is not relevant at the moment, *ma chérie*. What *is* important is that we not let this ruin the last day of our honeymoon."

I gazed into Luc's chestnut eyes as we walked, knowing that it was too late. The day had already been ruined for both of us. "What did Brigitte mean when she kept referring to all of your *secrets*? Is there something you haven't told me about why the two of you split up?"

"A relationship, a *marriage*, always takes two people. I was not perfect in my marriage with Brigitte, but I never betrayed her. She is just saying these things to make you doubt your decision to marry me. Brigitte has always been a very jealous person, and on top of that, she has a cold heart. But she is a good actress, and she made me believe she was different. You cannot trust the things she says, Charlotte."

"I'm sorry, Luc. Of course I trust you. I only wish you would've trusted me enough to tell me the whole story."

As we stopped at the crosswalk, Luc reached up to tuck a strand of hair behind my ears, then ran his finger along the curves of my face. "It is not that I didn't trust you; I just wanted to leave my past in the past. I promise you that I will not allow Brigitte to mess anything up for us. I will do what I have to do to handle her, but you and Adeline will always be my first priority. You must believe me, Charlotte."

"What about this Vincent Boucher character? Is he a threat?" I asked. "If this man was close with your family, aren't you creeped out that he's dating your ex? He must be at least twice her age, if not more."

As soon as the light turned, we headed through the crosswalk, passing by a group of American tourists, their loud voices grating on my already frazzled nerves. Normally I loved meandering down the Champs-Élysées, but today, I couldn't wait to get as far away from here as possible. The crowds, the cigarette smoke, and the excessive amount of dog poo muddying up the sidewalks were really getting to me.

"Brigitte's choices are none of my concern," Luc said. "Except if they have to do with Adeline. And Vincent Boucher was never *close* with my family. He knew my father, that is all. I haven't spoken with Vincent or his sons in years."

"Does he have something to do with why you don't speak to your father anymore?" Luc hadn't even invited his father to our wedding, and every time I'd asked him what the story was, he'd been evasive.

"No, that is a decision I have made for other reasons. But today isn't the day to talk about these things."

"When *will* be the day, Luc? When were you planning on telling me that the tiny blond bombshell splashed across the Metro billboards is your ex-wife? Were you going to wait until your four-year-old daughter pointed to her and said *maman*?"

"*Calme-toi, chérie.*"

"Please don't tell me to calm down right now. I just feel like there's so much you haven't told me. Like with the finances, for example. If you're not getting money from Brigitte, where *is* all this money coming from? I mean, you spent the past year as a full-time student putting yourself through grad school, you just went through a horrific divorce and custody battle that couldn't have been cheap, and now you're starting a job as a college professor. How are you paying for all of this if you're not putting it on credit?"

"I used to be in finance, remember? I am very smart with money, Charlotte. We are not in debt, I promise you. You will never have to worry about that. I will always take care of you."

"You're missing the point. I don't want to be taken care of. I just want you to be honest with me."

Just as Luc opened his mouth to respond, a piercing ring emanated from his jeans pocket. His eyebrows furrowed when he glanced at the caller ID on his phone. "*Merde.* It's Brigitte."

"Didn't she do enough damage for one day? She's already calling you?"

Luc sighed as the sharp ringing continued. "With her threats about Adeline, I am just worried—"

"I understand," I said. "Take the call."

"I'm sorry, Charlotte."

I squeezed his shoulder letting him know it was okay. But as my feet skimmed over the yellow leaves in the tree-lined park lining the Champs-Élysées, nothing about this situation felt okay. I needed to get some air, some space. And I didn't want to hear whatever Luc and his ex were going to be arguing about on the last day of *our* honeymoon.

Why couldn't she have just stayed in Australia? And why couldn't Luc have told me the truth about who she was? I felt like such a colossal idiot. Planning to go see that movie with Fiona—when all along I had no idea that Brigitte, my husband's ex-wife, was the leading actress.

And what was with Luc's connection to the Bouchers? There was definitely something fishy going on there: something he didn't want me to know.

I made my way to a bench situated underneath a fan of golden leaves that were shimmering in the early afternoon sunlight. I closed my eyes and inhaled the delicious scents of chocolate and hazelnut from the crêpe stand nearby.

I pulled out my phone to text Lexi. She'd spent the past few months in New York City getting her life on track after a rough hospital visit, and she'd just moved back to Paris with her boyfriend, Dylan. Lexi and I had certainly have had our share of hiccups as far as friendships go, but now we were closer than ever. Her blunt sense of humor could be really useful at a time like this.

I texted:

I could totally use a Nutella crêpe right about now. And a tall glass of wine. U around?

As I waited for her reply, I comforted myself with the thought that at least we were leaving Paris tomorrow. Luc would get this ex-wife situation under control, and we would go back to living out the rest of our twenty-nine-day honeymoon bliss in peace. There was no way I was going to let this girl ruin the wonderful life Luc and I had just begun to create together.

My phone buzzed. It was Lexi.

Girlfriend, u have no idea how much I need Nutella and wine right now. But u should be having steamy sex on last day of ur honeymoon. What's up?

Just as I was texting her back, Luc's lips landed on my forehead.

"I'm so sorry about that, *chérie.*"

The sincerity in Luc's eyes softened my response. "It's okay, Luc. She's Adeline's mother, so I know you can't just ignore her."

"Thank you for understanding." Luc held my hand, his eyes darting to the leaves on the ground which were now swirling with a gust of chilly wind that had swept through the Paris park.

"So what did she want?"

"She apologized for what she said to both of us earlier. And while Brigitte's apologies don't mean much to me anymore, she did sound rather sincere . . . well, as sincere as *she* can be."

"Remember, she's an actress. A good one, as you pointed out."

"I know this. I am not fooled. It is just that since she is back in France now and wanting to have visitation rights, we are going to have to deal with her more often."

"But didn't you tell me that Brigitte was doing drugs while she was living in Australia, and that's how you were able to get full custody of Adeline? How on earth does she expect to secure visitation rights if she's using?"

"She says she's clean now. Apparently she spent the last month in rehab."

"Of course she did." *Was it a prerequisite these days for all actors to go to rehab?*

"Regardless of whether or not she's telling the truth, as soon as she starts working with Vincent's lawyer, things could get ugly. I don't want to put you through that, or Adeline."

"So . . . what are you proposing we do?" *Can we deport her back to Australia?*

"Brigitte asked if we would join her and Vincent for a drink tonight at the hotel bar, and even though that is the absolute *last* thing I want to ask you to do tonight, it will only be for one hour, and it will give me a chance to see if she is telling the truth about cleaning up her life. And more importantly, it could help us avoid one more long and unnecessary legal battle."

"So you agreed to the drink?"

Luc nodded. "Like I said, it won't take long. Then you and I will have our romantic evening in the city. I have something very special planned for our last night."

I masked the spurt of rage and disappointment that boiled up inside my chest at the thought of spending even one hour with Luc's drop-dead gorgeous ex-wife and instead squeezed his hand. "It's okay. Whatever we need to do to protect Adeline."

Luc raised my hand to his lips and gave me three soft kisses. "Don't worry, *ma belle,* we have twenty-four more days of our *lune de miel* period. I promise to make them the best twenty-four days of your life."

I barely heard Luc's words, though, because I was already worrying about what I would wear to the bar tonight. Then I remembered my text exchange with Lexi. A dose of her feistiness—and her shopping expertise—was just what I needed.

At the same time, after everything that had just happened, I didn't want to leave Luc alone on the last afternoon of our honeymoon.

"What is it, *mon amour*?" Luc asked.

"If you have something special planned for tonight, I'm going to need something special to wear," I said. "Would you mind terribly if I met up with Lexi for a few hours this afternoon?"

Luc lifted a knowing brow. "This isn't a competition, you know. You will look stunning in whatever you wear."

"Luc, I'm not worried about Brig—" I began, but Luc stopped me from saying her name by planting his soft lips on mine.

Running his hands over my hair, he shot me a sweet grin. "Whatever you want, *chérie*."

"Thanks, Luc. I won't be long," I said.

"Of course, *ma princesse*. Have fun."

After Luc and I parted ways, I texted Lexi.

Where r u? Had run-in with Luc's ex and having drinks with her tonight. Urgent wine and shopping trip in order.

Not more than five seconds later, Lexi responded:

Meet me at Les Deux Magots in 30 mins. Not to worry. An hour of shopping with me and you will look so hot tonight, that bitch won't know what hit her.

Thank God for girlfriends.

THREE

"Luc's ex-wife is *Brigitte Beaumont*? Are you kidding me?" Lexi's gorgeous amber eyes widened in horror as I settled into our tiny sidewalk table underneath the green awning of Les Deux Magots Café.

"Dead serious."

"Now I understand the need for an afternoon wine binge. Here, drink this." Lexi handed me her glass, then shot the young French waiter a seductive smile. Not more than two seconds later, he was hovering over our table with a goofy grin on his face.

"We'll take a bottle of Bordeaux, *s'il vous plaît*," she ordered in French.

The waiter held Lexi in an awkward smile before bustling off in his long white apron.

"How on earth could he have left out that vital piece of information?" Lexi scoffed.

I took a massive sip of Lexi's Merlot, closing my eyes as the blackberry-flavored liquid sloshed down my throat, then quickly decided one sip wasn't enough.

"I know you guys got married really quickly, but her freaking face is plastered all over Paris right now. He had to have known you'd find out eventually," she said.

After two long gulps, I finally spoke. "I know. And you should see her in person. She looks like she's eighteen years old." The more wine I drank, the younger and prettier Brigitte became. "She's absolutely stunning. Bitchy, but stunning."

"Yeah, but bitchy and stunning doesn't equal intelligent, kind, loving, and beautiful, which is what *you* are—and which is why Luc married you."

When I responded by downing the rest of her glass in one fast gulp, Lexi's eyes narrowed in concern. "You're not regretting your decision to marry Luc, are you?"

"No, of course not. I'm totally in love with Luc, and this situation doesn't make me doubt his love for me either. I only wish he'd told me the whole story about Brigitte . . . and I feel like he's hiding more from me too."

"What do you mean?" Lexi asked.

I peered at the tables to either side of us, then leaned closer to Lexi before filling her in on Luc's secretive connection to the famous Boucher family. But she quickly cut me off.

"Back it up. Your husband *grew up* with the actors Nicolas and Marcel Boucher? This just gets juicier by the second. I have been in *love* with Nicolas Boucher since I was like fifteen. Oh, what I would do to that man if I ever got the chance to meet him . . ." Lexi's gaze trailed past me out to the bustling Boulevard Saint-Germain, where a man on a little blue scooter zipped through a red light.

"Focus, Lexi. We're not going to meet Nicolas because Luc doesn't even talk to him anymore."

"But Luc's ex-wife is dating Nicolas' dad. There's a chance we might—"

"Even if we could, you're with Dylan, remember? The guy you've been in love with for years who you've finally committed to and just moved to Paris with? That one?"

Lexi flicked the stem of the wineglass. "The one who fights with me nonstop about every little thing? Seriously, Char, I don't know if I'm cut out for this cohabitation business. Or this monogamy madness. How do *you* do it?"

Just then, the waiter came in for the save, a bottle of red wine and an extra glass in hand. Lexi thanked him with a bat of her long eyelashes and a wink.

"I didn't know you and Dylan were fighting. You seemed so happy together at our wedding last weekend," I said once we were left alone again.

"What wasn't to be happy about? We were in Annecy, the most charming, romantic town in the French Alps, drinking our faces off, watching your wild mother and crazy Aunt Liza dry hump Luc's unsuspecting uncle on the dance floor. Not to mention the look on your dad's face while this was all going down. Then when your mom yanked your dad's prissy girlfriend up to the dance floor, I almost died."

I plunged my head in my hands. "Ugh, don't remind me. I'm never inviting them anywhere ever again. Thank God I only have to get married once."

My parents had recently divorced after thirty years of a mostly unhappy marriage, and my mom was now living in Florida with my leopard-print-sporting, sleep-with-anything-over-fifty-that-walks Aunt Liza. And my dad was dating a woman named Jane, otherwise known as the Ice Queen of the Century.

My wedding had been the first opportunity I'd had to spend time with either of my parents since the divorce, and it hadn't been pretty. More like a soap opera on crack. Luckily the arrival of all of my closest girlfriends had kept me sane and focused on the real reasons for the family gathering: my unending love for Luc, and my decision to spend the rest of my life with him.

Of course the smooth French wine that flowed more heavily than the Lake of Annecy hadn't hurt in my quest to stay sane throughout the wedding weekend either.

"Sorry, I didn't mean to bring up traumatizing family memories," Lexi said before taking a long sip of her wine. "Besides the family drama and that random couple who crashed the cocktail cruise, your wedding was absolutely gorgeous, Char."

"That was so bizarre, wasn't it? Did I tell you that it turns out that couple was running from the police? Luc and I were stopped and questioned on the way to the reception. They thought we were helping them escape."

"Oh my gosh, that's insane! Do you know what they did?"

"I'm not sure, but I think it had something to do with a stolen painting. Whatever it was, it was crazy."

"Agreed," Lexi said. "But the craziest part of all is how much you and Luc love each other. I've never seen anything like it. I love Dylan, I do. But it's not like the two of you—and I don't think it ever will be."

"No relationship is perfect, though," I admitted, avoiding Lexi's gaze.

"Is there something else going on *besides* all of this ex-wife drama?" she asked.

"Just a few small concerns. I'm sure it's nothing," I said with a wave of my hand. I already felt bad enough that Luc hadn't been one hundred percent open with me about his ex; the last thing I wanted to do was make my girlfriends think I'd made a mistake in marrying him so quickly.

Lexi leveled a serious gaze at me. "Char, you've seen me at my absolute worst. You didn't judge me, and you didn't tell a soul." Lexi was referring to a scary hospitalization she'd had a few months back after a serious bout of depression. Besides her brother, I was the only other person she trusted with the whole story.

"I know that compared to Fiona, I might seem like the crazier friend," she continued. "But I am always here for you, and I will never judge you. You can tell me anything, Char. Trust me, these lips are sealed."

"Thanks, Lex," I said, realizing just what a wonderful friend Lexi had become over the past year.

"So, what else is worrying you?" she asked.

"Well . . . with our engagement happening so quickly, Luc and I haven't had a proper chance to sit down and discuss finances. I'm sure we'll get to it once we're back home in Lyon next week. But with the amount he must've spent on this luxurious honeymoon, I'm a little worried. I mean, he just went through a messy divorce and a long custody battle, and he's starting off a new career as a college professor. I asked him if he's getting alimony from Brigitte, and he denied it. He said he saved a lot during his years in finance, but what if he's putting us in debt and not telling me?"

Lexi cleared her throat as she crossed her hands over the table. "Char, when Fiona and I checked out of our hotel in Annecy after your wedding, we found out that Luc had taken care of the entire bill."

"You mean he paid for your and Fiona's hotel stay?" I asked.

"No, he paid for *everyone's* hotel stay. Not just ours," she said.

"As in my parents, our friends, his family? *Everyone?*"

"*Everyone,*" Lexi confirmed.

"But that must've cost him—or *us*—thousands of dollars. The hotel was practically sitting right on the Lake of Annecy. It wasn't cheap," I said.

"I'm sorry, Char, I probably shouldn't have rocked the boat even further, but after what you just told me, I thought you should know."

I wrapped my fingers around the stem of my wineglass and stared into the dark red liquid. Why wouldn't Luc tell me he'd taken care of the *entire* hotel bill? And where was he getting all of this money?

Lexi's reassuring voice interrupted my thoughts. "Luc's a really smart guy, and like he pointed out, he used to be in finance. Those guys make a lot of money. I'm sure he's saved a lot over the years."

"Of course," I said with a smile, but I couldn't deny the underlying doubt eating away at my insides. "I think this whole Brigitte situation has just gotten me all stirred up. We'll have the finance talk as soon as we get home, and I'm sure it will all turn out fine."

Lexi placed a hand on my arm. "Of course it will, Char. That man is so in love with you, he can hardly see straight. So what if he's a little secretive? There isn't a man on this earth who likes to open up about his past mistakes *or* his family drama. Plus, you have to remember, this is *France*. The rules are different here."

"So, having drinks with my husband's rail-thin, vindictive, drug-addict ex-wife and her sexy older boyfriend—who, by the way, my husband seems to hate—on the last day of our honeymoon just comes with the territory? If that's the case, then someone needs to write a detailed guidebook to French marriage. I'd be the first to buy it."

Lexi snorted. "*You* should write the guidebook, lady. Think about it, you already have a readership from your blog and from your *Bella Magazine* articles. I can only imagine your commentary on French marriage. It would be witty, sassy, and not to mention, *hilarious*."

"I don't know, Lex. After all of the drama I started last year with those blog posts, I don't want to do anything else to stir the pot."

Lexi raised a brow. "Char, it could be *so* juicy. I mean, excuse my French, but this shit is crazy. And you're living it! You can't keep this all to yourself. I know how much you hurt Luc last year with that blog, but you also helped *tons* of women in the process. And you made us laugh. The guidebook on French marriage could be the more mature you, writing about marriage in France from an American woman's perspective. I'd buy it, and I'm sure tons of other women would too. Whether we like it or not, we're all in this crazy game together."

"Hmm, I don't know. The last thing I need right now is more drama. And I will never again do anything to betray Luc."

"Char, I hate to burst your honeymoon bubble, but with the ex-wife back in town, things are bound to get a little hairy. You're going to need an outlet. And while I absolutely do not think you made a mistake marrying Luc, I don't want you to lose yourself in the marriage either. Women need to keep their independence. It's not healthy for us to do *everything* for a man and nothing for ourselves. Where would that leave us?"

"It would leave us wearing leopard-print bikinis and frolicking around old men at Florida pool parties, having no clue what in the hell we're doing with our lives. That's where."

Lexi stifled the smirk spreading across her face. "Your mom?"

"How'd you guess?"

"I hate to say it, but she's the perfect example. She gave up everything for your father—her identity, her passions, her career aspirations—all so he could cheat on her with a younger model and leave her high and dry thirty years later with no life of her own. I'm not saying Luc would ever do that to you, but you still need to keep your voice, Char. Keep writing. Keep your career, your goals, your dreams. Don't ever give any of that up for a man, no matter how much you love him."

"Luc isn't asking me to give any of that up for him. We had a bad experience with the blog, which was my fault, and—"

"Hold up, lady. You were only writing the truth about your experience. Luc was taking mysterious phone calls in the middle of the night and not telling you who it was. He would disappear for months at a time. Yes, of course now we know he has his daughter, and it was all related to the custody battle. But how could you have known that?"

"He tried to tell me, but I cut him off. I didn't want to be in a relationship. No serious discussions. Remember?"

Lexi waved her hand. "Details, details. The point is, the man withheld key information from you, and all you were doing was writing about your experience the way it unfolded from your perspective. You never mentioned names, so the way I see it, you did nothing wrong. And your posts were hilarious and helpful to women all over the world who are trying to survive this insane dating mess, not to mention anyone who's ever been cheated on."

"Thanks, Lex. I did really love writing the posts and especially the articles for *Bella Magazine.* A guidebook to marrying French could be really fun to play around with . . ."

"Well, promise me you'll think about it. I've lost enough friends to the demands of marriage and kids. I'm happy for you and your new life, I really am. And while I think Luc is amazing, and I really believe you two are meant to be together, he *still* hasn't been one hundred percent honest with you. I mean, he's a dude, after all. And if you need an outlet in the form of a spicy, hilarious commentary on the ins and outs of French marriage, well, then I'm all for it."

I laughed. "Fine, I'll *think* about it. But no promises." I peeked at my watch and at our half-full bottle of wine and remembered that besides our afternoon wine binge, we still had one *extremely* important task to accomplish. "We need to speed it up. I have to find the perfect dress for tonight, and I can't do it alone."

A conniving grin passed over Lexi's red-lined lips as she raised her glass to mine. "I may be a mess in every other area of my life, but when it comes to finding a dress to put the evil ex in her place, I am *so* your woman."

FOUR

With one sparkly silver stiletto in front of the other, I walked across our elegant suite to where Luc was standing at the mirror, buttoning his crisp gray shirt. I wrapped my arms around his waist and kissed him on the neck.

"*Bonsoir, ma chérie.* Let me see you." He flipped around and took a step back, his eyes combing the length of my silky black slip dress, his gaze stopping at the low-cut neckline. "Wow. You must go shopping with Lexi more often. This dress is absolutely stunning on you. No one will ever believe me when I say you are my wife."

Luc ran his fingers down the thin cami-straps and over the tops of my breasts, making me wish we weren't going anywhere tonight. His lips found that space between my neck and my collarbone that made me lose all control . . . and not long after, his hand slid underneath the short hem of my dress and up my thigh.

His husky voice tickled my ear. "*Tu me rends fou, Charlotte.*"

"You drive me crazy too, my sexy husband. But if you don't hurry up, we're going to be late."

"It's a shame because seeing you in that dress just makes me want to rip it off. *Right now.*" Luc's hand moved to the inside of my thigh, a little higher up this time.

I pinched his arm. "There will be plenty of time for this later on, but we have to go. You're the one who agreed to this lovely drink date in the first place, remember?"

Luc sighed. "*Oui*, I know. It will be quick, though, like I told you. Just an hour and then you will love what I have planned for us after. Although, I don't know if I will be able to get through the whole night with you looking like this. Seriously, Charlotte, you are incredible."

I smiled at my sweet husband, realizing that I had nothing to worry about. This man was head over heels in love with me, and nothing his bitchy little ex-wife could do would ever change that.

Well, not if this dress had anything to say about it.

Downstairs, we spotted Brigitte and Vincent seated across the chic hotel bar, already sipping on their wine.

My heels tapped against the dark oak floor, each step making my heart constrict inside my chest. Never mind all of that ridiculous self-talk upstairs about having nothing to worry about. Just the sight of Brigitte's profile, her high cheekbones, her endlessly long lashes, those seductive lips, made me want to pack it up and ship out.

Luc's hand found mine, his sweaty palm indicating that even though he looked as calm, cool, and collected as ever, he wasn't too jazzed about this meeting either.

Before I had a chance to hightail it out of there—slinky dress, stilettos, and all—Brigitte made eye contact. The expression on her perfectly made-up face morphed from slutty seductress to fake sweetness to . . . horror.

When she and Vincent stood to greet us, the reason for the horror registered.

We were wearing the same dress. *Merde.*

As icy kisses were exchanged underneath the crystal chandelier, I had to stop myself from stealing her wine and dumping it down the front of her dress. I knew this dress looked great on me, but on Brigitte—well let's just say that with the exception of my gentlemanly husband, every man's gaze in that bar was glued to her and *only* her.

"How adorable that you're wearing the same dress as me, Charlotte," Brigitte cooed in French, her dazzling smile slicing right through the armor I'd spent the *entire* afternoon building up. "I guess Luc's taste hasn't changed that much after all."

Vincent's deep voice interrupted the awkward silence that followed. "I must say, *both* of you wear the dress *quite* well. . . ."

It suddenly became clear that the only *other* man in the bar who wasn't mentally undressing Brigitte was Vincent. To the contrary, he didn't seem to be able to take his eyes off of *me.*

Oh, dear God.

I squeezed Luc's hand and raised my eyebrows at him.

He knew what that look meant. He immediately motioned for the server, then ordered us our own bottle of wine.

As soon as we settled into our seats, Brigitte crossed her slim, toned legs and leaned forward just enough so that her cleavage was on full display. As if I needed one more reason to hate her.

"So Charlotte, what do you do for a living?" Brigitte asked coolly.

I forced a smile. "I'm a teacher at this wonderful language schoo—"

"Oh, how cute," she cut in as her dainty hand landed on Luc's arm. "You know I never understood your desire to leave finance and become a professor, Luc. Maybe Charlotte understands this lifestyle better than I ever could." She shot a suggestive glance in Vincent's direction. "I needed more . . . I needed a *different* lifestyle."

"Yes, that was clear," Luc said, the sarcasm dripping from his tongue.

"Lucky for you, *ma beauté,*" Vincent chimed in as he ran his hand over Brigitte's knee, "the lifestyle you wanted is exactly what I can give to you . . . and more."

It was odd, though, that even as Vincent's hand ran inappropriately high on Brigitte's thigh, the look in his eyes was cold—dishonest, even. What was he doing with her?

Luc cleared his throat and sat up taller in his seat. "Well, we didn't come here to discuss your new choice in lifestyle *or* in partners," Luc said to Brigitte.

Brigitte's flirty eyes refocused on Luc as she pushed Vincent's hand off of her. "You're right. I need to speak to you alone for a minute, Luc. Charlotte won't mind, will she?"

Yes, you conniving little actress. As a matter of fact, I do mind.

Luc kissed me on the cheek, his whisper coming softly in my ear. "Just a few minutes so I can discuss the matter of Adeline with her. Will you be okay?" He looked from me to Vincent, the skepticism in his eyes palpable.

I summoned up every ounce of politeness I had in me and aimed the sweetest of smiles at Brigitte. "Of course. Now that the wine has arrived, I'll be just fine."

Luc winked at me, then stood and headed to the bar with Brigitte while I took the longest sip of wine ever known to man.

This drop-dead-gorgeous-famous-actress-ex-wife business was not made for the faint of heart.

Vincent poured himself another glass, his black-and-gray hair shimmering underneath the dim lights in the hotel bar.

"So, Charlotte, how long have you been with Luc?" he asked in French.

"We met about a year ago, and we actually just got married last week. I couldn't be happier."

Vincent ran his hand along his structured jawline, accentuating his salt-and-pepper five o'clock shadow. "I see. I imagine meeting the lovely Brigitte on your honeymoon was not exactly in your plans."

I couldn't help but smirk. "Not exactly, no." I wanted to tell Vincent that *lovely* wouldn't be the word I would use to describe Brigitte, but something in his tone told me that he hadn't really meant it either. "So how do *you* know Luc, Vincent?"

"Luc didn't fill you in on our family history? I am surprised. After all, shouldn't a husband and wife be completely transparent?"

When I responded with a cold look and another sip of wine, Vincent shot me a teasing grin. "Ahh, you're a feisty one I see. You mustn't take me so seriously, Charlotte. I have had *three* unsuccessful marriages. Clearly I am not the expert on this topic."

"Clearly," I said. "Anyway, you didn't answer my question. How do you know Luc and his family?" I wanted to know if there really *was* a story behind Luc's connection to the Bouchers, or if Luc was simply mad, and *jealous,* because this older, handsome man who his family had been friends with in the past was now dating his ex-wife.

"Luc's father Pierre and I were close friends in college, then after graduation, we worked together for a long time. In our late twenties, we started our own publishing company—the company *I* still own today. My sons, the actors, Marcel and Nicolas, grew up with Luc and his sister, Sandrine. Our families were quite close, but unfortunately, as good things always do, our business relationship *and* our friendship came to an end several years ago."

"Why is that?"

Vincent leaned a little closer to me, his leg brushing ever so subtly against mine. This man was smooth. I didn't move, though. I wanted to know the rest of the story.

"Pierre was the creative mind of the two of us. He directed the art and design teams of the magazines we created, worked with the photographers, the models, the writers. He had an eye for design, an incredible vision for story ideas that made our brand stand apart. In fact, even to this day, I credit much of my success to Pierre's extreme talent."

Vincent took a quick sip of wine before continuing. "Unfortunately, Pierre did not have the business or financial strengths that I possess, and by the time Luc and Sandrine were teenagers, he'd managed the family finances so poorly that they were nearly bankrupt. His beautiful wife Michèle had no idea, until . . ." He paused, an inquisitive look passing over his strong features. "Luc hasn't told you any of this?"

"I know that Luc hasn't talked to his father in years, but I haven't wanted to push him to tell me the details. I figured he'd tell me when he's ready."

"Then I'm not sure it's my place to continue on with the story." Vincent leaned closer to me, his broad shoulders and musky scent making me understand why Brigitte was so taken with him. There was something so powerful about his voice, his eyes, the way he held himself. But there was also something hiding behind that strong, intense gaze—something edgy and troubled.

Vincent moved in even closer, resting his hand on my knee. "What I *will* tell you is that Luc comes from a broken family, a family his *father* shattered. I don't know if Luc has ever recovered from what Pierre did to their family. I know from experience that Luc's mother never did."

"What do you mean you know from *experience*?"

"Luc's mother, Michèle, was my second wife."

Did I just hear him right?

Vincent had been Luc's *step-father*? And now he was dating Luc's twenty-five-year-old ex-wife?

Lexi was so right. France was playing by a *totally* different set of rules.

Not more than a few seconds after Vincent had dropped that colossal bomb, his cell phone rang.

"*Excuse-moi, Charlotte,*" he said, removing his hand from my knee. "I have to take this call."

As I watched Vincent walk over to a secluded corner of the bar, for the first time I really noticed the resemblance between him and his younger son Marcel, who was starring in *Le Problème avec l'Amour* with the lovely Brigitte. It wasn't so much that they shared the same facial features—it was more in the way they held themselves, and the way they dressed. They both exuded that bad-boy feel: a sexy darkness which *certain* women couldn't resist.

From what I'd seen of Vincent's older actor son, Nicolas, he was different—more secluded, more reserved, but every bit as handsome as his younger brother. Nicolas hadn't been in as many blockbuster hits as Marcel, and he seemed to shy away from the press for the most part. It was Marcel's face which was constantly splashed all over the front of every French tabloid, a new emaciated model or actress on his arm each time.

Like father, like son.

As Vincent talked in hushed tones back in the corner of the bar, I shot a subtle glance over to where Luc and Brigitte had been sitting, but Luc was already on his way back over to me.

Luc leaned down, wrapping a protective arm around my shoulder. "I don't want Vincent around you anymore, Charlotte. Please go up to the room and wait for me there."

"Could this have something to do with the fact that Vincent was *married* to your mother?" I whispered. "I don't know if this is normal in France, but it's sick that Brigitte would even consider dating your ex-step-father."

"I never considered him my *step-father*. He was married to my mother for only six months before she discovered that he was cheating on her. I haven't seen or spoken with him since then. But I am not surprised that he has *chosen* Brigitte."

"I don't exactly see this relationship lasting," I said dryly as I eyed Brigitte flirting shamelessly with the bartender. "Besides the fact that she's obviously using Vincent to get back at you, I get the feeling that Vincent isn't actually *in love* with Brigitte either."

"Of course he's not. He doesn't love any of the women he dates. He's a chauvinist, and he's only using the women for sex. I don't want you around him for another second, and I will never allow

Adeline near Brigitte as long as she is dating him. They are up to no good. Now please, Charlotte, go upstairs while I finish talking to Brigitte."

"How long do you think you'll be?"

Luc rubbed his forehead in his hands and mumbled a French obscenity under his breath. I'd never seen him this serious or this angry before. "I don't know. It could be a while. There are some things I have to find out from her. It has to do with Adeline, and it's extremely important."

"Will you please fill me in on all of this later, Luc?"

"Of course, *ma chérie*," Luc said as he brushed his thumb over my cheek and kissed me on the forehead.

Swiveling on my sparkly heel, I stalked out of the bar and focused my gaze straight ahead. I did *not* want to see the triumphant look Brigitte surely had plastered across her perfect little face as she watched me leave the bar alone.

When I reached the lobby, a whiff of the cool autumn breeze rushing in through the front doors of the hotel called to me. I turned away from the elevators and instead charged through the double doors, sucking in the chilly night air like it was water.

Leaning against the side of the hotel, I closed my eyes and tried to process everything that had happened in the past twelve hours. More importantly, I tried to tell myself that I hadn't made a mistake in tying the French knot so quickly. Clearly the huge secret Luc had kept from me last year—that he had a daughter—wasn't the only thing he'd been hiding. Yes, he'd told me that his parents had divorced when he was a teenager and that he and his sister hadn't spoken to their father in years, but he'd never elaborated beyond that.

This latest revelation—that media mogul Vincent Boucher had been in business with Luc's dad, only to later marry Luc's mother, and now was dating Luc's ex-wife—had my head spinning. I thought *my* family was out of control. *This* was a total mess.

What had I gotten myself into?

"You must be cold out here in that tiny dress." It was Vincent, his deep, cool voice rattling me from my thoughts.

I narrowed my eyes at him. "I'm fine."

He reached into the breast pocket of his gray suit jacket and pulled out a cigarette. "Would you like one?"

I shook my head. "Don't smoke. Even though it's practically a sin in France not to."

He chuckled. "*C'est vrai.* I like a woman who doesn't smoke, though. It's classy."

"Brigitte smokes, I assume?"

He raised a brow. "Are you implying that she's not classy?"

"Assume what you will—all I was asking is if she smokes."

A devious smile peppered his unshaven cheeks. "Only after sex."

"That's a detail I could've lived without."

"You asked." Vincent took a puff of his cigarette, then proceeded to eye me up and down. "You know, I wasn't lying in there when I said that you wear that dress *quite* well. Better than Brigitte, I must say. She is too thin to wear something like this. But you . . ." He trailed off, his intense gaze traveling up my body. "I understand why Luc married you so quickly. I would've too."

"As you pointed out before, you don't have the best track record with marriage. And judging by the way you're talking to me out here, with your girlfriend just inside, I can see why."

He shrugged. "What can I say? I adore women too much to be with just one." He took a step closer to me. "I hope I am not making you feel uncomfortable."

"I've been living in France long enough to be able to hold my own with overly forward French men. But since we're on the topic, what makes me just a little bit sick is that you were married to my husband's *mother,* and now you think it's acceptable to date his *twenty-five-year-old* ex-wife. *While* hitting on his current wife no less. As if this were all totally normal."

Another puff of smoke billowed from Vincent's lips. "The women in these scenarios have all been willing participants. In fact, Luc's mother, Michèle, was the one true love of my life. I loved her even before Pierre did."

"Interesting. Is that why you cheated on her?"

Vincent flicked his cigarette to the ground, a hardness settling into his jaw. "Luc may think he knows everything about what went on between me and his parents, but he is wrong. He was only a teenager then, only a boy."

"Cheating is cheating."

"Why don't you ask Luc about what his father did to him and his family before you judge my actions. You don't even know me, Charlotte. We only just met this afternoon."

"I've got a pretty clear picture already. And I know that my husband doesn't want me talking to you."

Vincent took another step closer, his hard eyes boring down on me. "Is that why he's inside drinking with his ex-wife, on *your* honeymoon?"

My cheeks blazed with heat. "What are you doing with Brigitte? I can see by the way you look at her that you're not really in love with her. Don't you think it's time you leave the women in Luc's life alone?"

"Brigitte and I have an arrangement that works for both of us, and as for love, well, she will never love me."

"Why is that?"

"Isn't it obvious, *chérie*?"

Suddenly Vincent cornered me against the wall, the strong scent of his aftershave making me dizzy as he ran a finger down my cheek.

"She's still in love with Luc. And she always will be."

FIVE

A loud car engine revved up behind Vincent, giving me an opportunity to step out from under his powerful hold.

The sleek black sports car came to a stop right in front of the hotel, causing a few giggly French teenagers passing by to stop and stare. Vincent walked toward the car, and within seconds, his ultra-famous, incredibly sexy older son, Nicolas Boucher, appeared.

You've got to be kidding me.

Dressed in dark, fitted jeans and a black sweater that accentuated his magnificently cut arms and chest, Nicolas gave his father a solemn nod then smiled at me.

Lexi was going to kill me.

"Who's this?" Nicolas asked in French as he ran a hand through the mop of dark hair that framed his rugged face.

Vincent placed a cool hand on my shoulder. I stepped away. I didn't care about being polite anymore. I didn't want that man's hands on me.

"This is Charlotte. And Charlotte, this is my oldest son, Nicolas."

Nicolas took a step forward and kissed me on both cheeks. After the second kiss, I noticed the cameras that had descended upon us. The paparazzi were back.

"So it's finished with Brigitte?" A chill laced through Nicolas' tone as he stared his father down.

"No, Brigitte is inside talking with your old friend, Luc Olivier. And *this* is Luc's new wife."

Nicolas' face paled as he looked from me to his father.

"*Mais qu'est-ce que tu fous*?" *What in the hell are you doing?* Nicolas growled in his father's ear.

Vincent gave his son a patronizing pat on the shoulder. "*Calme-toi, mon fils,*" he said sternly. *Calm down, son.*

Nicolas shrugged his father's hand off of him. "Are you coming to the premiere party tonight? This is a big night for Marcel. He really wants you to be there."

"I have to check with Brigitte first," Vincent said. "I have a feeling she may not be available tonight."

"She's *starring* in the film," Nicolas said, his tone annoyed. "She doesn't really have a choice, does she?"

"A woman always has a choice."

"Spare me your bullshit, Vincent. Are you coming or not? It starts in an hour."

"Excuse me for one moment while I go check with Brigitte."

Vincent and the overwhelming scent of his aftershave disappeared, leaving me alone on the sidewalk with Nicolas Boucher and three picture-hungry paparazzi.

Without warning, Nicolas grabbed my hand and led me to the passenger side of his fancy sports car. He opened the door and leaned into my ear. "You'll be safe from the photographers in here."

I hesitated. Luc thought I was upstairs in our hotel room. If he found out I'd been hanging with the Bouchers, let alone climbing into cars with them *while* being photographed, we'd be having serious words later.

"Please, Charlotte. There's something important I'd like to ask you before my father and Brigitte come back. And it will only take a minute." Nicolas did not possess the aggressive sleaze factor that his father did. The look in his eyes was sincere, and these camera-wielding maniacs weren't going to back off any time soon.

I climbed into the tiny car, hoping I wasn't going to create a massive marriage fight by doing this. But something told me that whatever

Nicolas was about to say wasn't going to creep me out the way his father had. I was also hoping that he could fill in some blanks as to what else had gone down between his family and Luc's, since it was becoming clear that Luc wasn't too eager to tell me the whole story.

Nicolas cranked up the heat, then swiveled toward me.

Suddenly a vivid scene from the last movie I'd seen him in flashed through my head. He'd played a troubled musician with a drinking problem. And in this particular scene, à la *Pretty Woman,* he'd made love to a woman *on* a grand piano.

Oh, God.

Focus, Charlotte, focus.

"*Ça va?*" *Are you okay?* he asked.

"Just a little warm. Could you turn the heat down?"

"Oh, of course. It's just that you had goose bumps on your arms. I thought you were cold."

"I was, but . . ." *But then I had a vision of your toned, naked body and a piano . . .* I reached for the door handle. "I'm sorry, I have to go find Luc."

Nicolas laid a warm hand on my arm. "Please, Charlotte. Just give me one minute."

I took a deep breath and forced the sex scene out of my mind, telling myself that Nicolas was a real person and that was only a *movie.* After Nicolas said whatever he had to say to me, I would get out of this car, find my husband, and we would forget any of this mess had ever happened.

"What do you need to ask me?" I said, registering the stress on Nicolas' handsome features.

"First, I want to apologize for my father. I hope he hasn't said, or *done,* anything inappropriate to you. Judging by the look on your face when I drove up, I assume it is too late for that."

"Your father's not very subtle, is he?"

Nicolas shook his head, his jaw tightening. "No, my father has never been able to keep his words *or* his hands to himself in the presence of a beautiful woman, no matter how complicated that might make his life. I am nothing like my father. I'm sure you picked up on this, but we don't get along very well. Anyway, I didn't ask you here to tell you the long story of why I don't care for my dad or for the way he treats women."

"So what *do* you want to ask me?"

Nicolas cleared his throat, nervously tapping his hands on the steering wheel. "I'm not sure how much Luc has told you about our friendship, or about our family history, but Luc and I were best friends in school—before my father screwed that up. I've been trying to get in touch with Luc for years, but he won't return my calls. He wants nothing to do with me or my family, and there's something important I found out recently. Something Luc *needs* to know. I'm aware that I am a complete stranger to you, Charlotte, but when my dad introduced you just now as Luc's wife, I knew I had to try to reach him through you."

"What is it?"

Regret traced Nicolas' brow, the lines around his stone gray eyes creasing as he spoke. "Luc's father didn't deserve to go to prison. He was innocent, and if Luc will give me a chance, I can prove it."

Tucking Nicolas Boucher's card safely into my sparkly clutch, I stormed into the hotel lobby. I didn't care if Luc was in the middle of negotiations with Brigitte.

It was time for him to tell me the truth about the family I'd married into.

But when I opened the fancy iron door that led to Le Bar 47, I bumped right into a fiery little blonde.

Oh joy. It was my favorite ex-wife.

Vincent was hot on Brigitte's trail, reaching for the pouty young actress. She huffed as she pushed past me, so forcefully I almost fell backward.

But I caught myself. I wasn't about to let her make even more of a fool out of me than she already had.

A harried, frantic look passed through her glassy green eyes as she stumbled over her four-inch heels. "It wasn't all my fault, you know," she slurred in French. "Luc was never home; he barely paid any attention to me. He had another woman on the side, I *know* he did. And then he gets me pregnant and—what did he expect me to do?" Tears now blurred those big baby eyes of hers, but she quickly wiped away her wounded look and replaced it with fire.

"He still loves me, you know. He always will, Charlotte. He always will."

"*Ça suffit.*" *That's enough,* Vincent said, taking her by the arm. "Go to the bathroom and get yourself together. You cannot show up to the premiere party in this state."

Drunk, raging, and emotional. I'm sure the paparazzi would eat that up in a second.

I turned to flee the scene, but Vincent laid a hand on my arm. I yanked it away. "Leave me alone, please. I have to go find my husband."

"It's unfortunate that we met under these circumstances, Charlotte. You are a beautiful, classy woman. I do hope our paths cross again."

I didn't grace him with a response. Instead I hightailed it the hell out of there. I hoped our paths *never* crossed again, but I had a feeling that Luc's complicated web of family drama—which I'd had no clue even *existed* until today—wouldn't disappear quite so easily.

Up on the third floor, I let myself into our suite. I wanted to see Luc's handsome face, hear him tell me this was all a bad dream—or at least explain to me why he hadn't told me that his father had gone to prison, and what in the heck the Bouchers had to do with it.

But instead of answers to my questions, I found Luc's black suit jacket tossed on the bed and heard his muffled voice coming from the other side of the bathroom door. I pressed my ear against the door but couldn't make out any of the short, tense phrases that flew from his lips.

Who could he be talking to?

Hoping he stayed in the bathroom a tad longer, I closed my eyes and concentrated on his words. Finally, after a minute of indecipherable ranting, I heard one sentence loud and clear.

"Charlotte won't know the truth until it's finished. It will only put her in danger."

I backed away from the door, my head suddenly dizzy with questions. What in the hell was going on? What would put me "in danger"?

If Luc walked out of that bathroom and saw me standing there, stupefied, he would know I'd been eavesdropping. After everything that had happened today, after everything he'd been keeping from me, I shouldn't have cared. But some bizarre instinct settled into my gut, and before I could fully evaluate my next best course of action, I found myself walking quietly back through the suite, opening the door, and closing it behind me.

Resting my head against the wall out in the dim hallway, I forced a few long breaths in through my nose, out through my mouth. My mom had always taught me to breathe like this when I was panicked. And even though after she'd left my father, most of her mom instincts had been sucked straight out of her, in that moment, I wanted nothing more than to see my mother's face, tell her everything that had happened today, and ask her what I should do.

In a rational state of mind, I would've walked right back into our honeymoon suite and demanded answers. I would've insisted that Luc spill all of his dirty family secrets and tell me who he was just speaking with so we could move on with our lives.

But with my key in the lock, Luc's mysterious words ricocheted through my jumbled brain once more. And I realized that being *rational* had never been my strong suit.

SIX

"*Chérie,* where were you? I thought you came back up to the room."

I smiled at Luc, revealing no trace of the panic that coursed through my body. "I just took a little stroll around the block. I needed some air. Is everything okay? You seem a little stressed."

"The talk with Brigitte didn't go so well. To be expected, I suppose . . . but still, this is not how I wanted to end our honeymoon."

Suppressing the urgent questions hanging on the tip of my tongue, I walked over to my husband and ran a suggestive finger down his chest. "Our honeymoon isn't over *yet* . . . we still have tonight."

Luc pressed my hand to his heart and sighed. "*Mon amour,* you are not going to be happy about this, but I have to take the train back to Lyon. Tonight."

My hand dropped from Luc's chest, my heart deflated.

"What's going on, Luc? Why do you have to leave?"

He paused for a split second before taking my hand once more. "It's Adeline. She has a really high fever and needs to go the doctor. I just spoke with my mother, and it sounds rather serious. I need to get home right away."

He was *not* just speaking with his mother—*was he?*

"Of course. I'll come with you," I said, before he could read the doubt in my eyes.

"No, *chérie.* Stay and enjoy the suite. After all, we are all paid up for one more night. You could invite Lexi over and order room service. I'm sure you'll miss her once we're back in Lyon and it could be nice to have one more girls' night before you officially start your new, domesticated married life." He grinned and kissed me on the cheek. "I will see you first thing in the morning."

I needed to hear the truth out of Luc's mouth before he left this hotel. We were *married* after all. We should tell each other everything. But my new husband was already grabbing his packed suitcase and heading for the door.

"Luc, we really need to talk. A lot has happened today."

"In the morning. I promise. I can't keep Adeline waiting any longer. I'm sorry." He kissed me once more on the forehead, then zipped out of our luxury honeymoon suite, leaving me alone, confused, and in desperate need of wine.

After conducting my second raid of the minibar, I pondered what Lexi had said earlier about keeping my voice and my independence . . . and about never becoming my mother.

As much as I hadn't wanted to admit it at the time, Lexi was right—I needed an outlet. During my year in Paris, my blog posts had provided just that. But as I'd learned the hard way, publishing details about my personal life online—even though the blog was anonymous—wasn't such a hot idea. Well, especially when I took away the anonymity by publishing an article under my own name in *Bella Magazine.*

Now that Luc and I were married, I had no intention of airing our clean *or* dirty laundry to perfect strangers, but that didn't mean I couldn't still reach out to women just like me who were navigating the tricky ins and outs of French marriage.

I'd only been married to a Frenchman for five days, and already I had loads of topics to explore: ex-wives, in-law drama, family secrets, and finances. Of course I couldn't forget about the good parts either: romantic dinners in the City of Lights, outrageously incredible lovemaking, chocolate croissants in bed—and the list could go on.

I pulled out the empty journal I'd been meaning to write in all week and gazed at the gorgeous cover photo of a man and woman kissing in front of the Eiffel Tower. I'd been in love with France since I was a little girl, and now here I was, living out my dream of marrying a sexy, sweet, adoring Frenchman and honeymooning in the most romantic city in the world. But there were clearly some lessons I had yet to learn about how marriage works, and specifically about how marriage works *in France.* If I was confused, I'm sure there were tons of other women just like me who could use a dose of wisdom and humor as they settled into their French marriages.

And so, as I sat alone in my Paris honeymoon suite, drinking wine and missing my new husband, I began composing chapter one of *The Girl's Guide to Tying the French Knot.*

SEVEN

"Helloooo," cooed a familiar voice from the other side of my hotel door. That didn't sound like Lexi . . . it sounded like—

"Fiona! Oh my gosh, what are you doing here?"

Lexi and Fiona tackled me with hugs as they barged into my hotel suite.

Fiona and I had become close friends while taking classes together at the Sorbonne in Paris, and she'd recently moved to Lyon with her doctor boyfriend and my former English student, Marc.

"Lexi called me after your shopping trip this afternoon and tempted me to take the train up to Paris for the night. She had a feeling you might need us." Fiona squeezed my shoulder, her sweet British accent making me smile.

I glanced over at Lexi, surprised and so thankful for her thoughtfulness.

"Lexi was right. If you girls hadn't have shown up, I may have spent the night in the hospital with a wine and chocolate overdose."

Lexi led Fiona into the suite and picked up one of the empty bottles and two crumpled chocolate bar wrappers. "I would say so, honey. Good thing we arrived when we did." Then she eyed me in my oversized *I Love Paris* T-shirt and black yoga pants. "You're not looking so hot. What happened after our shopping trip?"

"And where's Luc?" Fiona added.

"It's a long story, and I want to tell you girls all of it. I really do. But I need to get out of this hotel."

"Is *she* still staying here?" Lexi asked.

"Who?" Fiona said.

"You didn't tell Fiona about my run-in with the ex?" I asked Lexi.

Fiona stared at me, clueless.

"No, I figured it was your story to tell," Lexi said. "But I had a feeling that tonight might not go so well. Let's get you dressed so we can hit the town. This story will go *much* better with a cocktail."

"I couldn't agree more," I said.

Armed with two high-heel-clad friends, I strutted through the hotel lobby comforted by the fact that if there happened to be another ex-wife sighting, this band of stilettos would know *exactly* what to do. Regardless of the minor fallouts I'd had with Lexi and Fiona in the past year, I knew without a doubt that these girls had my back.

I only wished I could say the same about Luc.

After a swift walk up Avenue George V, we arrived at Bound, a chic bar full of twenty-somethings sipping expensive cocktails and staking out their next date. We headed straight to the bar and ordered three of those expensive cocktails for ourselves. This was no time to mess around.

Once we were settled in our corner table, cocktails in hand, the girls raised their eyebrows at me expectedly.

"So did I hear this correctly from what you said earlier . . . you met Luc's *ex-wife*?" Fiona asked.

I swirled my pretty blue cocktail around in my glass and took a massive sip before catching the girls up on some of the insane events of the day. I told them about the dress disaster, about Brigitte and Vincent's bizarre relationship, and about Vincent's sleazy advances. But when I got to Nicolas pulling up in his sports car and insisting that I get in, Lexi almost shot across the table.

"You were *inside* Nicolas Boucher's car? And you're just telling me this now? Charlotte, are you freaking kidding me?"

"Lexi has apparently been *in love* with Nicolas Boucher since she was a teenager," I explained to Fiona.

"Oh my God, Char, I'm hyperventilating over here," Lexi continued, her cheeks blushing crimson. "What was he like? Was he just as hot in person as he is on the screen? Are you going to see him again?"

Fiona placed her hand over Lexi's knuckles, which had turned white from gripping the table so hard. "Lexi, seriously, he's still just a *person*, like you and me. He puts his pants on one leg at a time—"

"Honey," Lexi interrupted, "in my little fantasy, Nicolas Boucher wouldn't be wearing *any* pants."

Fiona giggled then turned to me. "So, Char, the real question is, what did Nicolas ask you once you climbed in the car?"

Lexi's huge amber eyes drooped in disappointment.

"Don't give me that puppy dog look," I said to her with a laugh. "All right, if you must know, Nicolas is actually *more* handsome in person than on screen. When I got in the car, all I could think about was—"

Lexi, who'd been downing her cocktail so quickly you'd think her mouth was on fire, gripped my wrist. "The *piano* scene."

Fiona and I burst into laughter while Lexi lowered her voice. "Okay, I'm going to make a confession. After I saw that movie, I couldn't stop thinking about that crazy piano sex scene. And later that night, when Dylan and I were in bed together, I accidentally called him *Nicolas.*"

Fiona gasped, covering her hand with her mouth. "Lexi, that's taking it a little far—even for you."

Lexi threw back the rest of her cocktail. "Dylan wouldn't talk to me for a whole week. He thought I was cheating on him with someone named Nicolas. And to be honest, ever since I saw that film a few weeks ago, I *feel* like I've been cheating on him because I cannot stop thinking about that damn piano scene."

"Well, you're only human," I said. "I probably shouldn't say this, being newly married and all . . . but it was an *incredibly* hot scene."

Lexi raised her glass. "Cheers to that."

We all clinked glasses, then finished our first round of cocktails before signaling for the server. It was going to be a long night.

"Besides your little bedroom slip, how are things going between you and Dylan?" Fiona asked.

"It's been *interesting,* to say the least," Lexi said. "Basically, we have really amazing sex, but the reason the sex with Dylan is and always has been—so damn hot is because it's always make-up sex. We fight about *everything.* And even though he's a man, and we all know that men can be infuriating, it's not always his fault. I know this might surprise you ladies, but I've been known to be a little explosive when I'm angry, and unfortunately Dylan's the same way."

I didn't have any trouble believing that Lexi and Dylan could be explosive and dramatic. The first time I'd met Dylan was on New Year's Eve at the Hôtel Plaza Athénée, inside the fancy suite that Lexi had told me her parents paid for. What I didn't know at the time was that Lexi's parents died in a car accident when she was young, and she's suffered from major periods of depression ever since. The next morning, Dylan was gone and Lexi was locked in the bathroom sobbing.

"Do you think there's any hope that things will change?" I asked Lexi.

"I thought everything would magically improve when we moved in together." Lexi took a long sip of her pink cocktail. "Wishful thinking. Besides the sex, it's been a nightmare."

Fiona placed a hand on Lexi's shoulder. "If it makes you feel any better, Marc's mother, the dreaded Madame Rousseau, is coming to stay with us for *twelve days.*"

"Twelve days?" I gasped. In addition to being Marc's uptight mother, Madame Rousseau was our advisor at the Sorbonne the year before, and to put it in Fiona's typical words, she was a sodding old cow.

Fiona downed the last of her drink. "Yes! Twelve days! How will I survive?"

"This might be a good time to get a prescription for a strong sedative," Lexi said. "If you don't want someone to end up dead."

Fiona squared her gaze on me. "Now that it's clear that *all* of our love lives are a complete mess, let's get back to this Boucher brother business. While I think Nicolas is quite handsome, you know I prefer his younger brother, Marcel."

"Really?" Lexi said. "I wouldn't have pegged you for a Marcel type. He's so flashy, so teenage heartthrob, and *always* in the tabloids. Doesn't seem like your type of guy."

Fiona shot Lexi a sly grin, then shrugged. "We can talk about our Boucher brother preferences later. I want to know what Nicolas said to you once you got in the car, Charlotte."

"Oh, right. Well, Luc hasn't spoken with Nicolas or his family in years, since Vincent cheated on and divorced Luc's mother, I suppose. So Nicolas wants me to ask Luc to get in touch with him because he has something really important to tell him."

"Did Nicolas tell you what it is?" Fiona asked.

I hesitated. Did I really want to tell the girls about Luc's dad going to prison when I hadn't even asked Luc about it yet? When I didn't even know what he'd gone to prison for, or if it was even true for that matter?

The wine I had guzzled back at the hotel suddenly became best friends with the cocktail I'd just downed, making me remember that this was supposed to be the most romantic night of my honeymoon with Luc. But Luc had left me alone in our hotel suite, and I wasn't even sure if he'd been telling the truth about Adeline being sick. Not to mention the fact that he'd *omitted* the truth about where all of this insane money was coming from, Brigitte's famous actress status, his childhood connection to the high-profile Boucher family, his father going to prison, and most recently, his secret bathroom phone call.

Screw it. I couldn't possibly be expected to keep this disaster a secret. I would go nuts holding it all in.

"Okay, but you both have to promise never to tell a soul."

Lexi and Fiona both gave me serious nods and leaned over the table.

"All right, get ready for this. Nicolas said that 'Luc's dad never deserved to go to prison.' That Luc's dad was innocent, and that if Luc gives him a chance, Nicolas can prove it."

A stunned silence settled over the group. Lexi shot up from her seat and grabbed the waitress' arm as she passed by. "We ordered cocktails two minutes ago. We need them, *now*," she ordered in French.

As the scared waitress scurried toward the bar, Lexi sat back down and joined Fiona in her gaping stare.

"Luc's dad went to prison? Did Nicolas tell you why?" Fiona asked.

"No, I was too shocked to say anything after he dropped that massive bomb. Plus I had to get back in the hotel, and I wanted to hear the truth from Luc."

"So what happened next?" Lexi was on the edge of her seat now, gripping the table.

I reached into my purse, pulled out the little black card Nicolas had given me and slid it into the center of the table. "Nicolas said to call him if I wanted to know more."

"We *definitely* need to know more." Lexi picked up the card and held it high against the purple lighting in the club. "Fiona, you wouldn't happen to be up for a threesome, would you?"

I snatched the card from her hands. "No one will be having a threesome with Nicolas Boucher because I'm not going to call him. Not to mention the fact that you both have serious boyfriends!"

"Oh, just because you're married now means you can't have any fun?" Lexi said, holding the card tightly to her chest. "In all seriousness, Char, you have to call him to find out why Luc's dad went to prison."

"Wait, after you went back into the hotel, didn't you confront Luc about all of this?" Fiona asked.

I filled the girls in on Luc's sketchy bathroom phone call, and on how Luc had said Adeline was sick and had disappeared before I could get two words out of him.

Fiona crossed her arms, concern lining her eyes. "There's something Luc's keeping from you that will put you in danger? Are you absolutely sure that's what he said?"

I nodded, feeling that same panicky feeling rise up through my chest once more.

"This isn't good, Char," Fiona said. "Something really strange is going on—and I'm worried about you. I hate to say it, but I agree with Lexi. If Luc won't tell you what's going on here, you need to call Nicolas. You have a right to know the truth about the family you married into."

Lexi reached for my purse, then handed me my cell phone.

"Start dialing, honey. It's time for us to meet the sexiest man alive."

EIGHT

"I've never believed in God until this moment," Lexi whispered under her breath as she nodded toward the door. "*They're here.*"

"Who's *they*? I thought Nicolas was coming alo—" I began, but stopped when I spotted Nicolas *and* his tabloid star brother, Marcel, walking purposefully through the bar straight toward us.

If it weren't for the bumping bass in this swanky club, you could've heard a pin drop. Every female eye in that bar was glued to the sleek, sexy pair of brothers who'd only taken twenty minutes to leave the movie premiere party they'd been attending and zip over here to meet . . . *little old me.*

And for the second time that day, I wondered, *is this really my life?*

Lexi's sweaty palm gripped my knee. "If I faint, please tell Nicolas the only way to revive me will be mouth to mouth."

Fiona smacked Lexi under the table.

"Get it together, girls," I hissed through gritted teeth. A sweet smile quickly graced my lips as the men approached our table.

Nicolas placed a warm hand on my shoulder as he leaned in to give me a kiss on each cheek. "Charlotte, I'm so glad you called."

"Thanks for coming. I'm sorry to have pulled you away from the premiere party. You didn't have to—"

"We were happy to leave. Things with our father and Brigitte were getting *interesting* . . . as you can probably imagine." He nodded to his brother. "Charlotte, this is Marcel."

Shorter and thinner than Nicolas—but every bit as handsome—Marcel had a messy head of dark chocolate hair, a sexy five o'clock shadow, and brown eyes that could take most any girl from zero to naked in his bed in about two seconds.

He reminded me of a younger version of Vincent, just not *quite* as sleazy. Then again, we hadn't even spoken, so his sleaziness factor was yet to be determined.

I introduced the girls, and kisses—or *bisous*—were exchanged around the table, while *every other table* in the entire bar was watching this whole scene go down, no doubt wondering who in the hell *we* were to get to hang out with the ultra-famous Boucher brothers. Up until twelve hours ago, I would've been asking myself the exact same question.

Marcel took a seat in between Fiona and Lexi while Nicolas extended a hand to me. "Charlotte, would you mind taking a quick walk with me?"

I could actually feel Lexi deflating next to me, but when Marcel placed a hand on her shoulder and asked her if she'd ever done any modeling, she perked right up again.

"Girls, do you mind? I'll only be a few minutes," I said.

Fiona winked at me. "Not to worry. We'll be just fine here."

Nicolas took my hand and led me past the clinking of drinks and the excited chatter that circled the bar. "I have a car waiting outside. Is it okay with you if we talk in there?"

Before agreeing to his proposition, I promised myself I would never again think of the piano sex scene.

But oh God, that's all I can think about when I look at him!

And I love Luc, I really do. I would never do anything with Nicolas.

But that damn naked piano scene . . .

Stop it. I love Luc. Piano sex would hurt anyway. Like Fiona said, Nicolas is just a person. The piano sex wasn't even real.

But it looked so—

"Charlotte?" Nicolas repeated.

"Mm-hmm, yes of course!" I said, except I sounded more like a high-pitched squirrel. Suddenly I wished I hadn't downed that cocktail so quickly.

My steaming cheeks welcomed the cool night air that flittered past as Nicolas led me to a long black limo waiting at the corner. Apparently he was always riding in style.

Thankfully our invasive paparazzi friends hadn't found us yet. We slipped inside the dark limousine and Nicolas closed the door behind us.

"Did you talk to Luc yet?" He wasn't wasting any time getting to the point.

I shook my head. "No, Luc had to go back to Lyon tonight. It's Adeline, his daughter. She has a fever . . . or so he says," I mumbled under my breath.

Nicolas raised a brow. "You think he's lying?"

"What? No, of course not," I covered as I gazed down at my shimmering stilettos and realized the sparkles were blurring in the darkness. Maybe I'd had a bit too much to drink. . . .

"It's just that Luc has never mentioned this *minor* tidbit about his father going to prison, and now I'm not sure what to believe."

"Tidbit?" Nicolas repeated in a thick French accent.

"Oh, I'm sorry, I didn't realize I was speaking English."

"Never mind, it is not important," Nicolas continued in French. "I am really sorry, Charlotte. I never meant to cause any problems between you and Luc. I only want him to listen to what I have to say. Because the way things happened with our families, it was horrible. And if Luc only knew what I knew. . . ." Nicolas trailed off, gazing out the window at a group of young girls exiting the bar, but not seeming the least bit interested in them.

"Yes?" I prodded.

"It could change everything."

I looked Nicolas straight in the eye. "Listen, if you want me to admit to Luc that I've been talking to you and ask him to hear you out, I need to know what I'm getting myself into. What did Luc's father go to prison for?"

Nicolas shifted uncomfortably in his seat before finally spilling the beans. "When we were teenagers and our fathers were in business together, Luc's dad was found guilty of embezzlement. When the company was audited, they discovered that he had embezzled the equivalent of two million euros from their company. He was sentenced to a year in prison, leaving his family devastated—both emotionally and financially. Luc's parents got a divorce, and my father took that opportunity to swoop in and save the day."

Even in my semidrunken state, the sarcasm in Nicolas' tone was not lost on me.

"That's awful. Why would Luc hide this from me?" I asked.

Nicolas shook his head. "I'm not sure, but from what I remember of my friendship with Luc, he doesn't play dirty. He's an honest person. I don't think he would hide this information from you unless he had a good reason."

"Luc *is* a good man," I said. "I wonder though, do you think he's trying to protect me from something—something *dangerous*?"

Nicolas gazed back at me, perplexed. "Why would you think that?"

"Just something I overheard him saying on the phone today got me thinking that this could be more complicated than I thought."

"Luc has been through a lot with his family, and now with Brigitte. He hasn't had it easy at all, Charlotte. Maybe, like you said, he's been keeping this information from you to protect you, to protect your relationship. Maybe he just doesn't want his past to ruin your future together."

"Maybe, but he should've learned by now that our pasts will always catch up to us. The fact that I'm sitting in a limo with his former best friend and ex-step-brother, and that I had drinks with the lovely Brigitte and his ex-step-father—on what was supposed to be the last night of our honeymoon—is clear proof of that."

"True," Nicolas conceded. "What is important now, though, is that Luc knows the truth."

"So what *is* the truth? If Luc's dad didn't embezzle the money, then who did?"

Nicolas tapped his fingers nervously on the edge of the seat. "I'm afraid I can't tell you that, Charlotte. I need to speak with Luc first."

I pulled out my cell phone, brought Luc's number up on the screen, then handed it to Nicolas.

"Here's your chance."

Nicolas' dark gaze intensified as he took the phone. "Charlotte, after I make this call, you need to be aware that things might get complicated for a while."

I reached for the door handle. "And you don't call this complicated?"

Nicolas placed his hand on my arm. "No, Charlotte, I mean it. This is serious. Your name will be in the papers, you'll have reporters calling the house. This was a high-profile case back in the day, and opening it back up again isn't going to be easy—especially after the truth comes out. Just remember that no matter what happens, Luc is a good man. And judging from the little bit of time I've spent with you, I understand why he married you. You're smart and beautiful and . . . well, I don't want what I'm about to do to ruin what you have together. Promise me you won't let that happen."

"Nicolas, what you need to understand about me is that no matter what happens, I'm with Luc for the long haul. I love him unconditionally, and nothing you could say or do will ever change that."

As soon as I left Nicolas alone in the limo and stepped outside, a wall of flashing cameras descended upon me. I shielded my eyes and pushed my way past the intrusive photographers, but suddenly their attention shifted.

Marcel Boucher strutted out of the club like the superstar that he was with Lexi and Fiona pinned to his sides. Cameras flashed furiously as the paparazzi couldn't get enough—and apparently Marcel and the girls couldn't either. They all stopped to pose for the cameras, Lexi of course being the one to work it the most, before they finally made their way over to the limo.

Marcel reached for the door, but I placed a hand on his arm, stopping him. "Nicolas is making an important call. We should give him a minute."

Marcel tilted his head at me, a cocky grin passing over his lips. "Is that what you call it in English, *making a call*?" Then he shrugged my hand off of him and reached for the door once more. "Don't worry, I won't tell Luc," he whispered in my ear before slipping inside.

"That's not what's going on here," I said. But my protests were drowned out by my two giggling girlfriends climbing into the limo behind Marcel.

Peeking inside, I noticed Nicolas hanging up my phone, a disappointed look on his face. "No answer," he mouthed.

It had been well over two hours since Luc had left Paris, so he was definitely in Lyon by now. The fact that he wasn't answering his phone didn't bode well with me. Even if he was busy taking care of Adeline, he would've picked up his phone. He never ignored my calls.

The paparazzi vultures lined up at my back, the clicking sound of their cameras making me flinch. I could understand why celebrities lashed out at them—they were relentless.

Marcel was already passing around glasses filled to the brim with champagne when Lexi reached for me. "Come on, Char. We could all stand to blow off a little steam right now, don't you think? After everything that happened today, what's a limo ride around Paris and a little champagne going to hurt?"

Lexi was right. The damage of the day had already been done. Luc wasn't answering his phone, and the longer I stood out on that sidewalk, the higher chance I had of making it into every French tabloid first thing tomorrow morning.

I took Lexi's outstretched hand and climbed into the Boucher brothers' limo, where champagne flowed heavier than the River Seine, washing all of our troubles into a bubbly abyss.

NINE

"*Mmm . . . Nicolas, je t'aime.*" The breathy whisper came low and soft in my ear. An arm draped over my chest, pulling me in tightly. I tried to open my eyes, but the beating of drums against my temples forced my eyelids back to their natural state of closed.

"*Nicolas . . . Nicolas . . . Nicolas.*" It was that airy female voice again, whispering in her perfect French accent. Why was she calling me Nicolas? And why was she squeezing me so close I could hardly breathe?

I gritted my teeth as a wave of nausea swept through my core, and this time I forced my eyes open. Lexi lay sprawled across me, her eyelashes fluttering as she continued to whisper that name—*Nicolas, Nicolas*—over and over. I rolled out from under her tight grasp and peered down at my feet to find a set of silky black sheets bunched at my feet.

Black sheets?

I didn't have black sheets. And neither did Luc.

I peered around the sleek bedroom, my mouth unhinging when the most perfect view of *la Tour Eiffel* caught my eye through a stunning floor-to-ceiling window.

"*Nicolas, Nicolas, Nicolas,*" Lexi hummed.

Oh, God, it was all coming back to me.

Nicolas *Boucher.* The Boucher brothers.

Those gorgeous, sexy Boucher brothers.

The paparazzi . . . the limo.

And the *champagne.*

But what had happened after that first glass of bubbly bliss in the limo? I distinctly remembered saying to the girls right after we'd climbed in that we were only having one glass, and then we had to return back to my hotel room so my husband of five days wouldn't want to divorce me when all of this was through—*and* so we could get a little bit of shut-eye before my train back to Lyon in the morning.

My train!

"Lexi!" I hissed, shooting up from the bed, the threat of my gag reflex immediately making me wish I hadn't moved so quickly.

"*Oui, Nicolas, oui, je t'aime.*" With her eyes still closed, Lexi reached for me once more.

This time I grabbed her hand and squeezed it as hard as I could. "Lexi, get up!" I screeched. "I'm not Nicolas. We have to go, *now.*"

But Lexi didn't show any signs of life, except for her incessant murmuring of *I love you's* in French to the famous actor and my new friend, Nicolas Boucher, whose apartment I could only assume we were currently sleeping in.

At least the two of us still had all of our clothes on. But where was Fiona?

I gave up on Lexi and tossed the black sheets off the bed, kicking her butt in the process.

"Mmmm," she mumbled, curling into a tight ball and refusing to budge.

Feeling a mixture of cocktails and stale champagne tentatively sloshing around in my stomach, I scrambled to my feet and dashed out of the sleek bedroom. But just as I skidded around the corner in my bare feet, a catchy cell phone tone emanated from a room across the hall. A muffled male voice took the call, and when I crept up to the closed door, I recognized the voice as Marcel's.

Short, harsh responses shot from his lips.

"*Oui, je comprends . . . Non . . . Oui . . . Je sais . . . D'accord, je m'en occupe.*"

Okay, I'll take care of it?

What was this guy up to?

As soon as I realized Marcel's heated phone conversation had ended, I scurried away from the door. The slippery hardwood floors made that task a bit tougher than I'd anticipated, and my not-quite-sober butt plunged straight to the floor.

Merde.

A shirtless Marcel appeared in the doorway right at that moment, the disapproving look on his dark, handsome features tearing up any last shred of dignity I may have had left in me.

I needed to find Fiona, wake these girls up, and get the hell out of here.

Marcel lent me a hand without saying a word, the look in his brown eyes tinted with anger. "I need to speak with you, Charlotte. Please follow me."

Oh, God. Did he know that I'd been eavesdropping?

Marcel led me through a large living room decorated with two square black couches, a smooth black-and-white rug, and four rather scary modern art paintings splashed in red and black paint. The sleek, impersonal décor didn't fit with what I'd seen of Nicolas' personality the day before. And with no sign of Nicolas anywhere, that meant we'd spent the night in Marcel Boucher's Parisian bachelor pad.

Dear God.

Empty champagne and wineglasses littered the black coffee table, proof of our wild night—the details of which I could not remember for the life of me. Suddenly a splash of something pink and sparkly lying on the floor caught my eye. I lowered my gaze to find a lacy black thong lined with tiny pink jewels thrown carelessly next to the couch.

Please don't let that thong belong to any of my friends, I begged silently.

The freaky blood-red paintings in the living room were quickly redeemed when Marcel led me out to a beautiful balcony overlooking the River Seine. The early morning sun bathed the bustling city in a soft, orange glow, momentarily making me forget about all of the drama that had transpired since the day—and the night—before.

Somehow Paris always had that effect on me.

I scanned the rows of gorgeous Parisian apartment buildings across the river, watching as the green-and-white Six Train crossed the Seine on its way to Passy, one of my favorite shopping neighborhoods, and the quaint little *rue* where Luc had bought me the world's best *pain au chocolat* the day before.

Marcel lit a cigarette, then cleared his throat, snapping me out of my Paris haze and back to the present.

"What did Nicolas tell you last night in the limo?" Marcel's normally sexy jawline tightened as he blew a puff of smoke directly into my face. The charming, heartthrob actor who'd sauntered through the club last night had disappeared. Instead, standing before me was a jaded, pushy rich boy.

"He just wanted to talk to me about Luc. He was hoping to reconnect with him, that's all. Why do you want to know? What's this all about?"

Marcel took a step closer to me, the stench of alcohol and smoke on his breath making my stomach curl. "After you leave my apartment, I don't want you to talk to my brother ever again. There's more to our past with your husband than you will ever know, and if you want to keep your marriage intact, I suggest you stop digging and leave it alone. This is for your protection, Charlotte. *Tu comprends?*"

A chill slithered through my body as I took a step back from Marcel. The resemblance to his sleazy father Vincent was suddenly overwhelming. "Yes, I understand. Just show me where Fiona is and we'll get out of here."

"She is sleeping in my bedroom. I tried, but I could not wake her this morning. It was quite a night, you know." With a lift of his brow and another puff of his cigarette, the shirtless Marcel left me alone on the balcony, wondering exactly *what* had happened last night—and what or *whom* I needed protection from.

"Dude, I'm dying," Lexi said as she pushed her gargantuan black sunglasses up her nose and plopped her forehead on my shoulder in despair. "I haven't drunk that much since . . . since I can't remember when. What even happened last night?"

The mood on the Metro was somber as we all tried to keep our breakfasts down and wished we were about eight years younger. Passing the twenty-six mark really did reduce alcohol tolerance.

"It's best not to try to remember," Fiona said, pressing her cheek up against the cool window, her eyes drawn shut.

After Marcel's warning on the balcony earlier, I'd discovered the normally conservative and very British Fiona curled up in a topless ball underneath Marcel's sheets. Fiona's black dress crumpled up in one corner of the master bedroom and her heels and bra strewn in another confirmed my fear that outrageously high champagne consumption combined with Marcel Boucher's irresistible allure had led her astray. And I could only assume that the jewel-studded thong on display in Marcel's living room had belonged to Fiona, although I would never have pegged her to wear something so racy.

I'd helped her get dressed without saying a word, but the shame in her eyes had said it all. She loved Marc, her handsome doctor boyfriend, and they'd recently moved into an adorable apartment together in Lyon.

Fiona wasn't a cheater. It simply wasn't part of her character.

But, as I knew all too well, there are days when we look in the mirror and don't even recognize ourselves.

Fiona was clearly having one of those days, and if only I hadn't dragged her into my honeymoon mess, she never would've met Marcel and none of this would have ever happened.

Back on the Metro train, which barreled away from *la Tour Eiffel*, I squeezed Fiona's knee, hoping she knew I would never tell a soul what I'd seen this morning. And hoping that she knew how awful I felt about my part in it. Lexi eyed Fiona, then raised a brow at me. I shook my head in response. She nodded in understanding.

Sometimes girlfriends are telepathic like that.

Lexi squeezed Fiona's hand. "With situations like these, it's best to leave the past in the past. So the two of you missed your train back to Lyon, and our boyfriends and Charlotte's new husband are going to be pissed at us for a few days. We'll survive as long as we keep our mouths *shut* about this whole Boucher brother business. When the boys ask why we look like hell this morning, we tell them that we had a little too much to drink, then spent the night in Charlotte's luxurious honeymoon suite and overslept. That's all there is too it. Sound good?"

Deep gray circles swallowed Fiona's blue eyes as she finally lifted them to the group. "I'm in."

"Sounds like a plan," I said.

"It's settled then. This secret stays with—" Lexi stopped when her cell phone buzzed inside her purse. She glanced at the caller ID, but immediately silenced the phone. Red blotches splashed across her cheeks as she lifted her gaze back up to us. "What was I saying again?"

"The secret?" I prodded.

"Oh, right. Keep it quiet, ladies. For the sake of all of our relationships."

Lexi's phone buzzed once more, indicating a voice mail. A few seconds later, she practically jumped out of her seat when we reached her stop. "That's me!"

I shot her a questioning glance, but she dismissed it, kissed me on the cheek, and dashed out of the Metro, leaving two terribly hungover, memory-challenged friends in her wake.

TEN

Three hours and one more expensive high-speed train ticket later, the TGV pulled into the Part-Dieu train station in Lyon. Fiona and I grabbed our bags and rambled through the crowds in silence. The pounding of my temples was about all I could handle for the duration of our train ride, but there was something I needed to say to Fiona before we parted ways.

Just as we rounded a corner and the train station crowds died down a bit, I placed a hand on her arm. "Listen, Fiona, I just wanted to say I'm so sorry for getting you into this mess. If it wasn't for all of my ridiculous honeymoon drama, this never would've—"

"I'm an adult, Char. You don't have to take responsibility for this. Just please don't tell anyone what you saw this morning. Not until I figure out what I'm going to do about it anyway." Fiona's mouth quivered, her eyes watering up.

"Do you remember what happened after we got to Marcel's apartment?" I asked her.

Before Fiona could respond, the tabloid featured in the newsstand behind her head caught my eye.

"Oh, my God," I whispered, reaching for the magazine.

On the cover of the trashy French tabloid was a photo montage of my entire day yesterday. Our first encounter with Brigitte and Vincent outside the Château Frontenac Hotel, my private chat with Vincent, me climbing into Nicolas' fancy sports car, and finally our girls' night out stumbling into the champagne-studded limo with the Boucher brothers.

I flipped through the glossy pages to see what other prize moments they'd caught on camera. My heart sank when I discovered photos of me, Lexi, and Fiona following Nicolas and Marcel into Marcel's swanky apartment building late last night (a moment of which I still had no recollection) and another picture of us girls emerging from the same building early this morning, wearing the same skimpy dresses we'd been wearing the night before.

The translated headline read: "Another Wild Night for Bad Boy Marcel and Brother Nicolas." The article on the following page retraced the cover's photo montage with grossly inaccurate descriptions of what had gone down yesterday, including but not limited to:

Brigitte Beaumont leaves media mogul Vincent Boucher to reunite with hotty ex-husband, Luc Olivier.

Devastated by Olivier's infidelity, his new wife Charlotte Summers is seduced by the entire Boucher family. Which one will she choose?

Summers invites the girls to join her for a sleepless night chez Marcel. Will bad boy Marcel ever settle with just one woman?

A drunken Brigitte makes a scene at the premiere party of her new film, embarrassing Vincent and herself. She is later spotted fighting with Vincent in front of the Château Frontenac Hotel before storming off into the night, drunk and alone.

Well, that last one probably wasn't so inaccurate.

Those damn paparazzi hadn't missed a single moment.

"*Merde*," Fiona mumbled shaking her head.

"So much for our story of what happened last night," I mumbled. "I wonder if Lexi has seen this yet."

"Never mind Lexi. What about Marc, Dylan, and Luc? They're going to hear about this one way or another. What are we going to tell them?" I'd never heard Fiona's tone so desperate before.

I didn't even want to think about how we were going to explain these photos to our respective men.

Trying to whip up a story in my dazed, pounding head, I turned the page.

The final incriminating photo staring back at us made me realize I'd have to improve my story-telling skills if I wanted the four of us to get out of this unscathed.

The horrified gasp coming from Fiona's lips echoed my sentiment.

A photograph of two blurry silhouettes wrapped in a passionate embrace on Marcel's balcony was featured on the last page of the article. The picture had been taken at night, so it was impossible to make out *which* one of us was kissing one of the Boucher brothers.

Guilt washed over Fiona's pale blue eyes as she ripped the magazine out of my hands and snapped it shut.

"We need to put our sunglasses on and get the hell out of here before someone recognizes us," she ordered. "I won't lose Marc over these pretty boy actors. I just won't." Fiona flipped her dark sunglasses over her eyes and took off through the station.

"Fiona!" I called, grabbing onto her elbow. "I know after what happened this morning, you're thinking it had to have been you on that balcony, but we don't know for sure that it wasn't Lexi. She woke up murmuring Nicolas' name and saying she loved him in French."

"Right, but she woke up next to *you, not* in Nicolas' bed," she hissed. "And besides, neither of your significant others have a mother who will rake you over the coals for this, and who's arriving tomorrow to stay for *twelve sodding days*."

Fiona was right—Madame Rousseau, Marc's dreadful mother, would never forgive Fiona for this if she got wind of it. Judging by the fact that the wretched old woman had easily found out about my scandalous *Bella Magazine* article only a few months earlier, she'd be all over the fact that her precious son's new girlfriend's face was splashed all over the French tabloids.

"I have to get home to Marc. I'm telling him the truth," Fiona announced. "That's the only option."

"But we don't even know *for sure* what happened last night." I sighed, exasperated. "The balcony picture might not even *be* from last night for all we know. These are tasteless tabloids that specialize in distorting the truth."

Fiona looked as unconvinced as I was by my own words. "What about Nicolas? Do we know if he stayed the night? He wasn't there when you woke up this morning, was he?"

"No, he was already gone."

"You have his number; maybe you can call and ask him what he remembers about last night?" Fiona asked.

I thought of Marcel's harsh warning on the balcony earlier this morning to stay away from Nicolas. That there was more to the story than I knew, and if I wanted to keep my marriage intact, I needed to stay out of it.

I decided now wasn't the best time to freak out Fiona any further by telling her about that bizarre incident. "I'll see what I can find out," I said.

"God, what a mess," Fiona mumbled.

I leaned in and gave Fiona a hug before we went our separate ways.

Fifteen minutes later, I emerged from the Metro in Vieux Lyon, silently cursing the blaring sun as I started off toward Luc's apartment—which was technically *ours* now. A few blocks down the cobblestone stretch of rue Saint-Jean, my phone buzzed.

Expecting to see Luc's name on the screen, I was relieved to find my boss' number. That relief quickly evaporated when I realized that Jean-Sébastien *never* called me on the weekends.

Oh, God. Had he seen the tabloids?

I answered the phone and dove right in.

"Jean-Sébastien, I'm so sorry," I rambled in French. "You have to let me expla—"

"Charlotte, why are *you* sorry? What are you talking about?"

"Um . . . I . . . you mean you haven't seen . . . ?"

"Seen what?"

"Oh, never mind. Sorry! What can I do for you?"

A heavy pause traveled down the line. Why did I get the feeling that even though Jean-Sébastien clearly hadn't seen my trashy tabloid action, he wasn't calling to give me a promotion?

"Jean-Sébastien, what is it?"

"Your classes have been cancelled, Charlotte. In fact, I can't believe this is happening, but unfortunately, *most* of the classes this semester have to be cancelled. Our enrollment is lower than ever, and we've been in big financial trouble for the last several months. Apparently taking language classes for fun just doesn't fit into people's budgets anymore. That or I've done a horrible job at running this school." Jean-Sébastien's usual upbeat voice was completely deflated.

"But we're supposed to start class tomorrow. There has to be some way—"

"Unless a massive contract comes our way soon, we'll be forced to close down the school by next semester. I'm sorry, Charlotte."

I turned away from the direction of our apartment and headed down a skinny cobblestone alley toward the Saône River. I couldn't see Luc right now. Not yet.

"How long have you known about this?" I was careful to only allow a hint of panic to settle into my voice. I felt like screaming at the sky.

"I was hanging on until the last minute, hoping we'd have a high enough enrollment to at least make it through the semester. But we didn't. It was wrong of me to wait so long to tell you. You're an amazing teacher, Charlotte. You know you'll have my recommendation."

"Thank you. But what about you? Are you going to be okay? And your family?" Jean-Sébastien's wife, Marie-Élise, had just given birth to their second son and had decided to permanently leave her job to be a stay-at-home mom.

"I will figure out a way. But for now, there is little to no hope that the language school will survive in the long term. I'm sorry, Charlotte. I wish I could give you a different answer, but that's all I have for you today."

I plopped onto a bench facing the river, hung up my phone, and plunged my head into my hands. I *adored* my teaching job at the language school. How could this really be happening right now?

Plus, with all of the financial ambiguity between me and Luc, the last thing I wanted to do was start off our marriage jobless and completely dependent on him for money. After witnessing my parents' divorce and my mother's subsequent undoing, I'd vowed I would never be dependent on a man. I would always have my own career, my own way to support myself. And despite Luc's apparent savings from his days working in finance, he was still a professor with a young daughter, and potential future legal battles ahead of him with the One Who Shall Not Be Named.

Thinking back to my conversation with Lexi the day before, an idea popped into my mind. It was a long shot, but I figured anything was worth a try. As I sat facing the banks of the sparkling river, I drafted a quick e-mail on my phone to a contact back in New York. Then I picked myself off the bench, took a deep breath, and headed home.

It was time to tell my husband about my sudden lack of employment, deal with the tabloid mess, and find out why he never told me about his father going to prison. These were not exactly the topics I imagined we'd be discussing during our first week of marriage.

ELEVEN

Luc was comforting an extremely distraught Adeline when I walked into our little French apartment in the heart of Vieux Lyon.

His bloodshot eyes were weary as he lifted them to mine. "Look, Adeline. Charlotte's home," he said in French as he swiveled his daughter's tear-stained face in my direction.

"Hi, sweetie." I left my bags in a heap at the door and crossed the living room to where Luc was rubbing Adeline's tiny back as she sobbed into his shoulder.

My four-year-old step-daughter took one peek at me and cried even louder. "I want my mommy!" she howled in French.

Luc raised a brow at me, exhaustion seeping through his pores. "It's been an interesting day," he whispered. "I'm going to put her down to sleep . . . then we can talk."

I watched as Luc carried his little, crying girl into her bedroom and closed the door behind them. Besides her tears and the desire to see her *real* mommy, the thermometer and bottle of medicine that sat on the kitchen counter proved to me that at least Luc hadn't been lying about Adeline's fever.

Her cries grew softer as I quietly carried my bags back into our bedroom. But when I spotted a familiar French tabloid placed purposefully in the center of our bed, our honeymoon disaster and my girls' night out with the Boucher brothers once again staring me in the face, I felt like I could cry myself.

Obviously Luc didn't live in a cave. I just thought that with Adeline being so sick, there was a *slight* chance he wouldn't have gotten wind of this tabloid mess. And I certainly didn't think he would've left the incriminating evidence on our marital bed, but then again, what did I expect him to do?

So much for day six of supposed honeymoon bliss.

I'd just finished unpacking when Luc joined me in the bedroom. He sat on the edge of our bed, ran a hand through his messy brown hair, and gazed up at me with a look of complete exasperation.

"Is Adeline okay?" I asked, placing a hand on his shoulder. "I've never seen her like that before." In the short month that I'd known Luc's daughter, she'd never screamed for her mom, and she'd never turned away my comfort.

"She barely slept last night, and her fever was still high this morning, so I took her to the doctor. It's going down now, but she still doesn't feel well, as you can see. There's something else that's upsetting her, though."

"What is it?" I asked.

"Brigitte came over this morning."

My hand dropped from Luc's shoulder as I sat across from him on the bed. "She was here? In our apartment?"

Luc sighed. "Apparently she took the first train down from Paris this morning and decided she would show up on our doorstep unannounced. She claimed to be in town for work, and of course she wanted to see Adeline."

"Is she allowed to do that? She doesn't have visitation rights, does she?"

"Because of her past drug usage, she's not allowed to be alone with Adeline. But, she *can* spend time with her if it's supervised. And if she can prove to the courts that she's clean now, after her apparent month in rehab—which I have yet to receive proof of—it's possible that she could be granted regular visitation rights."

I tried not to sneer. "Do *you* believe she's fit to watch Adeline on her own?"

"Not as long as she has Vincent Boucher in her life. I told her as much this morning."

"I'm sure she loved that."

"Speaking of Vincent . . ." Luc nodded toward the magazine that had been lying between us on the bed, waiting to sabotage our brand-new marriage.

"Looks like you've become more acquainted with both Vincent *and* his sons," Luc stated dryly.

"I suppose Brigitte gave you that little gift this morning?" I guessed. "The photos don't exactly prove her newfound sobriety, do they?"

"No, they don't. But it is not so much Brigitte I am concerned with. It is my wife. What happened last night, Charlotte?"

I gazed down at the magazine and felt like ripping it to shreds, but instead I took a deep breath and looked at my new husband, the man I loved, and proceeded to lay down the law.

"I'm sorry about this, I really am. I clearly have some explaining to do. But so do you, Luc." I reached over and placed my hand in Luc's lap. "I promise I will tell you everything that happened last night, but in return, I need you to be honest with me too. We haven't even been married for a full week, and I find out that your ex-wife is *the* Brigitte Beaumont, that she's still in love with you, and that your father was in prison for embezzlement. It's a lot to take in, especially when it's not coming from your mouth."

"Which one of the Bouchers told you about my father?"

"Well, Vincent started the story at the bar, and Nicolas continued it later that night. Is it true?" I asked.

"Yes, back when I was in high school, my father and Vincent were in business together. My dad was found guilty of embezzlement and went to prison for a year. That is why my parents got divorced, and that's when Vincent moved in on my mother." Luc sounded annoyed, as if he'd repeated these exact words one hundred times before. My only question was: why hadn't he said them to *me*?

"The reason I agreed to talk with Nicolas inside his car yesterday is because he said he had something really important to ask me," I said. "He wanted to know if I could put you in touch with him."

Luc's jaw tightened before he spoke. "The ties between our families are forever broken, and there is nothing left for me to talk about with Nicolas."

"Nicolas said that your dad didn't deserve to go to prison, and that if you'll give him a chance, he can prove your father's innocence."

A long, heavy pause followed. Luc stared out the window for a few moments and finally turned to me. "That is impossible. Nicolas is just trying to find a way to get back into my life. Why? I do not know. But what he says about my father, there is no way it is true."

"What if he's right, though? What if he could prove your father's innocence? It could help your family heal. You could be in touch with your dad again. Maybe your mom would change her mind—"

"You have no idea what you're talking about, Charlotte. You need to stay out of this."

I really didn't want to lose my cool so early in our blissful honeymoon period, but the tone of his last comment sent me over the edge. "You're right, Luc. I have no clue what I'm talking about because you won't tell me anything! I have to learn it from a family of rich and famous sleazebags instead! In fact, Marcel gave me a similar warning this morning. He told me that I needed to stay out of it if I wanted to have any chance of keeping my marriage intact. Could you please tell me what is going on here?"

"The Bouchers are a toxic family, Charlotte. They ruined my family, and I will not let them ruin our marriage. But by the look of those trashy photos, it looks as if they've already infiltrated us. Am I right?"

"Are you asking if I cheated on you last night?"

Luc's silence was my answer.

I thought back through the random, spotty memories I had of the night before, and despite the fact that I couldn't remember certain key moments, like walking into Marcel's apartment, or anything that had happened once we arrived there, I was certain it hadn't been me kissing one of the Boucher brothers on that balcony. It didn't matter how many glasses of champagne I'd had, I would *never* betray Luc. And judging by the scene in Marcel's bed this morning and the underwear in his living room, I knew it had, unfortunately, been Fiona.

"No, Luc, I didn't cheat on you. I only called Nicolas last night because you wouldn't answer any of my questions when I came back up the hotel room. I wanted to find out why you'd never told me about your father going to prison, but instead all I found was my husband hiding in the bathroom taking some sketchy call."

"What are you talking about?"

"Please don't lie about this. I admit I was eavesdropping, but can you blame me after the events of that insane day? I heard you say that I wouldn't know the truth until 'it's finished.' That it would only put me in danger. The truth about *what*, Luc? What needs to be finished? And why on earth would I be in danger?"

Luc didn't deny anything this time. Instead he gazed at me apologetically and slid his hands up to my shoulders.

"I'm so sorry you've been dragged into this mess, Charlotte. That is exactly what I didn't want to happen. I never told you about my father or about Brigitte because I was hoping that my mistakes and those of my family wouldn't touch us. I wanted a fresh start for me, for us. It was wrong of me not to tell you those things, though, and I'm sorry. I understand why you went to Nicolas last night. You just wanted to know the truth, and I wasn't giving it to you."

"Who were you talking to on the phone, Luc?"

Luc hesitated, his eyes once again avoiding my gaze. "Just an old friend. Nothing you need to worry about, *mon amour.* The truth is that there *is* more to this whole Boucher family situation than I've told you, and unfortunately these are things that I am not able to tell you just yet. I know that is going to be hard for you to accept, but I'm asking you right now to trust me. Trust that I love you and that I will protect you, always. You must believe me, Charlotte."

"You're scaring me, Luc. I just want to know what's going on. I mean, how bad could it be that it would put me in danger?"

Luc ran a finger down my cheek and smiled. "It's not that bad. Just some unfinished business that you don't need to be involved in, that's all. Nothing for you to worry about. Now that we are back in Lyon, we can start our lives together. And I want nothing more than to make you the happiest woman on earth. I don't ever want you to regret marrying me. You are the love of my life, Charlotte. Do you believe me?"

"Yes, Luc, of course. I love you too. More than I can even express. Which is why I don't want us to have secrets from each other. That's not how a marriage should be. After all, both of our secrets were what caused so much trouble for us last year. I don't want to repeat the same mistakes."

Luc squeezed my hands, the look in his chestnut eyes sincere and full of love. "We won't, *chérie*. We won't. You just have to trust me, okay?"

I ignored the uneasy feeling in the pit of my stomach and nodded. "Okay, but what about Brigitte? We have to set some ground rules. She can't stop by unannounced and upset Adeline. I'm just beginning to build my relationship with your daughter, and I know Brigitte is her mother, but I don't want to lose the momentum."

"I will handle Brigitte. That is not your job. I didn't think she would return to France permanently, and I certainly didn't think she would try so hard to see Adeline. She was a neglectful mother, and while I hope for our daughter's sake that she can change, I honestly don't think it is possible. Only time will tell, though."

"You can't be so naïve to not see that she's still in love with you, Luc. That's why she's storming back in. She can't stand that you're remarried already. That you've moved on. Women are very jealous creatures—take it from one who knows—and a girl like Brigitte who's always used to getting her way . . . well, let's just say that she won't go down without a fight."

Luc kissed me on the forehead. "You will not be the one doing the fighting, though, *ma belle.* You understand?"

"We're married now, Luc. You don't have to fight these battles on your own. We're a team. I want to be here for you. I want to help." What I didn't say was that I wasn't about to let that raging little actress steal any more time away from my twenty-nine days of honeymoon bliss than she already had, but I figured that was implied.

"*Merci,* Charlotte. You see, *this* is why I married you." Luc leaned in and brushed his lips over mine, instantly making me remember all of the reasons why I married him too.

After his tingle-inducing kiss, he raised a flirtatious eyebrow. "I have something for you. Wait here." He walked over to our closet and pulled out a pretty white bag tied with a pink satin ribbon.

"Hmm, I think I know where *that's* from," I said.

Luc grinned and handed me the bag. "I was going to give you this on our last night in the hotel. Adeline is sound asleep . . . so if we're quiet, maybe we can make up for it tonight?"

"If you're lucky," I said with a smile. "But there are still a few things we need to talk about." It was time for me to come clean about my less-than-desirable employment situation, *and* I needed to ask him why he hadn't told me about paying the guests' hotel tab at our wedding.

Luc sighed, leaning his forehead into mine. "*Chérie,* to be honest, I'm exhausted after staying up most of the night with Adeline, and after all of this ex-wife business, I don't think I can handle one more thing." He pressed his lips to mine once more, his kiss lingering as he ran his hands down to the small of my back. "*Except* seeing you try on your lingerie. That is something I can handle."

"Oh, you can handle that, can you?" I lifted a brow at my adorable husband and couldn't help but laugh. If I was being honest, the *last* thing I felt like doing right now was discussing finances *or* the loss of my job.

"Open it, *chérie*," Luc prodded.

I opened the dainty gift bag from my favorite lingerie store in Lyon, Chez Isabelle. Inside, I found a delicate, silky pink slip that opened down the front. Three lavender bows tied across the opening, and a beautiful pattern of matching lavender lace trimmed the hem. Two sparkling amethyst-colored jewels studded the silky straps.

It was gorgeous, sexy, and exactly my style.

"I love it," I whispered back before giving him another kiss.

He wrapped his arms around my waist and trailed warm kisses up my neck. "Perhaps I can help you try it on?"

I pushed away all of the fears and doubts that had consumed my mind in the past twenty-four hours, and instead allowed my sweet husband to wrap me up in his warm embrace. Despite everything that had just happened, I felt so comfortable in his arms, so safe. If Luc couldn't divulge the details of this bizarre Boucher family business, I simply had to trust that he had his reasons, and that he was capable of handling it on his own. In the meantime, I was looking forward to making up for our missed night of honeymoon bliss.

"I'd *love* some help trying on my new lingerie," I said, squeezing his thigh.

He grinned as he slipped my shirt over my head and ran his strong hands up the length of my torso and over my breasts. He quickly unfastened my bra, stood me up in front of him, and unbuttoned my jeans.

"*Tu es magnifique, ma beauté,*" he whispered, kissing my navel and pulling my jeans down to my ankles.

I ruffled my hands through Luc's hair as he pulled me in closer and slipped his fingers in between my thighs.

"Luc, if you keep this up, I don't think you're going to see the lingerie on me. I won't be able to wait that long."

A sultry laugh escaped his lips as he stripped me completely naked, then slipped the silky nightie over my head, running his strong hands over my hips as he did so.

The smooth material felt cool on my skin in contrast to Luc's roaming hands, lighting a fire in my abdomen. I pulled him closer to me and ripped off his T-shirt. "One night without you was too long. Let's not make that mistake again."

Luc responded with a deep growl as he unbuttoned his jeans and let them drop to the floor. I fell backwards onto our cushy bed and let him have a look at me in my new lingerie. His sexy grin gave way to an even sexier dimple as he swiftly removed his underwear, then climbed over top of me and plunged his warm mouth onto mine.

My hips surged upward, melding with Luc's pulsing, toned body. I suddenly didn't care about anything that had happened over the past day and a half. Luc was my husband. He loved me unconditionally, and I loved him the same. I always would. Nothing would ever change that.

"*Mon amour, j'ai envie de toi*," Luc's husky voice whispered in my ear as he knelt in between my legs and ran his hands up the inside of my thighs, making me squirm in anticipation.

"I want you too, Luc." I grabbed his hips and pulled him back down on top of me. "*Now.*"

"A woman who knows *exactly* what she wants—there is nothing sexier." He hovered over me, his broad shoulders, ruffled brown hair, and lust-filled gaze almost too much for me to bear. "And what will you do if I don't give you what you want?" he teased.

I dug my nails into his back and pulled him closer. "I don't think you want to find out."

Luc laughed as he pulled a thin pink strap off my shoulder and ran his lips across the tops of my breasts. "I'll take my chances." He traced the outline of my nipple with his thumb, while his other hand slipped underneath the lace, his fingers immediately finding the spot that made me go *insane.*

I wouldn't let him get away with this.

Running my hand down his rippled abdomen, I reached lower and still lower until I found the spot that made *him* go crazy. I could hardly contain myself, though, as he slipped his fingers inside of me and pressed so deeply I had to bite my lip to stop from moaning. I matched his intensity with each stroke of my hand and watched as he closed his eyes and succumbed to the pleasure.

Suddenly he grabbed my hips and positioned me perfectly beneath him, then with an intense gaze that said *I love you, I want you,* and so much more, he thrust into me. This time I couldn't help but let out a low moan.

He pressed into me in slow, deep thrusts as he slipped the other strap off of my shoulder and cupped my breast in his hand. He lowered his face to my chest and ran his tongue over the tip of my nipple, the feeling of him inside of me, of his hands and lips on me, sending a ripple of pleasure through my core.

I took his face in my hands and looked him in the eye as he continued to move over top of me. "Luc, you are the only one who's ever made me feel this way."

That sexy grin reappeared, his sweet eyes lighting up as he leaned in to kiss me. He nibbled my bottom lip as he wrapped me tightly in his arms and pushed harder and firmer inside of me. "I want to see you," he said. "I want to see your gorgeous body on top of me."

Luc rolled to the side and hoisted my hips up and onto his, another muffled cry of pleasure escaping my lips as the length of him shot inside me. He pushed into me more forcefully now from below, his hands cupping both of my breasts, his eyes full of an intense desire, a longing, a love I'd never seen before in any other man's eyes. Luc's need to be with me and to love me made me lose all control, made me give myself to him fully and completely.

I rolled my hips back and forth over top of him, running my hands up his glistening torso and resting them on his firm chest.

Luc slid his hands underneath the slip that now bunched at my hips, then pulled me harder and faster onto him, his eyes closing as he bit his lip to hold back a moan. "*Charlotte, tu es trop belle. Tu me rends fou.*"

Nothing made me hotter than when Luc spoke French to me in bed. I leaned over him, kissing him with every ounce of wild passion that poured out of me, reveling in the perfect feel of his body, his love, his strength wrapped around me. He held me firmly against his pulsating body, thrusting into me almost violently as his breath quickened, his kisses, his touch becoming more urgent, more forceful. My core ached with desire until an explosion of pleasure set off inside of me. I muffled my cries into Luc's shoulder, my body resting on top of him as he continued to thrust faster and harder into me. Finally, I felt him grow firmer, his hands gripping my hips as he pushed one more time, going so deep I could hardly breathe.

Our bodies collapsed against each other, warm, sweaty, and totally and utterly in love. No one had ever made love to me the way Luc did. Every single time we romped under the sheets was different, incredible, mind-blowing, and *full* of surprises.

TWELVE

Hours later, a tiny knock on the bedroom door woke me from my sleep.

"Papa," Adeline's soft voice called through the night.

I shot out of bed, thankful that I'd put on a T-shirt and yoga pants before falling asleep. This whole living with a child situation was new to me—mostly in a good way, but new nonetheless.

"Are you okay, Adeline?" I whispered to her in French, noticing Luc snoring soundly on his side of the bed. I'd never heard him snore before; hopefully that wouldn't be one of our new *norms* in this whole marriage deal.

I refocused on Adeline's distraught face, the dim light from the streetlamp outside revealing a large tear running down her cheek.

"I don't feel good," she responded in French, clutching her fuzzy white teddy bear. "I want my daddy."

I knelt down, took her hand, and led her out into the hallway, closing the door behind me. "Your daddy is really tired, sweetie. He needs to get some sleep. How about I take you back to your room and read to you until you fall back asleep. Will that be okay?"

She stomped her little feet, her purple nightgown swaying back and forth. "*Non!* I want my daddy!" And then the tears came. Big, round, wet tears, streaming down her face.

I scooped Adeline up into my arms and carried her back into her bedroom. I didn't mind that she was kicking me the whole way. I wanted to try to make this right. Now that I was here to stay, it couldn't always be her daddy comforting her. I wanted her to learn to love me too.

I laid her down in her pink bed, flicked on the lamp, and sat down beside her, testing the back of my hand on her forehead to see if she was still running a fever. She didn't feel *that* warm, but then again I'd never done this before, so I really didn't have a clue.

She pushed my hand away and glared up at me, her almond-shaped emerald eyes tired, red, and sad. I'd always wondered where she'd gotten those beautiful green eyes; now, after meeting Brigitte, I knew. Adeline's smile, her nose, her normally sweet demeanor, all resembled Luc. But those eyes—*those* belonged to Brigitte.

I wondered if I would ever look at Adeline again and *not* see her mother looking back at me.

"I don't want you here," she said in French, turning her back to me and curling into a tight ball underneath her pink, fluffy comforter. "I want my mommy to come back. I want her to live here with me and daddy. *Not* you."

Maybe I should've woken Luc up after all. How do you even begin to explain divorce to a four-year-old?

I resisted my urge to rub her back and kiss her on the cheek, knowing she would just shrug me off and get even angrier. Instead I searched the room for something to help me with a three A.M. explanation of divorce and step-mothers to a sick, tantrum-throwing four-year-old.

Never in my wildest dreams would I have imagined that twenty-four hours after sleeping off a champagne hangover in Marcel Boucher's bachelor pad, I would be so happy to find a family of four stuffed penguins.

What has my life come to?

I grabbed the penguins from Adeline's overflowing stuffed animal bin and walked to the other side of the bed where she was facing the wall, her eyes purposefully squeezed shut.

"I know you don't feel like talking to me right now, so we're going to talk to your penguin family instead." I propped all four of the penguins up on the side of her bed. She kicked her little feet under the covers and kept her eyes closed.

"This is Daddy Penguin," I began. "And this is Mommy Penguin. One day Mommy Penguin and Daddy Penguin had a little baby penguin, and they named her Adeline."

I wanted to say, *Adeline is a stubborn little penguin who needs to open her eyes and pay attention because Charlotte Penguin is exhausted and doesn't feel like putting on a penguin puppet divorce show at three o'clock in the morning*, but I felt that a sarcastic penguin show wouldn't help matters.

Instead, I continued. "Mommy Penguin and Daddy Penguin love their little Adeline Penguin more than anything in the whole world."

Unfortunately, after meeting Mommy Penguin the day before, I could see that she *clearly* had her priorities, and her daughter wasn't one of them. Brigitte's little visit here this morning didn't fool me one bit. She was jealous that Luc was already remarried, and she wanted to get her little paws in here and screw things up for us. Again, I chose to bite my tongue and, instead, plodded onward.

"One day, Mommy and Daddy Penguin decided that they needed to spend time with other penguins so they could be truly happy. But that doesn't change how much they adore their sweet Adeline Penguin."

Adeline's eyes were open now. "But *why* do they have to spend time with other penguins? Amélie's mommy and daddy don't spend time with other penguins."

Amélie was Adeline's best friend. Of course Amélie's mommy and daddy didn't need to spend time with other penguins because her mommy wasn't a drunken, jealous, raging little actress who dated men twice her age and crashed her ex-husband's honeymoon.

I only hoped Brigitte would get her act together at least a little bit by the time Adeline was old enough to understand everything. Otherwise Adeline would surely see her mother acting out in the tabloids, and one day in the not-so-distant future, she would realize my penguin rendition of the way her family had broken up was not at all the truth.

"Every penguin family is different," I said. "And what works for one penguin family doesn't always work for another family. Having more penguins in the family can be more fun! I mean, don't you want to play with more penguins too?" God, I was really reaching here.

Adeline sat up, her little eyebrows scrunched in confusion, her long auburn hair sticking to her cheeks. "I guess so," she said hesitantly.

Whew.

"Me too! So when Mommy and Daddy Penguin decided they'd love to invite some more penguins into their life so that Adeline Penguin could have a bigger, better penguin family, that's when Daddy met Charlotte Penguin." I introduced the fourth and final penguin to the scenario, as Mommy Penguin took a nose-dive to the floor. Oops.

"Daddy Penguin fell in love with Charlotte Penguin, and as soon as Charlotte Penguin met Adeline Penguin, she fell in love with her too!"

"But Mommy still loves Daddy," Adeline insisted. "She told me that today. And *she* wants to live here. Can she move in too, so all four of us can live together?"

Hmm, seems I was getting more intel on what had gone down during the ex-wife's house call this morning from the four-year-old daughter than I was from my own adult husband. And what was wrong with Brigitte that she would *tell* her young daughter these things? No wonder Adeline had been a mess all night.

I brushed a strand of hair out of her eyes and put Charlotte Penguin in her lap.

"I'm sorry your mom told you those things and confused you today, sweetie. The truth is that while she loves you very much, and while your mom and dad will always care for each other, your mom has a very busy career as an actress, and she can't move in with us."

Adeline's face darkened, making me worry that I was doing this all wrong. Should I have left the parenting to Luc? Especially in these early weeks of our marriage?

Her thick lashes lowered as she gazed down at Charlotte Penguin in her lap.

"You see, I'm a really nice penguin too, and I love you and your dad *so* much," I said softly. "I promise that the three of us are going to have so much fun together. You just have to trust me. It's going to be wonderful."

She lifted those huge emerald eyes to mine, and just when I thought she was going to burst into tears or throw Charlotte Penguin in my face, she opened her little arms and wrapped them around me.

I don't think I'd ever felt my heart swell as big as it did in that moment.

Holding Adeline tightly against my chest, I kissed her on the forehead and made a silent promise to never abandon her, no matter how difficult this whole blended family business could be. She was only a little girl, and she deserved to be loved.

I knew what it felt like to believe like your mother didn't love you as much anymore, that she had other priorities, and that *you* weren't one of them. It was a hurt so deep, I couldn't bear to think about it. And *I* was twenty-six.

I could only imagine what it felt like to a four-year-old girl.

I knew I couldn't replace her mom. But as I rocked Adeline in my arms until she fell asleep, watching her tiny chest rise and fall with each breath, I recognized that deep down in my heart, I wanted to try.

After putting Adeline back to bed, I remembered the message I'd sent to my contact in New York earlier. Stifling a yawn, I padded out to the living room and opened up my laptop to sign into my e-mail. But to my disappointment, my in-box was empty. Which meant that when I awoke in only a few hours, the first things on my agenda were finding a job and coming clean with Luc.

Just as I was about to head back to bed, the Paris journal sticking out of my purse caught my eye. I definitely had a few new ideas to add to *The Girl's Guide to Tying the French Knot,* and I'd had so much fun writing the day before, I figured why not add to it? I grabbed a pen and got to work, making sure to add a note on how effective a penguin puppet divorce show can be when dealing with young step-children.

Come tomorrow morning, I'd have to find a real job, of course, but as the words flowed effortlessly from my pen, I couldn't ignore the little voice inside my head telling me that maybe, someday, this *would* be my real job.

THIRTEEN

Giggles filled my ears as a violent bouncing rocked my body and something hit my head.

"Charlotte, wake up! Tell me another penguin story, Charlotte. Tell me, tell me!"

Still clad in her purple nightgown, bed head and all, Adeline bounced up and down at the foot of the bed, then threw another penguin at my face.

"Charlotte, *wake up!*" she cried in French.

Oh, dear God. Where was Luc?

The loud squeaking sound coming from the ancient shower head in our minuscule bathroom told me he'd avoided the penguin massacre by hopping in the shower. I forced myself up and scooped Adeline into my arms.

"Looks like *someone* is feeling better today, hmm?" I said as I tickled her sides and gave her a kiss on the forehead.

"Tell me another penguin story. *Now,*" she ordered, her pretty green eyes turning all serious.

"Your dad has to get ready for work, and you have to go to school, so we'll do more penguin stories tonight after dinner, okay?"

Adeline lurched from my grasp and stomped her tiny feet on the bed. "*I. Want. It. Now!*" she screamed, hurling another penguin at me.

Too tired to deal with my penguin-wielding step-daughter, I grabbed my cell phone off the nightstand and shuffled into the kitchen. After only a few hours of sleep, a strong cup of French *café* was certainly in order.

Just as I got the espresso machine brewing, Adeline appeared in the kitchen, all four penguins in tow. She batted her thick lashes at me.

"*S'il te plaît, Charlotte,*" she begged in her sweetest, most adorable begging voice.

Wow, this girl had learned a thing or two about manipulation. I could only guess *who* she'd picked up these skills from.

"Adeline, I told you already. We'll have time for stories tonight. Right now we need to eat breakfast."

Tears pooled at the corners of her eyes, and she lifted her foot to begin her stomping tantrum.

"Wait!" I called out, remembering that I could play this manipulation game too. "Penguins like Nutella crêpes, don't they?"

Joy immediately replaced the tears as she jumped up and down, her auburn hair flying all over the place. "Penguins *love* Nutella crêpes!" she cried out.

Whew.

As Adeline seated all four penguins at the kitchen table alongside her, I poured my first steaming cup of espresso for the day (there would certainly be at least three more), then got cracking on my crêpe promise. In between batter pours, I checked my phone and found that a slew of text messages had come in from the girls between last night and this morning.

As to be expected, the news wasn't good.

Lexi: Hey ladies, has your boyfriend/husband seen our incriminating photos yet? Dylan isn't speaking to me. He's certain it was me on that balcony. I am certain that it wasn't. Which one of you was smooching Marcel last night?

Me: Lexi, how do you know it was Marcel on the balcony? The picture is too dark to tell.

Lexi: I have super X-ray vision. Kidding. I just know. So come on, fess up. Who kissed sex-on-a-stick Marcel Boucher?

Fiona: I don't remember anything after we arrived at Marcel's flat. By some stroke of magic, Marc hasn't seen or heard about the tabloids yet. Please, God, let him stay hidden under a rock until those sodding tabloids find their next victims.

Me: Don't you think it's strange that we don't remember anything? Could we have been drugged?

Lexi: Char, it's called memory loss induced by TEN glasses of champagne. You girls had at least that much. I still refuse to believe that whoever kissed Marcel wouldn't remember, though. Char, are you divorced yet?

I added another crêpe to the stack and quickly texted the girls back.

Me: Still married as of this morning. Was up until 4 a.m. performing a penguin puppet divorce show. Don't ask. I don't remember anything either. So sorry I got you all into this mess.

Two minutes later, my phone buzzed again.

Lexi: Don't apologize. I haven't had that much fun in ages. Dylan and I are always fighting these days, and I needed to blow off some steam. Sucks we got caught, but at least we're famous now. Still desperately want to know who was on that balcony . . .

Fiona: Screw famous. Marc's evil mother Madame Rousseau just arrived for her twelve day visit and shoved a copy of that heinous tabloid in Marc's face. Life = officially over.

Oh, God. What a disaster. After my horrific run-ins with Madame Rousseau the year before, the thought of having her in my home for twelve days and, worse, having her as a potential future mother-in-law made me nauseated. Not to mention the fact that she would make Fiona's life pure hell now that those photos had been released. Poor Fiona.

I gave Adeline and her penguins a Nutella crêpe, then hightailed it back to the bedroom to have one more look at that tabloid. How did Lexi know for sure that it was Marcel on the balcony? As far as I knew, I was the only one who was aware of Fiona's late-night tryst with Marcel, so how could Lexi be positive it hadn't been Nicolas?

I found the magazine lying on the floor next to our dresser and flipped to the incriminating balcony photo.

I held it under the light, but it was still too fuzzy to make out. It appeared as though the guy had dark hair, which meant nothing because both Marcel and Nicolas had dark (fabulous) hair. The photo was mainly of the guy's back, so you couldn't see more than a dark, blurry silhouette of the girl.

Which meant that hopefully Fiona would be in the clear.

"Do you know who's in that photo, Charlotte?" Luc's voice startled me so much I dropped the magazine to the floor.

I turned to find him wrapped in a towel, his light brown hair a messy, wet mop on his head. He looked exactly like he had the first day I met him, towel and all. And in that moment, as I considered betraying my friendship with Fiona to tell him the truth, I wished I could zap myself back in time to that very first day and do a few things very differently—one of those things being the last forty-eight hours.

But since time travel and memory erasing weren't an option, I opted for the truth.

"It was Fiona and Marcel."

"Fiona?" he asked incredulously. "Are you certain?"

I nodded, immediately feeling horrible for telling Luc, even though he *was* my husband. "I'm sure. Please, Luc. You can never say anything. She had too much to drink, and she loves Marc. It was a mistake."

Luc shrugged his shoulders as he plucked the magazine off the floor. He stared at the picture once more, then tossed the sickening tabloid into the trash.

"I would've thought for sure it was Lexi," Luc said. "And how are you so sure it wasn't Nicolas? It's impossible to see."

"Just trust me, Luc. It wasn't Nicolas."

"Why? Were you with him?"

"What? No, of course not!"

"How do you know? If you drank so much that you don't remember, how do you know what you did or didn't do that night, Charlotte?"

I'd thought after our talk the night before and the incredible lingerie and love-making session we'd had, that Luc believed me. That we were finished with this tabloid argument.

"You're right, Luc. I drank too much, and I don't remember everything. I was really stressed out after what had happened with us, and after everything I found out about you, but still, there's no excuse. I'm sorry for landing our lives in the papers, and for the fact that I don't remember everything. But I would *never* have cheated on you, Luc. We're married now, and I'm madly in love with you. Please, don't ever doubt that."

Luc ran his hand through his wet hair and walked up to me. "I'm sorry, Charlotte. I know you. I'm just upset that the Bouchers have infiltrated my life again—*our* lives. I will handle all of this, though. You can trust me, okay?"

I nodded, that uneasy feeling once again biting at the pit of my stomach. "Luc, can you tell me what it is you're hiding from me? It will be so much easier if I know the truth."

Luc walked to the window and gazed out, his silence answering my question.

Finally, he spoke. "There are some things you can't know right now, Charlotte. You need to leave it alone." The edge in his tone made me flinch. What in the hell was going on?

Just as I was about to break the news about my canceled classes, Adeline zoomed into our bedroom, a walking advertisement for Nutella. Her entire face was smeared with the sticky chocolate spread, and the two penguins she was holding had chocolate-covered mouths as well.

Luc raised an eyebrow at me, then knelt down beside her. "Chocolate for breakfast?"

"Like father, like daughter," I said, taking Adeline's hand. "Come on, Adeline, let's get you cleaned up."

Luc laid a hand on my arm. "I'm sorry, Charlotte. I didn't mean to get angry."

"It's okay," I said. But nowhere inside of me did it really feel okay.

"Do you need a ride to the language school?" he asked.

"There's something I need to tell you about the language school, actually," I said.

"Come on, Charlotte," Adeline whined, tugging on my arm.

After our tabloid argument and Luc's purposeful omission of the truth, it probably wasn't the best time to go into the story about my recent job loss. Especially on the first day of his new university teaching position.

"I'm running a little late," Luc said. "Can we talk tonight?"

"Of course," I said, relieved. "I hope classes go well for you today. Are you nervous?"

Luc smiled his sweet, charming smile, dimple and all. "Finance 101 with a bunch of eighteen-year-olds—should be a slice of cake."

"You mean a *piece* of cake?"

"I never said I was teaching English." He laughed before heading back into the bedroom to change.

While Adeline pulled me into the bathroom, visions of a daylong nap danced through my head. But first, I had to get a job.

FOURTEEN

After Luc left to take Adeline to the *crèche*—France's version of day-care or preschool—and begin his first day teaching at the university, I took the Metro to my adorable studio apartment by the Perrache train station.

I'd only had my apartment for a little over four months and hadn't yet tackled trying to get out of my one-year lease since Luc and I had decided to get married so quickly.

And, if I was being honest, I loved the idea of keeping my own space for just a little while longer. Luc's tiny two-bedroom apartment in Vieux Lyon was charming, but with two adults and an extremely hyper four-year-old, it was beyond cramped. How would I squeeze all of my clothes into that minuscule closet of his?

More important, how would I continue paying the rent on my apartment if I didn't have a job?

Opening my laptop, I signed into my e-mail and proceeded to refresh it obsessively over the next two hours, hoping for a message from the New York contact I'd emailed the day before: Beth Harding, an editor at *Bella Magazine.* I'd written two articles for her in the past year, and I was praying she'd be able to offer me something more substantial than the occasional article.

I interspersed my ten thousand refreshes with a job search for language teaching positions in Lyon. But, as my e-mail remained empty of new messages and my job search turned up a big, fat nothing, I resorted to a Google search on Brigitte Beaumont and the Boucher family.

Loads of photos and article links filled the page. As I scrolled through them, I discovered what I already knew I would find: more tasteless coverage on my night with the Boucher brothers, on Brigitte and Luc's supposed "reunion," and Brigitte and Vincent's relationship turmoil.

As I clicked on one of the articles, a photo I did *not* expect to find made me understand why the papers thought Luc and Brigitte were back together.

If I'd taken this photo, I would've made the same statement.

Luc and Brigitte were sitting outside, having a drink at La Cave des Voyageurs, a wine bar just down the street from our apartment in Vieux Lyon. I immediately recognized the location because that bar had been one of Luc's favorite places to take me since we'd gotten back together.

Yesterday, Luc had told me that Brigitte had taken the train down to Lyon just that morning to see Adeline. This picture had clearly been taken at night, though. Had Luc lied to me? Could Brigitte have left the film premiere party early on Saturday evening, ditched Vincent, and taken the train down to Lyon late that night to see Luc?

In the photo, Brigitte had her impossibly thin legs crossed toward Luc, one spiky heel resting against his leg, and her dainty hand touching his arm.

Nothing about Brigitte's demeanor surprised me in the least. It was the same slutty, evil, overly forward performance I'd witnessed when we'd met.

It was the look on Luc's face that made a giant knot form in my stomach.

He was smiling. Smiling his sweet, loving smile. Dimple and all. Right at Brigitte.

On the last night of *our* honeymoon.

Where was the feverish, sick Adeline while her two divorced parents were out enjoying a lovely evening with wine, flirtation, and laughs?

I pulled out my cell phone and realized I'd put it on silent. There were two missed calls from Luc already.

He'd probably seen the photo and was calling to explain.

I threw the phone back into my purse and decided to let him sweat this one out a little bit. Besides, I was too upset to have a coherent discussion.

I slammed my laptop shut, stormed out of my apartment, and went to the only place that would calm me down at a time like this.

Endless racks of lacy French lingerie welcomed me as I walked into Chez Isabelle.

As I'd learned from the past year living in France, the French were masters of cuisine, *café*, *pâtisseries*, art, charm, romance . . . and as I'd more recently discovered, they were also incredibly skilled at making the most beautiful pieces of lingerie I'd ever laid eyes upon.

"*Bonjour, Charlotte,*" a female voice called out to me as I lost myself in the never-ending rows of silky satin and lace.

It was Isabelle—the owner of this heavenly store. With her wavy, sandy-blond locks that stretched all the way down her back, her vivacious curves—which she *never* hid—and her sparkling sapphire eyes, she was even more gorgeous than the lingerie she sold.

And while I wasn't here to add to my own collection—especially not after my recent loss of income—the sight of a grinning Isabelle surrounded by beautifully cut nighties and bras somehow gave me a small amount of comfort.

It was the little things in life.

"*Bonjour, Isabelle,*" I said with a smile.

We were on a first-name basis because of the excessive amount of times I'd visited the store since Luc and I had gotten back together over a month ago. And after a few lengthy dressing room chats, Isabelle and I had discovered we had much more in common than our shared affinity for lingerie. For starters, we'd both been cheated on more times than we could count *and* both of our parents had recently divorced.

"You'll never guess who called me today," she said with a click of her tongue. Isabelle's father was British, so she spoke perfect English in addition to her elegant French.

"Oh, I bet I can," I said. "Your slimy, cheating ex?"

She lifted a brow. "How'd you know?"

"Cheaters—they're all the same," I said with a wave of my hand. "He wants you back?"

She nodded, placing a hand on her hip. "*Begged* me. It was the most pathetic speech I've ever heard . . . and I've heard *a lot* of them."

"I hope you didn't give him the time of day."

"Oh, don't worry. I shut him up real fast when I told him that the sex with my new man is the best I've ever had."

"Are you sure we weren't sisters separated at birth?" I said. "I did the exact same thing last year to my cheating ex."

"Feels extraordinary, doesn't it?" Isabelle said with a mischievous twinkle in her eye.

I grinned as I lifted a transparent black slip from the rack. "It does. Sometimes a little revenge is necessary."

"Taking your lunch break to shop?" she asked.

I glanced at the price tag and sighed. "It's more of a *permanent* lunch break, if you know what I mean."

"Did something happen with your teaching job?" Isabelle asked, concern sweeping through those big blue eyes.

I filled her in on my jobless status while I proceeded to pile her latest collections over my arm. "I shouldn't be shopping at a time like this, but it's not for me. I need to buy a few pieces for my girlfriends. I got them into a bit of a mess this week, and I have to do something to make it up to them. Although, if their boyfriends break up with them, I don't know how much they'll be needing new lingerie."

Isabelle added a saucy violet bra to my rapidly growing pile. "A girl *always* needs new lingerie, regardless of her relationship status."

"I knew you'd understand."

"Sounds like you've had a rough few days, my dear. How about forgetting your troubles and playing lingerie model for an hour or two? Most of these pieces just arrived yesterday, so I haven't had the chance to see them on anyone yet. . . . " Isabelle paused while her gaze combed the length of my body. "And you're just the woman to do it."

I opened my mouth to protest, but Isabelle grabbed my shoulders, turned me around, and prodded me toward the dressing room.

"I'm not taking no for an answer, Charlotte. I saw the papers yesterday. You are clearly in need of some lingerie therapy. And while you're trying these on, I want to hear *everything.*"

Fifteen pieces of lingerie and an hour of venting later, Isabelle's normally twinkling eyes had taken on a curious expression, and she'd gone silent.

Finally, after a few moments, she spoke. "That's quite the story," she said softly before turning toward the front of the store. "Would you excuse me? I need to go make a call."

A whiff of Isabelle's flowery perfume lingered in the chic dressing room as I thought about the bizarre look on her face. I hadn't known her *that* long . . . maybe I'd shared too much. Perhaps Isabelle wasn't feeling too sympathetic to my outrageous story, considering my voluntary involvement with the Boucher brothers. I slipped off the bra and changed back into my clothes. Even though we'd already confided quite a bit in one another, perhaps airing my dirty laundry hadn't been the best plan. Plus, she was working—something I needed to be doing.

I plucked up the two pieces I'd chosen for Fiona and Lexi, then headed to the counter, but Isabelle was nowhere to be found. A door at the back of the store was cracked open, and Isabelle's tense voice filtered out. I couldn't make out what she was saying, and not wanting to be nosy, I pulled out my own phone and checked once more to see if I'd received any e-mails from *Bella Magazine.* I really needed a shot at that job.

But instead, I found a text in French from Nicolas.

Saw the papers yesterday. We need to talk. Please call when you can.

Sighing, I deleted the text. I genuinely liked Nicolas, and from the little I'd spoken with him, I could tell he was different from his shady, fame-hungry brother and father. He seemed sincere, and I wished Luc would just talk with him to set things straight and find out what Nicolas had to say about Luc's father. But after Marcel *and* Luc's warning to stay out of their family feud, I knew the last thing I should do was return Nicolas' call.

On the other hand, maybe he could shed some light on what exactly had happened during our night of champagne-induced debauchery at his brother's house.

Isabelle's sharp tone was still traveling from the back room, so I figured now was as good a time as any to get the scoop from my new famous actor friend.

Nicolas picked up on the first ring. "Charlotte?"

This time was much easier knowing Nicolas was on the phone, and I wouldn't have to see him in all his gorgeousness and be reminded of that brazen piano sex scene.

"Hi, Nicolas. I just got your text. What's up?" I asked in French.

"I understand I am probably the last person you want to speak to after the photos that have been released, but I'll be in Lyon next week, and I was wondering if we could meet."

Anxiety knotted up my stomach. Things with Luc were already bad enough. Meeting with Nicolas would only exasperate an already dramatic start to our marriage.

"Is it something we can just talk about over the phone?" I asked.

"No, I have something I need to give you. In person. It's important, Charlotte. I wouldn't have gotten in touch otherwise."

"Okay, but we need to meet somewhere the paparazzi won't follow you. Having my life mocked by the tabloids isn't really helping out my blissful honeymoon period."

He laughed. "Of course. I'll be at the bar at La Cour des Loges Hôtel in Vieux Lyon next Friday at seven P.M. I'll be sitting in the back, having a drink by myself. I know the owners, so they'll make sure no one bothers us."

"Are you sure?"

"Yes, you can trust me."

I wondered how many times Luc had said those words in the past twenty-four hours. I only hoped Nicolas would follow through with his promise.

"Okay, I'll see you there," I said.

"*Merci,* Charlotte. *À demain.*"

"See you tomorrow, Nicolas."

As I hung up, I was startled to find Isabelle standing at the counter, that mischievous gleam back in her eye.

"Hot date with one of the sexy Boucher brothers?" she asked with a raise of her brow.

"Oh, no. Just some unfinished business from this weekend apparently. I'm not really sure what in the hell is going on to be honest."

"Welcome to the party," she said with a laugh. "Sorry about running off like that earlier." Isabelle threw a lock of her shiny blond hair over her shoulder. How did she get her hair to look that perfect every day? Maybe she had a professional stylist hiding in that back room too.

"No worries," I told her with a smile. "Sorry for venting so much. I didn't mean to take up your time. I'm sure you have work to do."

Isabelle waved my apology away with her hand and laughed. "Absolutely not! I wanted to hear all of the juicy details. I just remembered that my daughter's ride from school had canceled this morning, and I had to call to rearrange. That's all."

"You never mentioned you had a daughter," I said as Isabelle began ringing up the lingerie.

"I have three of them," she said with a bitter laugh. "Keeps life interesting, especially since their father has nothing to do with us."

"I'm so sorry."

"Oh, don't be. Like I told you, I do have a special man in my life at the moment, and things are getting quite serious."

"That's wonderful. But still, my ridiculous tabloid problems must seem so trivial to you."

Isabelle wrapped Fiona's night-blue slip in her signature pink tissue paper. "Not at all. With the loss of your job, a husband who's keeping secrets, and a crazy ex-wife in the mix, your problems sound anything but trivial." She tied a thick pink ribbon around Fiona's gift package, then lifted her gaze to mine. "I want you to know you can always talk to me about anything, Charlotte. It's been difficult keeping friends with everything I have to do for my daughters, but I really like talking with you."

"Thanks, Isabelle. That means a lot."

She smiled sweetly as she handed me the gift bags. "And to be honest, I've never met anyone who's as in love with lingerie as I am. I think it was fate that brought you to me."

I laughed. "Actually, it was Luc. Right after we got back together, he bought me a gorgeous piece from your shop, and I've been hooked ever since."

"Well, go home and give that husband of yours a big kiss from me. And make up with him already. You two are newlyweds. You have the rest of your lives to fight."

I wanted nothing more than to make things right with Luc, but the question still remained: how far would Brigitte go to worm her way back into his life? And how far would *he* go to protect our marriage?

FIFTEEN

After spending the afternoon back at my apartment sending out résumés, I decided to walk back to Vieux Lyon to give myself a little more time to think. Two little white lingerie bags dangled from my arms—one for each of my girlfriends. Hopefully these sexy pieces would bring a little bit of spice back to their bedrooms after the mess we'd made in Paris.

I headed down rue Victor Hugo, a bustling pedestrian walkway that cut right through the heart of Lyon. A young French couple strolled along in front of me, stopping to kiss nearly every ten feet, then whispering sweet French nothings into each other's ears. The French were never short on romance, but were they *so* romantic that they were incapable of being faithful? A quick glance at the newsstand to my right reminded me that I had a very important question to ask Luc tonight regarding *his* faithfulness.

I jetted past the kissing couple *and* the tabloid shots of my husband and Brigitte Beaumont, made my way through the crowds of French teenagers who'd just gotten out of school, and walked into Bellecour—the giant, red sandy courtyard situated in the center of the city. Storm clouds hovered over the majestic, white Fourvière Basilica, towering over Lyon from its spot high up on the hilltop. Minutes later, a chilly fall breeze whipped past me as I strolled across the sparkling Saône River, which led me to the charming cobblestoned streets of Vieux Lyon.

I was expecting to find Luc waiting at home with an explanation the minute I walked in the door to our minuscule French apartment.

But instead of an apologetic husband, I found Luc's mother, Michèle, playing penguins with Adeline on our living room floor.

So much for day seven of pure honeymoon bliss.

"*Bonsoir, Michèle.*" I walked over to give my mother-in-law the customary *bisous* on each cheek.

She stood without smiling, without saying a word, then gave me the iciest set of kisses I'd ever received.

Adeline proceeded to pummel me with penguins as Michèle eyed my lingerie gift bags. "Busy day at work, I see?" my chic mother-in-law said in French.

"Oh, these are just gifts for a few friends." I didn't think it would be a good idea to tell Luc's mother that her new daughter-in-law had just lost her teaching position. We could save that fun conversation for another day.

She arched a brow at me, the gaze shooting from her dark brown eyes bleeding disapproval. "You Americans certainly are interesting."

"Grandma has been playing penguins with me all afternoon!" Adeline jumped up and down in pure excitement, her pretty auburn hair bobbing over her tiny shoulders.

I placed the bags in the hall closet, then leaned down to give Adeline a hug and a kiss. "That's wonderful, sweetie!"

Adeline trotted off with her penguins while Michèle placed a hand on her hip and continued eyeing me as if I was an alien who'd stormed into her son's life without warning. To give her some credit, we *had* only just met the night of the rehearsal dinner, and she'd seemed more than blindsided by the swiftness with which Luc and I had tied the knot.

In my experience with French women, it took some time to get them to warm up to you, to trust you. They weren't as bubbly and fake as American women could sometimes be, but once you'd earned their trust, you were in their good graces forever. As I'd learned from the women in my former host family, underneath that chic, mysterious façade, French women could be some of the warmest, most genuine friends you could ever make.

Judging by the glacial stare Michèle was giving me, I realized it might take quite a while before I unearthed *her* warm side—if she even had a warm side.

"Where's Luc?" I asked. "He should be home by now from his first day at the university."

"He was offered an extra course at the last minute, so he'll be teaching nights now too," she responded coolly. "When he couldn't reach *you*, he called me to pick Adeline up from the *crèche*. In fact I'm glad it worked out this way because there's something I need to say to you."

Michèle peered down the hallway to make sure Adeline was playing in her room, then took a step closer to me, her small frame and rigid facial features exuding a fierceness I'd not yet seen in her.

"My daughter Sandrine brought to my attention the recent mess you've made in the tabloids. Luc made a huge mistake marrying that slutty actress Brigitte. All she cares about is fame, money, and sex. Luc has spent the past year working to get Adeline back and build a stable environment for her. The last thing he needs is another flaky, irresponsible wife screwing up the life he's created for his daughter."

"Madame Olivier, I'm nothing like Brigitte. I'm in love with your son, and I love Adeline too. What happened this week . . . if you'll just let me explain—"

"I don't care what happened this week. Your behavior is inexcusable. If you want to be a part of *this* family, you will stay away from the Boucher family, and you will do everything in your power to keep Brigitte away from my granddaughter *and* from my son. Luc has a soft heart, and if he thinks Brigitte is sober again, he will let her back into Adeline's life—and back into his. That woman will ruin your marriage, and she will ruin your life."

"Luc won't let that happen. He doesn't love her anymore."

Michèle narrowed her eyes at me and let out a sinister laugh. "I love my son, Charlotte, don't get me wrong. But you mustn't be oblivious to the fact that while French men are charming, being faithful is *not* their best quality." She swiveled on the heels of her tall brown boots and headed toward Adeline's room. Just as she reached the door, she peered back over her shoulder. "Trust me, I know."

Adeline had already been in bed for a few hours when Luc's key turned in the door that night. I was curled up on the couch, watching France's version of *Entertainment Tonight* paint a tumultuous history of Brigitte Beaumont's stormy relationships—including her dramatic divorce with Luc—and her struggle with drug and alcohol addiction. They concluded the story by posing the question: *Will Brigitte reunite with her ex, Luc Olivier?*

Luc's eyes narrowed as he grabbed the remote and switched off the television.

"What do you think? Will Brigitte win back the love of her ex?" I asked, unable to mask the weariness in my voice.

Luc shook his head at me as he shrugged his bag off his shoulder and walked across the tiny living room. "Why are you watching these horrible shows, Charlotte? They're only going to upset you." Placing his bag inside the hall closet, he peered around, then raised a brow at me.

"You went lingerie shopping today? At Chez Isabelle?"

"Don't get too excited. It wasn't for me; I bought a few gifts for the girls."

Luc closed the closet door, then sat down on the couch next to me. "I want you to know that *I* will always buy your lingerie for you. That is my job, as your husband. You never need to buy it for yourself, okay?" While his offer was sweet, his voice was a little too forceful.

I raised a curious brow at him. "That's nice, honey. But sometimes I like to shop for myself too."

Luc nodded. "Of course, *mon cœur*. It's just that . . ."

"What is it?"

He shook his head and smiled. "Nothing. It is nothing, *ma belle*. Now tell me what is upsetting you."

I hugged my knees to my chest, overwhelmed with feelings I did *not* want to have so early on in our marriage—or ever, for that matter. What if Luc wasn't the honest, trustworthy man I thought he was? I didn't want to call attention to what I'd seen today, but there was no skirting around the issue of the suggestive photograph of Brigitte and *my* husband splashed all over the tabloids.

"I saw the photo, Luc. The one of you and Brigitte at La Cave des Voyageurs. Why didn't you tell me about Brigitte coming down to Lyon the last night of our honeymoon?"

"Because she didn't," he said firmly. "Brigitte stopped by the next morning, like I told you."

I grabbed my laptop off the coffee table and pulled up the photo. "So how do you explain this?"

Luc examined the picture, his eyes fatigued. Too bad if he was tired. Maybe he shouldn't have lied to his new bride about where he'd been that night, when he should've been with me.

"I haven't been to La Cave des Voyageurs with Brigitte since we were married," Luc said. "This must be an old photo that they used again, just to create drama."

I crossed my arms and raised a questioning brow at my husband.

Luc sighed. "I'm telling the truth. Adeline was sick, and I was home taking care of her that night, just as I told you." Luc pointed at the photo. "Look at that awful, tight black T-shirt I'm wearing in the photo. Brigitte always wanted me to wear those kinds of clothes. I would never wear that now. And Brigitte isn't wearing that black dress you both had. She's in a skirt."

I leaned in to get a better look at the incriminating picture. Luc was right. He wouldn't be caught dead in a shirt that tight.

But even more so, he wouldn't have taken Brigitte out for a drink, and he wouldn't have lied to me about spending time with her. I felt ridiculous for even questioning him.

"Ugh. I'm sorry, Luc. I just saw the photo and freaked out," I said quietly. "When was this even taken?"

"This must've been taken back when we were married, when we'd come down to Lyon to visit my mom and sister."

"Why would they print it now?" I asked.

"Charlotte, these paparazzi are vultures. They don't care about our lives. They don't care that we're real people, trying to have a healthy, happy marriage. The more drama they can fabricate, the more material they'll have for the future. It's sick." Luc closed the web browser and laid a hand on my knee. "The only way we're going to get through this rough patch is if we trust each other. I would never go out with Brigitte alone without telling you. I don't love her anymore. No matter what these papers and TV shows are making you believe, I don't love her. I love you."

I thought about what Luc's mother had said to me earlier—about the Frenchman's inability to be faithful. I had a nasty history with cheaters. In fact, *every single man* I'd dated before Luc had cheated on me. But he was different from all the rest. I was certain of it.

And I didn't care what his mom had said—Luc would never betray me.

I laced my hands around the back of Luc's neck and looked into his handsome eyes. "I know you love me, Luc. And I feel awful for even questioning you about this. I'm sure having Brigitte back in Adeline's life isn't going to be easy for either of us, but I'm in this for the long haul, so I want you to know I'll do everything I can to help you through it."

"Thank you, *mon amour.* Let's start by ignoring the tabloids, no?"

I giggled as I kissed him on the cheek. "We will be a tabloid-free house from this day forward. You have my word."

As Luc leaned in and brushed his soft lips over mine, I felt a little bit of the tension in my chest releasing. And as he cradled the back of my head in his hand and traced his fingers up my neck, I remembered once again the way it felt to be in his arms, to trust someone with every fiber of my being.

Even though *I* was more than willing to let go of all of the drama that had happened these past few days and move forward in our new, exciting life together, I knew that Luc's ex-wife had other plans.

As I ran my fingers through Luc's hair and kissed him back with that intense passion I'd *only* ever felt with him, I reminded myself that Mademoiselle Brigitte Beaumont *clearly* didn't know what she was up against.

SIXTEEN

Friday morning marked day eleven of honeymoon "bliss" and day five of unemployment hell.

I still hadn't heard a word from Beth Harding, the editor at *Bella Magazine* in New York who I'd contacted in the hope of securing a long-distance staff writing position. As a result, I'd spent the past four days hiding out in my apartment submitting résumés to every English teaching and translating position I could find. Unfortunately, though, the pickings seemed to be exceptionally thin.

In my breaks between online job hunting, I'd spent one too many hours gossiping with Isabelle among her shop's lush racks of lingerie. Okay . . . I *may* have broken down in a weak moment and bought myself the most gorgeous raspberry-colored bra, but I could only go into that store so many times and walk out empty-handed. In addition to my lengthy gossip sessions with Isabelle, I'd also spent time every day writing ideas in my Paris journal for my *Girl's Guide to Tying the French Knot* book. I'd certainly learned my lesson from the disasters my blog had created, so instead of including personal stories, I was envisioning it as more of a humorous commentary on French weddings, French honeymoons, French in-laws, and French husbands. I would need to interview more women to have a complete picture of course, but so far, I was having a blast writing it.

On the home front, Luc had worked late every night this week, which left me to pick Adeline up from the *crèche*, make her dinner, and play endless games of penguins with her until she'd throw her nightly "I don't want to go to bed" fit and beat me with said penguins until I caved and allowed her to stay up for another half hour.

By the time Luc returned home from the university each night, sometimes as late as ten thirty, I was already passed out—meaning we *still* hadn't found a time to discuss our finances *or* my job situation. In the mornings, Luc was always rushing out the door, and he'd been more stressed and tired than I'd ever seen him. I couldn't imagine dropping the unemployment bomb on him when we only had two minutes to talk.

Plus, the thought of a complete financial merger taking place so early in the marriage didn't sit well with me. That's never how I'd imagined my marriage to be, and from what I'd witnessed in my parents' union, it was a recipe for disaster. I was hoping that by the time Luc and I *did* have the talk, I'd already have another job lined up.

In other news, Fiona was still entertaining the dreadful Madame Rousseau in her small Lyon apartment while trying to convince her boyfriend that she hadn't been the girl kissing one of the Boucher brothers on Marcel's Paris balcony that night—when in fact we both knew she had been.

Lexi and Dylan's fights had escalated from bad to worse since our romp through the French tabloids, and I had a sneaking suspicion that Lexi's celebrity crush on Nicolas Boucher was turning into more than just a crush.

As for Luc's secret past with the Boucher family, he still hadn't opened up any further, and I'd stopped questioning him. I wanted to trust that whatever was going on, he had it all under control. The problem was, I couldn't stop thinking about his words from that mysterious bathroom phone call he'd made on the last day of our honeymoon. What on earth could be going on that would put me in danger? And if I was in danger, what about Adeline? And what about Luc?

My meeting with Nicolas was to take place in one week, so if Luc didn't tell me before then, I figured I would find out soon enough.

Back in my apartment, I signed into my e-mail, ready to gear up for another day of job hunting and writing. But when I opened my in-box, excitement flooded through me.

Finally, Beth Harding, the editor I'd written for at *Bella Magazine,* had responded.

Hi Charlotte,

So sorry for my late reply. Congrats on the wedding! I can't believe you married Half-Naked French Hottie and that this all stemmed from your Bella Magazine *article in August. I'm thrilled we could play a part in your finding and marrying the love of your life. I guess I should stop calling him Half-Naked French Hottie now that he's actually your husband. Luc is a good name too, and doesn't make him any less hot.*

I'm sorry to hear about your job at the language school. But I think I have some news you will be excited to hear. . . .

Bella Magazine *is starting up a French version, and I have been given the lovely task of flying to France to help them prepare for the release of their first issue. The really great news is that the magazine is headquartered in Lyon. This all happened rather quickly, and I actually flew in last night. I know this is last minute, so as long as someone hasn't scooped you up by now, I'd love for you to come in today at ten* A.M. *for an interview with the editor-in-chief, Mireille Charbonneau. I can't promise anything of course, but our US readers loved your articles so much that I'm sure that will hold some weight here.*

Regardless of what happens, I would love to finally meet you in person.

P.S. Are you working on anything new on the writing front? If you are, send it my way!

All the best,

Beth Harding
Editor, Bella Magazine

I responded to Beth immediately, telling her that of course I was interested and that I would be there at ten sharp. *Bella Magazine* in Lyon? Could this be any more perfect?

I also sent her a quick description of my book idea for *The Girl's Guide to Tying the French Knot,* hoping that once I'd written a solid portion of the book, Beth might be willing to take a look and put me in touch with some of her contacts in the publishing world.

Closing my computer, I smiled at the thought that hopefully I wouldn't have to break the job news to Luc because there wouldn't be any bad news to share.

Twenty minutes and one wild closet raid later, I took a look at myself in the full-length mirror. With my black pencil skirt, violet button-down shirt, tall black pumps, and long, wavy brown hair, I felt I'd nailed the chic, sassy, professional look that encompassed *Bella Magazine.*

Underneath, I was wearing my favorite black bra from Chez Isabelle just for that extra boost of confidence.

With my résumé in tow, I jetted down the skinny, winding staircase in my apartment building, being careful not to take a nose-dive in my tall heels, then ran out to the corner to hail a cab. After three available taxis passed by without a second glance, I jutted my hip out to the side and showed a little leg. Within seconds, a cab swooped across two lanes to pick me up.

Sometimes it paid to be a woman.

The new offices of *Bella France* were located in the only skyscraper in Lyon, nicknamed *le crayon,* or *the pencil,* because of its sharp pencil-like point at the top. This was my first time inside *le crayon*, and as the elevator shot me up to the eighteenth floor, I hoped I would be spending a lot more time here.

Inside the lobby, a glossy black sign reading *Bella France* hung high above the receptionist's smooth white desk.

"Mademoiselle Summers, I presume?" she asked in French.

"Yes, I'm here to see Beth Harding and Mireille Charbonneau," I responded, noting the strong scent of perfume wafting from her side of the desk.

She nodded, giving me a curt smile. "Beth is in a meeting at the moment, but Mireille is expecting you. Follow me, please." Standing, she revealed a lanky, rail-thin body propped up on the tallest set of black stilettos I'd ever seen. I wondered if she modeled for the magazine on the side.

I also wondered if she had ever eaten in her life.

I followed the thinnest girl alive through a set of glass double doors, the scent of fresh paint swirling underneath my nose as we walked down a long hallway. Two women dressed in chic black dresses and four-inch heels showed off their perfectly accessorized outfits as they rolled a rack of wispy scarves, short skirts, and skimpy tops toward us.

A man dressed in skinny jeans and pointy black boots trailed the girls. "Move it," he squealed in French. "She'll be here in ten minutes!"

I smashed myself against the wall as the girls broke into a wobbly stiletto jog and Monsieur Skinny Jeans snapped at them to move even faster.

If I landed this job, I would definitely need to spice up my wardrobe—and practice running in four-inch heels.

We passed by the art department and several smaller, bustling offices where writers were tapping away on their computers, making calls, and prepping for *Bella France*'s first issue.

Squeezing past two more sets of moving racks of designer clothing being hurled down the hallway, we finally reached the editor-in-chief's office.

My heart sped up as I took in the excitement buzzing in the air. The receptionist-slash-model who led the way knocked on Mireille Charbonneau's door. She waited a moment, then knocked a second time, and finally a third.

A shrill voice sounded from inside the office, prompting her to open the door and announce my arrival. "Charlotte Summers is here for her ten o'clock appointment."

"Send her in."

The girl ushered me ahead of her, then swiftly closed the door at my back.

Mireille Charbonneau sat at a long glass desk in the center of her pristine, chicly decorated office. The impressive floor-to-ceiling windows behind her looked out over the entire city, while colorful *Bella Magazine* covers splashed the other three walls.

Mireille sat back in her chair, crossed her thin legs, and lowered her stylish black glasses as she gave me the once-over. Her dirty blond hair was pulled up halfway, creating that disheveled but sexy look only French women could pull off. Her full lips pursed in a near frown as she waited for me to speak.

"*Bonjour, Madame Charbonneau. Je suis Charl—*"

"I know who you are," she responded in English, her thick accent strangely full of suspicion. "Please, have a seat." She nodded toward the two stiff white chairs that faced her desk.

"Thank you." I smoothed down my skirt, taking note of her impossibly thin body with curves in all the right places. God, sometimes French women were such a mystery. Would I ever truly fit in here?

"I received your CV from your editor in New York, Beth Harding," Mireille said, switching into French. "She has spoken very highly of you, so I took a look at the pieces you wrote for *Bella Magazine.*"

"Thanks so much for taking the time to read them," I said with a smile. Even though Mireille had yet to show even a hint of kindness in her thickly lined eyes, it did seem like we were at least headed in the right direction. "What did you think?"

"What I *think* is that it is quite pretentious of you to assume that writing two freelance articles for the US version of our magazine would qualify you for a staff-writing position at *Bella France.* I have personally hand-selected each of our writers, and all of them have years of experience writing fresh, relevant copy that will appeal to our readers." Mireille snatched up a piece of paper from her desk. "From what I see here in your CV, you have been teaching French and English for the past several years. You have established a career as a teacher, not as a writer, Miss Summers, and your inquiry has been nothing but a waste of my time."

I wasn't sure how long my mouth hung open as I stared back at Mireille in astonishment, but it was long enough for me to imagine pointy red horns growing from that messy mop of hair on her head.

"I'm sorry I've wasted your time," I said, standing to leave.

"I didn't tell you to leave yet, Miss Summers."

"I wasn't going to wait for your permission," I snapped. I didn't owe this woman anything, and I certainly didn't owe her the courtesy of staying around for further humiliation.

She raised a brow at me, seemingly intrigued by my attitude. "You didn't think I'd call you in simply to tell you that your writing proposition is laughable, did you?"

"That's certainly what it seems like," I said. "Do you have something else to say to me? Because if not, now you're wasting *my* time."

A sadistic chuckle left her lips as she slipped off her glasses and stood to meet my gaze. "Beth Harding is quite insistent that we find something for you to do here, and as it turns out, our new publisher is in need of someone to translate outgoing and incoming correspondence from our sister magazine in the States. I noticed on your CV that you have some experience in this field, no?"

"Yes, I was a translator for a publisher back in DC."

"At the request of both Beth Harding and our new publisher here at *Bella France*, I put in a call to your former employer. Contrary to what I thought I might hear, they informed me that you were quite competent. Our publisher would like to interview you himself, of course, but I wanted to get a first look. Make sure you had what it takes to deal with a man of his . . . *stature*." She eyed me up and down once more, her judgmental gaze lingering on my outfit.

"And?" I asked, trying to ignore the feeling that this chic, forty-something, bitchy woman was mentally undressing me with her eyes.

"If he likes you, you'll start today." She tossed my résumé back onto her desk and strutted past me. "Follow me."

Mireille hauled some serious ass in her pointy heels while I struggled to keep up with her. I wondered if the magazine offered a stiletto speed-walking course during training. If they did, I'd be the first to sign up.

Inside the publisher's massive corner office, a tall black chair on the other side of the room faced a magnificent view of the city. As Mireille cleared her throat, the chair slowly swiveled around.

With his jet-black hair and that slight peppering of gray making him look mysterious, distinguished, sexy, and sleazy all at the same time, there was no mistaking the infamous Vincent Boucher.

"Vincent, this is Charlotte Summers," Mireille said in French. "She's interviewing for the translating position."

The right corner of Vincent's mouth slid up into a sly grin. "Thank you, Mireille. I'll take it from here."

A flash of apprehension appeared in Mireille's cool eyes as she looked from Vincent back to me, and finally left us alone.

Vincent didn't even wait for the door to shut before he combed my body with his intense hazel gaze. "Charlotte *Olivier,* what a pleasant, beautiful surprise."

Suddenly Vincent's words from that first meeting outside of our Paris honeymoon hotel rushed back to me. He'd said that he was opening up a new magazine which would be headquartered in Lyon. Then he'd asked Luc if he still had family down that way.

How could I have forgotten?

"I think there's been a mistake." I mentally shook off Vincent's greasy stare and turned for the door.

"There hasn't been any mistake, Charlotte. You need a job, don't you?" Vincent's voice was smooth, strong, practiced.

I stopped with my hand on the doorknob. Yes, I desperately needed a job, but *not* from the one man my husband hated with all his heart and soul.

"I'm offering quite a generous package for this position. With Luc being a meagerly paid university professor and Brigitte initiating custody hearings again, it would not be wise for you to turn your back so quickly on this opportunity—at least not until you hear what I can offer you."

I thought of Jean-Sébastien, my supervisor at the language school, and how distraught he'd been over the closing of classes. I thought of his wife Marie-Élise and their two small sons. I thought of my mom who'd had no interests of her own and no career to fall back on after years of being dependent on my father. I thought of Luc and his refusal to tell me the whole truth on what was really going on with the Boucher family. And I thought of my own dismal financial outlook.

There were a million and one reasons why I should not dignify Vincent Boucher's proposition with a response.

But there were also just as many reasons why I needed this job right now.

If I was going to do this, Vincent was going to have to play by my rules.

I flipped around and marched up to Vincent's desk. "I'm not oblivious to the fact that you seem to have a personal vendetta against my husband and his family . . . and that for some reason, you're dead set on stealing all of the women in his life: his mother, his ex-wife, and now here you are offering me a translating job. Oh, but I'm sure that's just a coincidence."

"Your point?" He leaned back in his chair and lifted a brow, completely unfazed.

"I don't want to know your reasons for wanting to hire me. I don't care. What I do want is to secure a translating contract, but the only way this will work is if *I'm* dictating the terms."

Vincent plucked a pen and notepad from his desk. "And those terms would be?"

"First, this is purely a business relationship. I'm in love with my husband, and nothing you say or do will turn me against him. So don't try. Also, the contract will be with the language school I work for. They have other qualified translators on staff, so if at some point it's time for me to move on, you'll have your pick of some fantastic language specialists. Lastly, I would like to submit a few pieces for consideration for the magazine, and I want written confirmation from you that after this translating contract ends, I will be considered for a full-time staff writer position."

"Finished yet?" Vincent asked as he scribbled down the last of my demands.

I sat down in the cushy black chair facing his desk and placed my hands in my lap. "Yes, I think that's all."

He chuckled. "You're quite the businesswoman, you know that?"

"Well, if you really need a qualified translator *that badly*, I would hope you'd consider my small list of demands."

He glanced over the list once more. "The only request I will have a hard time meeting is number one. Beautiful women have always been my weakness, as you well know."

"Must be tough for you working in this estrogen-dominated environment every day."

He laughed. "You have no idea, Charlotte. You have no idea."

"I'd like to know a little bit more about what this translating position will involve, what types of hours you'll need me for, and how much money we're talking." I wanted to show Vincent that I was serious about keeping things all business.

Okay, there may have been a *tiny* part of me hoping that in working for Vincent, I would find out what was really going on between Luc and the Bouchers, and that I could actually *help* Luc, so that whatever he was facing, he wouldn't be facing it alone.

"Since we're opening up as the sister magazine to *Bella*'s US version, there is quite a bit of correspondence between my office and theirs, and as you probably noticed the first time we met, my English is terrible," Vincent said with a charming grin.

I'd never understood the phenomenon of twenty-something girls going for much older men, and I hated to admit it, but with Vincent, I understood. Just one intriguing gaze from him screamed power, charm, sex, and mystery. Not that a man like him was *my* cup of tea—but I understood why a woman like Brigitte would fall prey to Vincent's charms.

"I'll need you to translate incoming and outgoing e-mails, sit in on conference calls with me and, occasionally, accompany me to events and photo shoots," Vincent said. "Working for a magazine can be very glamorous at times, but it is also a business. And with the amount of money we have at stake with this new venture, there isn't much room for error. You'll need to be extremely accurate—*and* discreet. Can you handle that, Madame Olivier?"

I nodded, wondering *what* exactly I would have to be discreet about. "Of course."

"There is one more thing, in addition to your translating and interpreting duties," Vincent said.

Okay, if this was where he asked if I would give him a blow job under the desk every afternoon, the deal was off. "Yes?"

"I would like for you to spend a couple of hours a week teaching me English."

I wondered how it was possible in all of his years of business that Vincent had never properly learned the English language, but now wasn't the time for that question. At least he hadn't asked me for the unthinkable.

"Yes, for the right amount of money, of course I can," I said.

Vincent jotted something down on his notepad, then flipped it toward me.

The amount staring back at me took my breath away. This contract would surely buy Jean-Sébastien a few more months with the language school, and it would encourage him to begin bringing in more outside translating and teaching contracts. This contract would also buy *me* at least a few more months of full-time pay before I had to figure something else out. Hopefully that something else would include a writing position at *Bella France,* which—if the stars aligned—would provide the perfect platform for me to complete and publish *The Girl's Guide to Tying the French Knot.*

I smiled up at Vincent. "I think we have a deal."

"Is Luc going to be a problem?" Vincent asked.

As I imagined the uncomfortable task of telling my husband about my new job, a knock at the door interrupted us.

Mireille strutted in, one hand on her hip. "She's here, and she's already flipping out at the photo shoot. The *Bella US* crew is trying to tell her what to do, and she can't understand anything they're saying. She's requested to see you immediately." Mireille shot Vincent a dramatic eye roll, then slammed the door behind her.

"*Oh là là . . . les femmes,*" Vincent mumbled under his breath as he stood. "Do you have anywhere to be this afternoon?"

"Not for a few hours anyway."

"Some of *Bella Magazine*'s English-speaking staff have flown over to help us get our first issue up and running, and to be sure we stay within the *Bella* brand. I haven't understood a word these people have been saying all week. It will be nice to have you there to translate today if you're ready to get started. Don't worry, I'll have my legal assistant draw up your contract as soon as we're finished with this. We will, of course, be sure to include *all* of your terms."

"Thank you," I said, standing to meet Vincent's gaze. "Where are we headed?"

"We have a very high-profile actress posing as the cover model for our flagship issue, and we're needed at the photo shoot." Vincent headed for the door. "As Mireille said, this actress doesn't speak much English either, so your services will be extremely useful today."

Excitement flooded through me as I followed Vincent down the long hallway. I just landed a job making more money than I'd ever made in my life! I was going to be able to help Jean-Sébastien keep the language school open, *and* I was going to have a shot at an exhilarating writing career when this was all over.

Plus, in the meantime, I would be attending glamorous photo shoots!

In the business sense, at least, Vincent Boucher suddenly didn't seem *that* awful.

Now the only thing I had to worry about was how I was going to break the news to Luc.

Vincent opened the door to a massive room filled with lights and photographers. But when I spotted the actress posing in the middle of this cover-shoot frenzy, I realized that telling Luc about my new position wasn't the *only* thing I had to worry about.

Working with the rail-thin, gorgeous blonde who was shooting her pouty gaze at Vincent had *not* been part of our deal.

Vincent leaned into my ear. "If you're really serious about writing for the magazine one day, you were bound to cross paths with the lovely *Brigitte* at one point or another. I figured it might as well be today. Still in?"

I pushed my shoulders back and held my chin up. "Of course I'm in."

But as Brigitte Beaumont's cool green gaze landed on me, I wondered what in the hell I'd just gotten myself into.

SEVENTEEN

"What is she doing here?" Brigitte hissed into Vincent's ear.

Vincent motioned for me to join them, which was obviously the last thing I felt like doing. Bolting out the door and never looking back sounded like a much more viable option at this point.

But I wouldn't let her ruin this for me.

More outrageously fashionable magazine staffers swirled frantically around the room as I walked toward my nemesis. Of all people to be posing for the cover shoot of *Bella France*'s first issue, why did it have to be Brigitte?

Vincent placed a heavy hand on my shoulder while Brigitte continued her evil stare-down. If she was already throwing a fit at the shoot, I couldn't imagine that having me here would do anything to improve the situation.

Was Vincent asking for a petty catfight? Did he get off on this kind of stuff?

"Brigitte, I'm sure you remember Charlotte Olivier," Vincent said calmly. "I know you've been having some problems working with the English-speaking staff here at the shoot, and Charlotte is here to help. She's *Bella France*'s new translator."

I could almost see the icicles forming in Brigitte's stone-cold eyes as she crossed her arms over her chest and stuck her bony hip out to the side.

"Is that going to be a problem?" By the lack of affection in Vincent's tone as he addressed Brigitte, I wondered if there was still trouble in paradise.

"Of course it won't be a problem," Brigitte said, but the evil pout splashed across her heavily made-up face certainly said otherwise.

"Wonderful," Vincent remarked, ignoring his girlfriend's defiant attitude. "I have some business to attend to, so I have to be going. Charlotte, I'll need you to stay for the duration of the shoot and deal with any translation issues that come up. In the meantime, I'll have my legal assistant draw up your contract, and Mireille will show you to her office as soon as this wraps up."

Brigitte shot Vincent another distressed look and opened her mouth to speak, but Vincent cut her off. "You're a professional actress now, Brigitte. I suggest you start acting like one." Then he turned on his heel and walked out of the room, leaving a steaming little blonde in his wake.

Another impeccably dressed woman walked up to us, her warm smile and kind eyes a welcome sight.

"Beth Harding?" I guessed.

"Charlotte." Her grin widened as she held out her hand. "It's so good to finally meet you in person."

"You too," I said. She had no idea how happy I was to have a friendly face in this landmine of Luc's past.

"I just heard the good news about your job offer!" she said, patting me on the shoulder. "You work fast, girl. I know you were looking to write for the magazine, but just give it a little time. Translating will be a great way to get to know everyone here."

"Thanks, Beth. I'm excited to see how it all goes." Excited wasn't *quite* the right word, but I didn't feel like filling Beth in on why I wasn't jumping out of my skin at the moment.

"We're still receiving reader mail about your latest article," Beth said. "Women want to know what happened after you confessed your love to Half-Naked French Hottie, and now to think you've married the guy already! What a story. We'll have to squeeze in a follow-up piece once you've been hitched for a little while. I'm sure you'll have some more juicy gossip for us on the ins and outs of French marriage."

Clearly Beth had no idea that Brigitte was Half-Naked French Hottie's (aka: Luc's) ex-wife.

But when I glimpsed the expectant look on Brigitte's clueless face, I remembered—she didn't understand a thing we were saying.

That's what *I* was here for. Hmm . . . this could turn out to be fun after all.

"Do you speak French, Beth?" I asked.

She sighed. "I wish. But no, I barely speak a word. I wasn't even supposed to be the one making this trip, actually, but my supervisor had to cancel at the last minute, so they sent me. I'm so glad they did, though."

"What are you two talking about?" Brigitte asked in French.

"Oh, we were just discussing how that top looks a little too tight on you, and your forehead could use a little more powder," I said. "It's great when the lights bring out your natural shine, but we're not going for the *greasy* look, if you know what I mean."

Luckily my French lie didn't register in the slightest with Beth as she kept gabbing. "You really are a woman of many talents, Charlotte Summers. I absolutely love your book idea on the guide to tying the French knot. With your voice, I have no doubt it's going to be fabulous. Send it over to me once you've written an outline and the first three chapters. I may be able to put you in touch with a few of my contacts in the publishing world."

"Thank you, Beth. That would be amazing!"

Brigitte nudged me this time.

"Beth was just asking me if I'd ever done any modeling. She thinks I'd be great for one of the *Bella*'s next cover shoots," I told Brigitte in French.

I knew I was absolutely terrible, but I just couldn't stop myself. I only hoped no one else was listening to my purposefully botched interpreting job.

Brigitte puffed out an exasperated breath, then marched over to the makeup artist, where she proceeded to throw a fit. Oops.

"Another high-maintenance actress," Beth noted, watching Brigitte spin a toddler-worthy tantrum across the room. "I've been in this business for ten years, and every time I encounter one of these spoiled brats, I count the days to retirement."

I chuckled, feeling only slightly bad for having contributed to Brigitte's latest outburst. From what I'd already seen of my husband's ex-wife, I was certain she would've gone off the handle with or without my prodding.

"I have some tricks of the trade that will calm that entitled little darling down real fast," Beth said. "In fact, I don't know what I'm doing being an editor. Instead, I should be teaching a course on how to tame wild, young actresses. Follow me."

Thank God for Beth.

Four hours later, we wrapped up the photo shoot, and to my surprise, Brigitte hadn't tried to tackle me or pull my hair out at any point throughout the day. That was mostly due to Beth's superb dictations of exactly the right things to say to Brigitte to force her to focus on the shoot, rather than on her constant roller coaster of needy, irrational emotions.

As the day wore on, Brigitte even seemed to forget that it was *me,* the woman she hated most in the world, doing the talking.

The prissy little star didn't bother to thank me after she'd finished, though. In fact she didn't thank the photographers, the designers, the makeup artist, or Beth. Instead, she grabbed her Louis Vuitton bag and pranced out of the room checking her cell phone the whole time.

I couldn't even begin to imagine this woman being a full-time mother to Adeline. She didn't seem to have a motherly bone in that stick-thin body of hers.

"Thanks for your help today, Charlotte," Beth said as I helped her clean up. "I couldn't have done this without you."

"You're welcome. I'm so glad I got the chance to meet you in person, and I can't thank you enough for putting in a good word for me here, and for your help with my book."

"Of course." Beth stepped closer to me, lowering her voice. "Listen, I'm heading back to the States this weekend, and I'd love to have an English-speaking contact over here at *Bella France* to keep me posted on how things are running. Would it be okay with you if I touch base from time to time?"

"Of course. I'd be more than happy to give you updates."

Beth cast a curious glance around the room before continuing in a whisper. "Our publisher over at the New York office has a few concerns about certain staff members here."

"Oh?"

Beth nodded as we slipped behind one of the hanging racks of clothing. "Do you know Vincent Boucher very well?"

"I've only met him once before I got the job today, but I can't say that I know him all that well." I didn't feel that it was appropriate to divulge Luc's family drama with the Bouchers to Beth just yet, especially since it didn't seem to have anything to do with Vincent's current publishing career.

"I know you'll be working directly underneath him, so if you notice anything out of the ordinary going on around here, I trust you'll keep me in the loop?"

"Of course," I whispered back. "Is there something specific you're worried about?"

"Vincent is an incredible publisher, don't get me wrong. We've watched his career explode in recent years. He was very much in demand, but there's just something *off* about him. I mean, I know this is France, and things are different here, but still. Am I making any sense?"

I nodded. "Yes, I completely understand. I'll keep my eyes peeled."

"Thank you, Charlotte. Now go sign your contract so you get paid for all of the hard work you put in today."

"Thanks," I said, wondering how in the world I was going to spin all of this to Luc at the end of the night. I would worry about that later. First, it was time to sign on the dotted line, then call Jean-Sébastien to tell him about the massive contract I'd just scored for the language school.

EIGHTEEN

"Thanks so much for coming, Sandrine," I said, leaning in to give my new sister-in-law *bisous* before letting her into our apartment.

"Of course. It is never a problem to watch my adorable niece." Sandrine's short, silky brown hair framed her heart-shaped face as she gave me the once over. "*Maman* tells me Luc has been working late with his new teaching position?"

"Yes, he took on some night classes, and with everything that's been going on this week, we haven't exactly had much time to talk. I thought it would be nice to meet him out for a late dinner. I really appreciate you coming on such short notice."

"Only an American would think eight o'clock is late for dinner." Even though she was smiling, Sandrine's commentary on our cultural differences felt cool . . . and slightly judgmental. She was a lot like her mother.

I grabbed my keys off the counter, watching the way Luc's sister's wispy frame stalked through our living room.

"You know, I've seen the papers." Sandrine picked up a photo of me and Luc off the coffee table, running her fingers around the black frame. "And of course I spoke with *maman*."

I tucked my keys into my purse, contemplating my response. It was clear that Sandrine and her mother had been wary of my sprint to the altar with Luc, and to be honest, I couldn't blame them. They barely knew me, and Luc's last marriage had ended in complete disaster. It would take some time for them to learn that they could trust me and to comprehend that I was nothing like Brigitte.

Unfortunately, I'd already started off on the wrong foot by landing myself in the tabloids with the dreaded Boucher family.

"There's more to the story than the photos you saw in the papers, Sandrine," I told my sister-in-law.

She sighed, placing the photo back on the coffee table. "There's always more to the story with the Boucher boys. And now that Brigitte has aligned herself with Vincent, who knows what trouble is around the corner for poor Luc. *Quel désastre.*"

I walked over to Sandrine and faced her square on. "There's something going on between Luc and the Boucher family that he's hiding from me. You wouldn't happen to know what that might be, would you?"

Sandrine crossed her arms over her chest. "I imagine you have heard by now that our father went to prison?" Bitterness lined Sandrine's tone as she pursed her thin lips.

I nodded. "Yes, I know about your father. And I also know that your father going to prison and breaking up your family is the reason Luc hasn't spoken to him in years."

"No, that is why *I* have chosen not to talk to our father in years. Luc and I have never seen eye to eye on this matter."

"What do you mean? Luc still wants to have a relationship with your dad?"

Sandrine shook her head, a dry laugh escaping from her lips. "It is happening all over again."

"What is?" I asked. "What's going on, Sandrine?"

"Luc and his secrets. When will my brother learn that secrets like this destroy relationships?"

I stared back at my sister-in-law, remembering Brigitte's words outside the Château Frontenac Hotel on that fateful day when our honeymoon was completely ruined.

"Luc Olivier, you and all of your secrets were never cut out for marriage . . . as your little Charlotte will soon find out."

"What isn't Luc telling me?" I pressed.

"Luc never believed our father was guilty, Charlotte. And he is still in touch with him. He doesn't even want me to know, but this summer, I overheard Luc speaking to our father on the phone. And by the way Luc was talking and laughing, I could tell they speak often. I understand why he would hide this fact from me and my mother considering neither of us want anything to do with the man after what he did to our family. But I don't know why Luc would hide this fact from you, his wife, and I refuse to lie for him."

"Thank you for telling me," I said, trying to make sense out of all of this. "What I don't understand, though, is that when I tried to tell Luc that Nicolas Boucher thinks your father was innocent, Luc said that was impossible. He gave me the impression that he honestly believes your dad was guilty, and that he blames him for breaking up your family."

Sandrine raised her brows at me.

"You're saying Luc's been lying about all of it?" I said.

Sandrine nodded slowly, then lowered her voice. "Nicolas Boucher told you he believes my father is innocent? How interesting. He is probably just saying that to make up for what he did to Luc, and for what Vincent did to our mother, of course."

"I know about Vincent cheating on your mom, but what did Nicolas do to Luc?"

Sandrine placed a dainty hand on her hip and leveled her gaze at me. "Before Brigitte came along, Luc was madly in love with a girl named Marion. He was going to propose to her, but then he walked in on her kissing Nicolas. As if what Vincent did to our family wasn't enough, Nicolas had to steal the girl Luc was planning to marry. Only a week after the breakup, Luc met Brigitte. They married before he had any clue what he was getting himself into."

I'd never even heard Luc mention the name Marion before. And why was it that I was hearing the stories of my husband's past from everyone's mouths but his?

Sandrine surprised me by placing her hands on my shoulders. "You must understand that my brother has a past, Charlotte. It is a long, dark past that he doesn't like to talk about. There are secrets even I don't know—things I will probably never know. But that doesn't matter, because *you* are his wife. And while French men do not always make the most *faithful* of husbands, I have never seen my brother look at another woman the way he looks at you. Not even Marion, and definitely not Brigitte.

"He is truly in love with you, and I suspect this is why he rushed to marry you only three weeks after proposing. He carries too many secrets around, and he knew that once you spent more time with him, those secrets would begin to drive you mad, and you would eventually leave him for someone else. Just like Marion did. And just like Brigitte."

Sandrine squeezed my shoulders and lowered her voice to a whisper. "Don't let my brother get away with living like this any longer, Charlotte. Do whatever you have to do to find out what he is hiding. I agree with you—there is more to the story with the Bouchers than either of us know. Brigitte's new relationship with Vincent cannot be a coincidence. If you don't want to see this marriage crumble before it even has a chance to start, you'll have to take things into your own hands."

"What do you suggest that I do? I've confronted Luc, and he's told me flat out that there's something going on that he can't tell me about, but he told me to leave it alone," I said. "Marcel even threatened me, telling me the same exact thing: drop it or else. And I overheard Luc on the phone on Saturday telling someone—an old friend, apparently—that if I knew the truth, it would only put me in danger."

Sandrine shook her head, anger seeping through those big hazel eyes of hers. "Let me ask you a question, Charlotte. Do you know for sure that Luc is teaching night classes?"

I opened my mouth to tell her that yes, of course Luc is teaching nights now. He told both me *and* his mother that the university had a few last-minute course openings that they offered to him. And with more custody battles on the horizon with Brigitte, now certainly wasn't the time to turn down extra money.

But the skeptical look flashing through Sandrine's eyes told me that Luc's word might not be as trustworthy as I'd once believed it to be.

"You deserve the truth," she said. "And Adeline deserves a mother who won't be prancing around the tabloids with a different man on her arm every week."

Suddenly Adeline bounded out of her bedroom, dressed head-to-toe in fluorescent pink princess attire. She threw her arms around Sandrine, while I ignored the queasy feeling that settled in my stomach at the thought that Luc might even be lying about his night classes. What else would he be doing in the evenings?

Could the fact that Brigitte was in Lyon for the *Bella France* photo shoot have something to do with why Luc was coming home late every night?

Was he seeing his ex-wife and lying to me about it?

Sandrine looked up at me as she hugged Adeline. "You better go. You're going to be late for your eight o'clock dinner."

As I walked down the narrow set of stairs in our old apartment building and exited onto the smooth cobblestones of Vieux Lyon, I hoped Luc's sister wouldn't mind staying longer than I'd originally asked her to.

Because I wasn't leaving that restaurant until Luc told me the truth.

It was nine o'clock on the eleventh night of what was supposed to be our twenty-nine days of honeymoon bliss, and as I sat alone at a candlelit table in the corner of Les Fines Gueules—one of our favorite restaurants in Vieux Lyon—I downed my second glass of wine and wondered if by *bliss,* Luc had actually meant to say honeymoon *hell.*

I checked my phone for the hundredth time that hour, but still no missed call or text from Luc. I'd tried him three times already, to no avail, and I wasn't about to keep blowing up his phone if he couldn't even have the decency to let me know he was going to be an hour late to our dinner date.

Sandrine's words grated on me as I took in the sickeningly sweet French couple cooing over each other at the next table.

Luc and I had only been married for eleven days. *Eleven days.*

That should've been us acting all lovey-dovey at that table, making other restaurant patrons want to vomit.

I finished my glass of wine and decided I wasn't going to put myself through this misery for another second longer.

After taking care of the bill and leaving the server an extremely generous tip considering I'd only ordered two glasses of wine, I stormed out of the restaurant and down rue Saint-Jean. I needed to blow off some steam before I locked myself in our apartment for the night with Adeline. And Sandrine surely thought we'd be out for another two hours at least, so I could afford some time to myself.

Along my brisk evening walk, I passed by the Smoking Dog Pub, a lively English bar I used to frequent with my girlfriends during my study abroad days as an undergrad. A mixture of French and English cries blasted through the open door as I poked my head in to see if anyone I knew happened to be in the crowded pub. I'd had enough wine by myself. I could use a pint of cider and a few friends to cheer me up right about now.

But inside the rowdy bar, all I found were memories of a different time—a time when I was only twenty years old, having the time of my life, and that life did *not* revolve around a man. Although I did have a boyfriend waiting for me back home during my semester abroad in Lyon, I'd never felt so free, so alive, and so excited about life as I did in those days. I'd come to Lyon to study the French language, but this beautiful, exciting city had offered me so much more. It had shown me that I was just fine living on my own, making new friends, and discovering a new culture *without* a man by my side.

When I moved back to Lyon on my own only four months ago, this old, charming city brought me that same joy, that same fervor and excitement. How had I let it slip away so quickly?

Here I was, distraught and confused yet again, over a man.

This time, though, that man was my husband. And I loved him more than I could even express. I loved his sense of humor and what an amazing father he was to Adeline. I loved how he fed me chocolate in bed, and how I'd never felt safer than I did when I was wrapped in his arms. But all of Luc's secrets were threatening that safety. And worst of all, they were making me question my quick decision to run—not walk—down the aisle.

Letting the pub door slam behind me, I took back off down rue Saint-Jean, wrapping my scarf tighter around my neck as a chilly September breeze whipped between the stone buildings and sent a shiver down my spine.

My love for Luc was stronger than anything I'd ever felt before. And I wanted our life together in Lyon to be just as amazing as I'd imagined it when I professed my vows to him only a week and a half ago.

But no matter how much I loved Luc, I refused to spend my days and nights wondering where he was, if he was telling me the truth, or if he was still seeing his ex-wife. Clearly I wasn't a saint, and I had some explaining to do regarding my career change and my recent interactions with Vincent and Brigitte, but standing me up on a Friday night without even a call or a text was simply unaccepta—

"Charlotte! Charlotte, wait!"

I flipped around to find Luc chasing after me down the cobblestones, his hair a ruffled mess atop his head. "Charlotte, I'm so sorry to have kept you waiting."

I pulled my phone out of my bag and flashed it in his concerned face. "Ever heard of picking up your phone when you're going to be over an hour late? I'm not just some girl you're dating, Luc. I'm your wife."

Luc took my hand and led me farther away from the restaurant where he'd stood me up, from the pub that made me long for different days, and from our apartment where Sandrine would be tucking Adeline into bed any minute now.

"Where are we going?" I asked, struggling to keep up with him.

He flashed me a mischievous grin, revealing that sexy dimple in his right cheek that always made me forget how to be mad at him.

"You'll see," he said.

Damn that dimple. He will not get away with this.

NINETEEN

Twenty minutes later, Luc and I were sliding into a red leather booth at Le Nord, an upscale brasserie situated on the Presqu'île of Lyon.

On the metro ride over, Luc had shown me the dead battery on his cell phone as well as the course syllabi for the evening finance courses he'd been asked to add to his teaching schedule this week. Luc explained that several students had lined up to ask him questions after class, which was the reason for his one-hour delay.

The look in his chestnut eyes had been sincere as he explained his way out of the dog house, but what he didn't know on our quick metro ride over was that I had a slew of questions ready to unleash as soon as we sat down to eat.

"*Une bouteille de champagne*," Luc ordered from our tall French waiter, who was clad in a crisp white shirt, a spiffy black vest, and a long white apron.

As we waited for our bubbly flutes that would hopefully ease a little bit of this newlywed tension, I folded my hands over the pristine white tablecloth and smiled sweetly at my husband.

Then I cut the bullshit. "Why did you lie to me about your relationship with your father?"

Luc took a long sip of his water before speaking. "What are you talking about, Charlotte?"

His immediate denial of the truth made me want to kick him underneath the table, but the classy French couples seated around us stopped me from committing a childish act of violence.

"Your sister informed me that you still talk to your father, and that you do, in fact, believe he was innocent. Interesting how you've told me the exact opposite, don't you think?"

Luc's expression remained deadpan, but I noticed his nostrils flaring just the slightest bit.

I'd caught him.

"I'd really love to move forward with our twenty-nine days of honeymoon bliss, so if you could just tell me the truth now, that would make everything so much easier." I was just about to take a gulp of water when the waiter returned with our bottle of champagne, pouring us each two fizzy glasses.

Thank God.

I took two long sips, then waited for Luc to fess up.

"*Chérie,*" he said, reaching for my hand across the table.

I pulled away, wrapping my fingers instead around the stem of my champagne flute. With all of Luc's lies, my hand felt safer there.

"Luc, honestly, if you expect me to be your partner, your *wife*, I need you to tell me what's been going on. *All of it.*"

Luc cleared his throat, then cast a quick glance around the brasserie. "In return, will you tell me why you have been lying to me about losing your job at the language school?"

The last drink of champagne I'd just downed caught in my throat. How did he know I'd lost my job?

"There's a reason I've been holding back, and I'm sorry," I said after a brief coughing fit. "I was planning to tell you tonight, but first I want to know what is going on between you and the Boucher family, and why you've lied to me about your relationship with your dad."

The server appeared at our table just before Luc began to speak. Since when were French waiters so attentive?

"*Madame, Monsieur, vous avez décidé?*" he asked.

I was tempted to tell our server I'd like an order of honest husband with a side of the truth, but instead opted for the chicken in a mushroom crème sauce which sounded so much more elegant when pronounced in French—*le poulet de Bresse à la crème et aux champignons.* Luc ordered *la quenelle,* a Lyonnais specialty, and as soon as our waiter zipped off to the next table, I resumed my somber stare.

Luc could woo me all he wanted with fancy dinners, sexy dimples, and mind-blowing sex followed by creamy squares of chocolate, but none of that mattered when my own husband wouldn't even tell me the truth.

Luc leaned over the table, lowering his voice. "If I told you that soon you would know everything, that this whole mystery would be over, and you would fully understand why I couldn't give you all of the answers *right* at this moment, would you trust me?"

I took another sip of champagne and raised my brows. "What do you mean by *soon*?"

"I don't have an exact date for you, but I can assure you that within the next month, everything will come to light, and you will know what I cannot tell you right now regarding the Boucher family and my relationship with my father."

"But I'm your wife, Luc," I said softly. "You should be able to tell me anything."

"It is true that there are things you don't know about me, Charlotte. But that doesn't change how much I love you."

"Could one of those things be that you have an ex-girlfriend named Marion who you were once madly in love with and planning to marry, but then Nicolas Boucher stole her from you?"

The corner of Luc's mouth twitched as he nodded slowly. "Sandrine told you this as well, I assume?"

"Yes, it was Sandrine. And I have to be honest, I'm having a really hard time with the fact that I have to learn the details of your past from my sister-in-law," I said before taking another gulp of champagne. "I know we got married really fast, and there are bound to be pieces of our lives we haven't talked about yet, but do you honestly believe a relationship, a *marriage,* can survive with all of these secrets?"

Luc crossed his arms over his chest and sighed. "Let's not forget that I'm not the *only* one keeping secrets here. For the past week, you have been telling me you were teaching at the language school, and yet that is not in any way the truth. Am I correct?"

I shifted uncomfortably in my seat, wishing I'd been honest with Luc from the start about my job. I couldn't be so angry at him for hiding things from me if I was doing the same thing.

"I'm sorry I didn't say anything—I tried a few times, but you were too exhausted and stressed from everything that's been happening this week, so I never found the right time."

The hard look in Luc's eyes softened a bit, so I continued.

"Last Sunday afternoon, right after I saw the pictures in the tabloids, I received a call from Jean-Sébastien. Apparently the language school hasn't been making enough money for a while now, and he was in denial about the whole thing. They had to cancel most of the classes for this semester and potentially close down altogether by next semester, *but* I may have found a temporary solution to buy him *and* me some more time."

"And what would that be?" Something about Luc's accusatory tone told me he already knew the answer.

"Wait, how did you find out about my job at the language school?" I said. "Did Brigitte tell you?"

"How would Brigitte know?" Luc asked. "Have you been talking to her?"

"Have *you* been talking to her?" I countered.

Before either of us could break the tension that had settled over the table like a thick fog, the server appeared with our creamy plates of French cuisine.

"*Merci, monsieur,*" Luc said as the waiter refilled each of our champagne glasses to the brim.

The aroma of chicken marinating in a creamy mushroom sauce flittered past my nose, making my stomach growl. But before I took a bite, I wanted answers.

"So, how did you know I'd lost my job?" I asked my husband once more.

Luc folded his napkin over his lap, then picked up his fork and knife and cut a piece of *quenelle*. "On Monday, I tried calling you to let you know I'd agreed to teach night classes and that I would be late. You didn't pick up your phone all day, so I called the language school and spoke with Jean-Sébastien. He told me about your canceled classes. I didn't bring it up until now because I figured you were upset and that you would tell me when you were ready. Plus we've had enough on our plate between the tabloid photos, Brigitte initiating another custody battle, and me working late every evening." Luc took his first bite, washing it down with another sip of champagne.

"That's exactly why I hadn't brought it up yet," I said. "In our first week and a half of marriage, we've already had enough drama to last a lifetime. The last thing I wanted to do was tell you that in addition to paying lawyer fees and gearing up for another dramatic legal battle with Brigitte, right as you're starting your new university job no less, you're going to have to support your new wife while she looks for another job. But, what I was planning to tell you tonight over dinner is that you won't have to worry about that now because I've found a job." I finally let out the breath I'd been holding and took a bite of my chicken. The creamy mushroom sauce melted in my mouth, making me realize how hungry I was.

"First of all, *chérie*, I am happy to support you, to take care of you in every way, and that means financially too," Luc reassured me. "We are husband and wife now. You don't have to do everything on your own anymore."

"I know, but it's not healthy for a woman to depend solely on her husband for income. Look at what happened to both of our mothers. Your mother was left in financial ruin after her divorces with your father and with Vincent. And as for my mom, during her thirty years of marriage with my father, she never kept her own career or followed her dreams, and now she's in her fifties, single, and has no clue what she's doing with her life."

Luc set his champagne glass down and covered my hand with his. "I will never do those things to you, though, Charlotte. You will never be left alone like your mother, or like mine. You will always have me to depend on, to trust, to take care of you if or when you need it. I am nothing like *either* of our fathers." Luc's deep, reassuring voice drowned out the sounds of clinking wineglasses and French banter swirling through the restaurant.

I thought of what Luc's sister Sandrine had just said to me. That despite the problems we were facing, Luc had never looked at any woman the way he'd looked at me. That he truly was in love with me.

"You do believe me, don't you?" he asked.

"Of course I do. But we haven't sat down and had a real finance discussion since we've gotten married. I have no idea how much money you've saved or how you've managed your finances up to this point. You told me that you put aside a lot during your years working in finance, and that you're smart with money, but even still, how on earth were you able to afford paying the *entire* hotel bill for all of our wedding guests? And if you do have so much money, why were you living so cheaply in a college dorm last year? Some of this just isn't adding up."

"To answer your question about the wedding, I knew that your family and friends had all made a huge financial sacrifice to fly to France on such short notice, and I thought the least I could do was help them with the hotel bill."

"Why didn't you tell me?" I said.

"I don't think it's right to bother women with such matters," Luc said. "I want you to trust that I have it all under control. I am nothing like my father, who, as you now know, managed the family finances so poorly that he left my mother in complete financial ruin. I have learned from his mistakes, and I would never put us in debt, if that's what you're worried about."

"Luc, this isn't the olden days. I *want* to be involved in those types of decisions. And of course I don't think you're like your father, but until you're completely, one hundred percent honest with me about everything, you have to understand where I'm coming from."

"I do understand because you haven't been honest with me this week either," Luc said. "What is this new job you've already found?"

"All right, here goes." I swallowed nervously and looked Luc straight in the eye. "Before I go into the specifics, you need to know that this job will make it possible for Jean-Sébastien to keep the language school open."

Luc set his fork down, giving me his full attention.

"I signed a contract today with *Bella France,* the new French version of *Bella Magazine*, to be a translator and English teacher for their new publisher, with the promise that they will consider me for a full-time writing position in the not-so-distant future."

The hope in Luc's eyes vanished as he drew his lips into a tight line. "In other words, you signed a contract to work for Vincent Boucher."

"How did you know that Vincent was running *Bella France*?"

"Oh, you are on a first-name basis with him now?" Luc snapped.

"Please don't be like that. I think that man is just as much of a sleazebag as you do," I said. "So how did you know already?"

Luc tapped his finger on the stem of his champagne glass. "You must remember that on the day Vincent and Brigitte so kindly crashed our honeymoon, Vincent told us that he was heading up a new magazine based out of Lyon. I didn't want that man anywhere near my family, let alone *my wife,* so I did some research and found out he was starting up the new *Bella France* here in Lyon."

"Well, I, on the other hand, had absolutely no idea *he* was the publisher when I went in for an interview. But he made me an offer

I couldn't pass up, not for myself or the language school. The amount of money he's offering will keep the school open for at least a few more months, giving Jean-Sébastien time to secure other outside translating and teaching contracts like this one until he can get enrollment back up again. And you know that Jean-Sébastien's wife just had their second baby."

"Of course. It is nice of you to want to help him, but it's not your job to take care of other people's families. You need to be thinking of *our* family first—of you, me, and Adeline. And signing a contract to work directly underneath Vincent Boucher will serve no other purpose than to tear us apart. How could you not understand that?"

"I would understand more if you would tell me the entire truth about your involvement with Vincent and his sons."

"I am not involved with them in any way," Luc snapped.

I raised a doubtful brow at him and went back to telling him about the job. "I obviously knew you wouldn't be happy with this, but you also need to understand that this could open huge career doors for me. And as much as I love teaching, to be honest, I wouldn't mind making a career switch into something that pays a little better. Something more exciting. You should've seen how everyone buzzed around that magazine today. The energy in that place was so motivating. Regardless, you'll be relieved to know that I worked with their legal department and asked them to rewrite the contract to allow for a thirty-day trial period. That way if this is a complete disaster—"

"Which, with Vincent, it *always* is," Luc cut in.

"Then I'm clear to leave after thirty days," I finished.

"Vincent can do a lot of damage in thirty days, Charlotte. I know a writing career sounds glamorous, but you can seek that out at another magazine. With Vincent, you simply have no idea what you're dealing with." A hardness settled in Luc's jaw as he stared down at his plate, not touching his food any longer.

"There's more," I said.

Luc's gaze lifted slowly to mine, almost as if he were forcing himself to stay calm.

"After I accepted Vincent's offer today, my first assignment was to do some translation work during *Bella France*'s first cover shoot. And of course, as luck would have it, Brigitte was the cover model."

"You're telling me you spent the day translating for both Vincent *and* Brigitte?"

"Yes. I didn't do this to upset you, Luc. Honestly I—"

Luc's jaw tightened as he wiped any last traces of kindness from his eyes. "Charlotte, you have no idea what you're dealing with here. Please, finish out your thirty days, then take your magazine writing dreams and your teaching and translating abilities elsewhere. I promise you, I have enough money to support both you and Adeline while you're looking for work. *D'accord?*"

I nodded slowly, then took a long sip of my champagne before asking Luc one last question. "Luc, you do know that this isn't normal, right? To keep secrets from your wife, especially during the very first weeks of a marriage."

"In the weeks that come, the truths you are searching for will come to light," Luc said firmly. "And in not telling you certain things right now, I'm only trying to protect you. Very soon, you will understand everything, I promise. And in the meantime, you must try the *fondant au chocolat* for dessert. Trust me, *ma belle,* it is simply divine." Luc's gaze finally softened as he flashed a devious grin my way.

That French husband of mine wasn't stupid—he knew that there were only two things in this world that would shut me up: sex and chocolate.

Fifteen minutes later, my secret-keeping husband and I were devouring the most decadent dessert I'd ever tasted. A volcano of hot, melted dark chocolate poured out of a moist chocolate cake, each sinful bite that hit my tongue making me realize that if Luc wouldn't give me the truth just yet, at least he could give me orgasmic chocolate.

Later that night, after Luc had fallen asleep and my chocolate haze was beginning to wear off, I lay awake thinking about what Luc had said to me over dinner. That the truths I was searching for would come to light. That in keeping secrets from me, he was only trying to protect me. And that I needed to have faith in him . . . and just wait it out.

While I believed Luc had only good intentions, I also wasn't one to sit around and wait for the shit to hit the fan. And by the anger that boiled over in him every time I mentioned Vincent Boucher's name, I could only assume that whatever was going on behind the scenes between Luc, Vincent, and Luc's father, was big . . . and potentially dangerous.

Now that I would be spending quite a bit of time in close proximity with Vincent, I figured it wouldn't hurt to do a little investigation of my own. And maybe, whatever I found out would actually help Luc . . . and help me to be able to place all of my trust in him once again.

In the meantime, since there was no way this confused head of mine was going to allow me to sleep, I fetched the Paris journal from my purse and crept out to the living room to write the introduction to the most life-altering chapter in my guidebook: "*Le Fondant au Chocolat* and What It Can Do for Your Marriage."

> *In a previous chapter, we've already discussed the point that hot sex doesn't fix everything (yes, even if your husband is an incredibly sensual French lover). Well, tonight I discovered something that doesn't fix everything per se, but it comes pretty damn close:*

Le fondant au chocolat.

In case you've never tried this magnificent dessert, allow me to elaborate.

First you have a moist, warm, gooey piece of chocolate cake (not American chocolate cake—I'm talking chocolate cake à la française, *which automatically makes it a rich, chocolaty culinary masterpiece). Typically this magnificent cake is in a circular shape, but any shape will do.*

Now, for the best part: inside the best piece of cake you've ever tasted, you will find an explosion of melted dark chocolate. Not just a little bit, either—think molten lava in chocolate form overflowing from the center of the cake.

This dessert is literally a volcano of chocolate, and it will sweep away all of your marriage troubles (guaranteed to work for at least one evening, and possibly more, depending on the severity of your marriage issues).

The heavenly fondant au chocolat *may very well be the key to surviving a rocky start to your marriage (French or otherwise).*

I recommend eating this decadent, sinful dessert with your husband anytime you want to spice up the pleasure level in your relationship, and especially if you are at odds with each other.

The magic of le fondant au chocolat *is that in just one little cake, you will find peace, romance, and orgasms without all the work. Happy indulging!*

TWENTY

It had been almost one week since my dinner at Le Nord with Luc, and the high from the delectable *fondant au chocolat* dessert that we had drowned our troubles in had officially worn off. Nothing had "come to light" as Luc had promised me it would, and every night when he returned home from his long teaching days, he *pretended* that everything was fine, but I knew him better than that. I could see the stress lines around his eyes, the worry tracing his brow. One night, when I'd surprised him but putting on the sexiest piece of lingerie I owned from Chez Isabelle, he was too worn out to take me up on my offer—which was *so* not like Luc. And as much as I was truly beginning to worry about him, I was also tired of being left in the dark.

Now, more than ever, I was determined to get to the bottom of all of this.

As I hurried into the elevators inside *le crayon* on what should've been day seventeen of honeymoon ecstasy, I reminded myself that I was also determined to make this new career path work out. After a brief discussion with Jean-Sébastien last Friday to inform him of the new contract I'd scored for the school, I would do almost anything to prove myself at *Bella France*. Not only to save the language school I loved so dearly and help Jean-Sébastien and his family in the process, but also to pave the way for my future magazine and, *hopefully*, book-writing career.

I strutted into the chic offices of *Bella France* wearing my tallest pair of black stilettos and a sleek black dress that accentuated my curves, while still being work appropriate. The silky red scarf I'd wrapped loosely around my neck served two purposes: hide my cleavage—I hadn't forgotten who my new boss was after all—and bring my outfit up to par with all of my super stylish coworkers.

The same ultra-thin receptionist—or model wannabe?—who'd greeted me each morning stood from her pristine white desk, then silently eyed my outfit for at least ten seconds. I wondered if she was calculating how many more kilos I weighed than her. I was tempted to rest my hand on her bony shoulder and tell her not to worry, that I weighed far more than she probably ever had, and I would never out-stage her because I loved buttery croissants and baguettes and creamy camembert cheese—God, did I forget to eat breakfast?—way too much to give a damn about trying to be *that* skinny. Luckily we were able to skip that awkward conversation as she finally cracked a cool smile, then nodded for me to follow her through the shiny glass double doors into the whirlwind of fashion, design, and story ideas that made up the brand-new offices of *Bella France*.

"Monsieur Boucher is busy on a conference call," the receptionist said in French as she stiletto-sprinted down the hallway. "Mireille has requested to see you first thing. She will get you set up with everything you need to get started today."

I hadn't met with Mireille since that very first disaster of a meeting last Friday, and as we neared her office, I realized I'd rather jump into a snake-filled pit than deal with her again today. Or ever for that matter.

But just before we reached Mireille's door, the girl turned to me with a curious gleam in her eye. "I have to ask, is it true that you're the same Charlotte Summers who wrote the blog *Sleeping with Paris,* and who wrote those two articles for *Bella Magazine*'s US version?" she whispered.

"That's me," I said, wondering if she was about to tear into me the way Mireille had done the week before.

"My friends and I loved your blog!" she whisper-squealed, pinching my arm. Then she pulled me out of earshot from Mireille's office. "Is it true that you married Half-Naked French Hottie, and that his ex-wife is Brigitte Beaumont, that bitch actress who's been running around here all week like she owns the place?"

I couldn't help but laugh. "Yes, I married him—which makes me Charlotte *Olivier* now. And as for Brigitte . . . no comment," I said. I'd spotted Brigitte dashing in and out of the magazine offices almost daily since I'd begun, holding secret meetings with Vincent and having hissy fits over the photos that had come back from her shoot. She thought her forehead looked too shiny in all of the pictures.

Oops.

The receptionist chuckled, then extended her impeccably manicured hand out to me. "I'm Chantal. It's so exciting to have you on board. I hope you get to stay. We could use some positive energy around here. Mireille is a little scary, if you know what I mean."

I giggled. "Yes, I know exactly what you mean."

"She's already threatened to fire four people since I started!"

"Wow, that's really harsh," I said, feeling my nerves sloshing around in my stomach. Or was it the three glasses of red wine and the bar of Lindt dark chocolate I'd devoured while writing the night before?

Chantal nodded for me to follow her back to Mireille's office. "We better go. She's waiting for you. And she hates when anyone is late."

"Does Mireille know now about my connection to Brigitte?" I asked.

"She knows *everything,*" Chantal whispered before knocking on Mireille's door once, twice, then a third time, just as she had the week before. "*Bonne chance,*" she whispered to me as Mireille's shrill voice permitted her to open the door.

As soon as I spotted Mireille Charbonneau's slim, yet perfectly curvy frame standing in front of her floor-to-ceiling windows, arms crossed, severe black glasses rimming her narrowed eyes, I actually wished I could just head straight to Vincent's office instead. I was going to need more than luck to deal with this woman.

"Charlotte, I need to speak with you," she said, nodding for me to sit. I hesitated, not wanting to get comfortable. I felt like she was itching to fire someone, and by the way she was staring me down, that someone was most definitely going to be me. My only comfort was in the fact that Vincent had been the one to hire me, and I'd already signed a thirty-day contract, so technically, I didn't think she had the authority to fire me . . . *yet.*

"Is there a problem?" I dared to ask as I took a seat.

She stalked toward me, eyeing me the whole way before sliding a hip onto her shiny glass desk. "I understand you have recently married Brigitte Beaumont's ex-husband. You neglected to tell me this last week when we first spoke . . . and every day that you have been here since."

I nodded, swallowing my nerves and facing her straight on. "Yes, I had no idea she would be here, and I didn't want to make a big deal out of it."

"Well, your translation efforts during the photo shoot last week certainly could've been a little more professional, do you agree?"

Just as I was about to apologize for my pettiness, I noticed that Mireille wasn't shooting me that menacing glare any longer. The scary editor-in-chief of *Bella France* was grinning—and that grin was turning into a full-on evil laugh.

"You were brilliant," she said. "Most actresses are high maintenance to an extreme, but Brigitte Beaumont is a nightmare. When Vincent told me he was going to bring her on as our first cover model, I almost quit this job. He promised me it would only be for the first issue, then we'd be finished with her, thank God. The way you handled her was impressive, especially considering this is personal for you."

"Thank you," I said, trying to mask my shock at Mireille's kindness.

"Don't get too excited," she said. "This does *not* mean I'm going to hire you for a writing position any time soon, even though you convinced Vincent to agree to that possibility once your translating contract is up." She crossed one thin leg over the other, revealing a pair of scarlet stilettos that perfectly matched my scarf.

I didn't expect Mireille to change her mind about giving me a chance on the writing front, but I at least hoped she would take notice of the effort I'd made to be a little more stylish today.

"As you are most certainly aware, Vincent's weakness is beautiful women. Brigitte is perhaps his most pronounced weakness . . . but as of today, *that* will be over." She gazed wistfully out the window, her eyes sparkling with hope.

"I don't want to overstep my boundaries, but I'm not totally convinced that Vincent is finished with Brigitte," I said. "She's been in to see him every day since I started, and she doesn't even work here."

"Oh, don't be fooled by Vincent's flirtatiousness. Monsieur Boucher is a master at reeling in attractive young women who will be beneficial to him—in a purely business sense, of course—then letting them go when they are no longer of use. Brigitte means nothing to him." The way she spoke of Vincent's feelings toward Brigitte made me wonder if Mireille didn't have a little something for that sleazy publisher of ours.

"In fact," Mireille continued, "we will be seeing a lot less of Mademoiselle Beaumont around here. Vincent has just called her into his office to end their little love affair."

"Really?" I said. "I don't imagine that's going to go over too well." I wondered if that also meant that Brigitte would be left without Vincent's powerful lawyer, who'd already initiated custody hearings with Luc. This could be the best news I'd heard all week.

Mireille slid off her glass desk and took a step toward me. "Did Beth Harding ask you any questions about Vincent's *professionalism* when she was here for the photo shoot last Friday?"

I pinched my eyebrows together, faking confusion. "No, she didn't," I lied. "Why do you ask?"

"She mentioned some concerns to me that she and the *Bella Magazine* US publisher had about Vincent's attitude toward women at the office. It was laughable, actually. I mean this is France—the rules are different here. We aren't nearly as *prude* as our United States counterparts."

"The rules are definitely different here, as I'm learning pretty quickly," I said, wondering where she was going with this.

Mireille flipped her tousled blond hair to one side as she shot a penetrating gaze my way. "That's what I wanted to talk to you about, Charlotte. I understand that today is your first formal English lesson with Vincent. You will be working in close proximity to him, and it is important that you know he is *taken.*"

"You and Vincent are together?" I clarified.

"We've been keeping it quiet until he ends things with Brigitte, but I thought it was important for you to know. I don't want you getting the wrong idea about his kindness toward you."

Kindness wasn't exactly how I'd put it, but it was hardly worth getting into an argument over semantics.

"I know you already have a relationship with Beth Harding, and she thinks quite highly of you. If she comes to you, you need to know that just because Vincent and I are in a relationship does not mean that anything unprofessional is going on here. This is the way of the world, or at least it is the way of the world in *France.* Your American colleagues may disagree, but that is none of their business. I earned my position here at *Bella France* by being one of the most competent, talented editors in my field, and my connection with Vincent only helped me learn of this exceptional opportunity."

A smug smile spread across Mireille's pale face. "Since you'll be working directly under Vincent, I figured it was best to keep you in the know . . . just so you don't get any ideas."

"Mireille, I'm married," I said flatly.

"And since when has marriage stopped anyone from having an illicit office affair?"

"That's not really my style."

She nodded in approval. "Good. I was just testing you." Her eyes combed my black dress, resting on my hips. "You're not really Vincent's type anyway. I knew I had nothing to worry about."

Nothing to worry about? Granted, I hadn't known him that long, but from what I'd learned so far, Vincent was the *last* man any respectable woman should be entering in a relationship with. He would destroy Mireille, just as he'd destroyed Luc's mother, and just as he was going to destroy Brigitte.

It was only a matter of time.

After my meeting with Mireille, I took a swift right down the long corridor which led to Vincent's secluded corner office. Our lesson wasn't supposed to begin for another ten minutes, but after my little chat with Mireille, I had other reasons for heading to his office early.

On my way, I noted how Vincent had his own wing of the floor entirely to himself. Clearly the man liked his privacy.

Just as I neared his door, I heard Brigitte's unmistakable, high-pitched voice snapping at Vincent.

I scanned the hallway to make sure no one was coming, then pulled out my cell phone and pretended to mess with it as I inched closer to the door.

"What were you thinking bringing Luc's new wife in to work here?" Brigitte screeched in French.

"I needed a translator, and Charlotte Olivier just happened to be looking for a job at the magazine," Vincent replied coolly. "Fate has a way of working itself out like this sometimes."

"She's too much of a good girl for you, Vincent. She'll ruin everything," Brigitte spat.

"Why don't you let me worry about Charlotte, and you keep on doing what I've asked you to do." Vincent's voice was powerful, controlling, calculated.

The coast was still clear, so I continued pushing random buttons on my cell phone while I eavesdropped.

"You've humiliated me, and I'm not sure I want to keep playing your game," Brigitte said. "I can do just fine on my own."

"Oh, is that so?" he snapped back. "What if Luc were to find out the truth about you? And the press? Your career would be over before it even began, and you'd never see your daughter again."

"Two can play at this game, Vincent. One word out of my mouth about *les bijoux* and your career—and your entire life for that matter—will be over."

Les bijoux? What did any of this have to do with *jewels?* Was Vincent some kind of jewelry thief or something?

A pounding sound emanated from inside the office, followed by Vincent's deep, growling voice. "Don't you *ever* threaten me. We both have a lot at stake here, and that's why you'll keep your mouth shut."

"Marcel neglected to tell me that you were such a cruel bastard when he cut me into your little operation," Brigitte said.

Operation? What in the hell was going on here?

"That's funny, because what Marcel told me about you was exactly right. He said you were a greedy little slut who was hungry for attention, and that you were willing to do *anything* to score more drugs and more money. Which is *exactly* why we chose you."

Oh, shit.

A loud smacking sound followed by another pounding noise came from inside the office. Brigitte whimpered, making me think that Vincent had just slapped her across the face and possibly shoved her against the wall, but then a rustling noise and a low moan made me think otherwise.

Were they . . . ?

"Marcel thinks I'm his, but he's wrong." Brigitte's breathy, seductive voice was difficult to make out, so I gave up on trying to look innocent and instead pressed my ear against the door.

"I've always been yours, Vincent. Ever since I saw you walk on set that day, it's always been you that I wanted. And Marcel is right. I am a greedy little slut. But I'm *your* greedy little slut."

What in the—?

"That's right, *ma chérie*. You are the most beautiful of *mes bijoux*, the most cherished asset I have, but I need you to keep your promises to me. I need you to find out what Marcel is hiding. Keep letting him *believe* that you are falling for him, that you are finished with me, and I know my son—he will open up to you. After all, what man could resist these . . . and this . . . and this?"

Another smacking sound followed by Brigitte's devious giggle proved more than ever that Luc was right: this woman had no business being around Adeline, *especially* while she was involved with Vincent and whatever sketchy *operation* he had going on.

"No one can work this business like you can, Brigitte. My associates have been telling me what a *natural* you are. Of course I already knew this, but it wouldn't hurt to show me one more time, would it?"

More giggling and rustling traveled through the thin walls, then came Vincent's voice, except it was all business this time.

"Chantal, something has come up. I won't be able to attend my English lesson with Charlotte. I'll be on an important call, so please hold all calls and visitors for the next hour."

By the lack of words and the heavy breathing, growling, smacking, and moaning that followed, it became absolutely clear what was happening on the other side of that door—and even clearer why Vincent had chosen such an isolated location for his corner office.

TWENTY-ONE

Later that afternoon, I was sipping a glass of Chardonnay inside Pain & Cie, my favorite café situated on the Presqu'île of Lyon. I'd texted Fiona to meet me for an emergency briefing, gossip, and advice session (over wine and dessert, of course), and I'd texted Lexi to tell her we'd put her on speaker phone. Plus I had gorgeous Chez Isabelle lingerie to give Fiona, and I wanted to make sure my friends hadn't been kicked out of their respective homes after our tabloid debacle the week before.

Halfway into my glass, as I was lost in thought trying to decode the sick and bizarre interaction I'd heard between Brigitte and Vincent, I spotted Lexi flying up the stairs to the second floor of the café where I'd blocked off a corner table.

"Lexi! What are you doing here?" I asked as I stood to give her a kiss on the cheek.

"What? A girl can't take the train from Paris to see her best friends?"

"Of course! But I obviously thought you were in Paris when I texted you. When did you get to Lyon?"

"Only a few hours ago. Dylan and I haven't stopped fighting since the tabloid mess, and I just had to get out of there for a few days. Plus I had to come talk Fiona down off the cliff. When I spoke to her last night, she was actually considering poisoning Madame Rousseau's coffee. I figured stopping our sweet British friend from serving a life sentence for premeditated murder was probably worth the trip."

"Poor Fiona," I said, but I couldn't stop my giggle. "Things must be desperate if she's plotting the woman's murder."

"Hey, no judgment here," Lexi said, shooting a flirtatious glance at our handsome French waiter. "Fiona is a saint. I know Marc is wonderful, but that mother of his is a total deal breaker."

"Speaking of deal breakers, I'm so sorry if those stupid tabloid pictures are the reason you and Dylan are fighting. Are you guys going to be okay?"

Lexi waved off my apology. "This isn't your fault, Char. That man and I are always fighting; I'm just not sure how long this type of relationship can last. And there's something else . . ." Lexi trailed off, a mischievous gleam in her eye.

"What is it, Lex?" I suddenly remembered Lexi's mad dash off the Paris Metro after she'd received a mysterious call and wondered if she was finally going to fill me in.

Before she could spill, Fiona bounded up the stairs.

"I hope you girls are planning on staying here for a while." Fiona plopped into her seat and blew out an exasperated sigh. "Because you couldn't pay me enough to make me return to the hell that is my life right now."

"I heard about your murder attempt on Marc's lovely mother," I said with a grin.

"I haven't attempted it . . . *yet,*" Fiona said.

"You know you're more than welcome to stay with me and Luc if it gets too unbearable," I said. "Adeline isn't too into sharing right now, but I'm sure we'd figure something out."

"Thanks, Char," Fiona said, the dark circles under her eyes telling me she probably hadn't been getting much sleep lately. "But the Wicked Witch of the West is leaving tomorrow, thank the heavens."

After we put in our afternoon wine and dessert orders, Lexi turned to me. "So what's going on?"

"Before I spill the beans on the latest turn of events, I need you two to promise that you will not breathe a word of this to another living soul," I whispered over the table. "And I'm talking no one. Not even the boyfriends."

Lexi and Fiona simultaneously crossed their fingers over their hearts. "Promise," they both said.

"Did you two choreograph that or something?" I asked with a laugh.

"We're just really in tune with each other," Lexi said impatiently. "Which is why we won't tell a soul. Now spill it, honey."

I proceeded to fill the girls in on some of the events that had gone down at *Bella France* that day, including Mireille's belief that she was in an exclusive relationship with Vincent, followed by Vincent and Brigitte's talk of operations and jewels, and the icing on the cake: their kinky sex session inside his office.

Our berry crumble tarts had arrived by the time I finished unloading the latest outrageous gossip, but the girls couldn't have been less interested in their desserts.

"This is insane," Fiona said. "What do you think they're up to?"

"Money, drugs, jewels—sounds like some sort of organized crime operation," Lexi said.

"With Brigitte as Vincent's pawn," I added.

"It sounds like you have more than enough proof that Brigitte is unfit to have partial custody of Adeline," Fiona said. "Are you going to tell Luc about all of this?"

"Yes, I have to. He's teaching nights now, so it's hard to find any time during the week to really talk, but I'll wait up for him tonight."

"Wait," Lexi finally spoke. "What kind of contract did you sign? I know you want to score a writing position with the magazine at the end of all of this, but to be honest, I wouldn't touch this situation with a ten-foot pole if I were you."

"I didn't sign on the terms Vincent and I had originally agreed upon. Instead, I'm there on a thirty-day trial period. That way I'll receive enough money to hold me over and keep the language school up and running temporarily, but if things are still out of control after the initial thirty-day period, I can leave and have no further obligation to Vincent or to the magazine."

"Does Vincent know about the thirty days?" Fiona asked.

"I'm not sure, but if he has a problem with it, all I have to do is mention what I overheard today, and I think he'll let me do whatever the hell I want."

"Char, this guy sounds dangerous," Fiona said. "And whatever he's up to with Brigitte does not sound like something you want to associate yourself with. Are you sure you want to go through with this? I mean, hasn't the Boucher family caused us all enough trouble lately?"

"I've already signed on the dotted line, so there's no going back now. I want to find out exactly what Vincent, Brigitte, Marcel, and Nicolas are up to, and what Luc has to do with all of it. There's still something Luc is refusing to tell me about his past with the Boucher family, and I'm tired of being left in the dark," I said. "So, if he isn't going to open up to me, I'll just have to launch my own investigation."

"What makes you think Nicolas has anything to do with this?" Lexi asked.

"He got in touch with me last Monday after he saw the pictures of all of us in the tabloids. He said he's going to be in Lyon this week, and he wants me to meet him at the bar inside La Cour des Loges Hôtel tomorrow night. He says he has something important he needs to give me. Whether he's involved in Vincent and Brigitte's sketchy dealings or not, he clearly knows something. And despite Luc and Marcel's warnings to steer clear of Nicolas, I have to find out what he knows. I feel like something really big is going on here, and I refuse to let me *or* Luc be blindsided when the shit hits the fan. Learning that Brigitte Beaumont is my husband's ex-wife was enough of a surprise for me this year."

Fiona's eyes widened. "I can't thank you enough for telling me this outrageous story. Seriously, Char, your life is like a soap opera. I can't wait to find out what Nicolas is going to give you."

"I'm sure he's just trying to help," Lexi said, her tone defensive. "He doesn't seem like the kind of guy who would get wrapped up in his father's messes."

Fiona arched a brow. "Lexi, do you know something about Nicolas that you're not sharing with us?"

When Lexi pushed a strawberry around on her plate and refused to make eye contact with us, I had to ask, "Lexi, was it you and Nicolas on the balcony that night? Is that why you were so intent on saying it was Marcel? To point the finger in the other direction?"

"No, it wasn't me," Lexi said. "I swear on my Jimmy Choos, I was not kissing Nicolas Boucher on the balcony that night. So which one of you was it?" A sly grin crept up on her full red lips.

Fiona clenched her stomach and suddenly looked as if she might be sick, so I launched in for the save.

"I have a theory," I said. "Remember how one of the pictures in the tabloids showed Brigitte storming off alone that night after making a fool of herself at the premiere party with Vincent?"

Lexi nodded, while Fiona's panicked eyes focused on her full glass of wine.

"Well, think about the conversation I just overheard between Brigitte and Vincent. Vincent instructed Brigitte to keep seducing Marcel so she can find out what he's hiding. What if it was Brigitte on the balcony with Marcel that night?" I was really reaching here, but the sudden relief that washed over Fiona's face made my fake little theory worth it.

Lexi gazed out the window of the café, lost in thought. "You may just be right," she said after a few seconds had passed.

"Then it's settled. We'll tell the guys that I overheard Brigitte today at the office admitting to being in the balcony photo with Marcel that night. Hopefully this will get the men off our backs," I said, feeling quite satisfied with this new solution. Fiona desperately needed something to appease both Marc and his impossible mother, and hopefully this would do the trick.

"Oh, and I have something else that might help." I retrieved the dainty lingerie bag from underneath the table and handed it to Fiona. "Lexi, yours is back at my apartment because I didn't know you'd be here. Do you want to take the Metro back with me so I can give it to you?"

Lexi peeked down at her shiny silver watch. "You're so sweet, Char. I have to run, actually, but maybe I can swing by tomorrow?"

"Of course," I said, eyeing her tight red top and dangly earrings. "Where are you headed?"

That naughty gleam sparkled in Lexi's eyes once more as Fiona peeked in her lingerie bag.

"What is it, Lexi? What were you going to tell me earlier?" I asked her.

Lexi swiped the last bite of her tart off the plate, then opened her wallet and left some euros on the table. "Oh, it was nothing," she said, but I knew my friend better than that. She was definitely hiding something.

And by the way she'd been defending Nicolas, I was almost certain I knew what it was.

"Remember, Lex, keep it zipped," I reminded her.

With one hand on her hip, she shot me a sassy look. "Char, honey, the only thing I'll be doing with these lips in the near future is kissing a hot man. All right, ladies, I have to run," she said. "Have fun with that lingerie tonight."

"Oh, I sure will, while my boyfriend's mother snores all night in our bed and I'm sleeping on the couch with Marc sprawled out on the living room floor," Fiona scoffed. "Thank you, though, Charlotte. This is gorgeous. I'm sure it will come in handy as soon as that old cow is out of my apartment."

With her contagious laugh and a flip of her long, silky dark hair, Lexi weaved through the skinny aisles of the café, leaving me alone with Fiona.

I took another bite of my delicious tart, watching as Fiona's normally cheery gaze turned from bleak to desperate. "Fiona, it's all going to be okay. You can tell Marc *and* his evil mother that it was Brigitte that night up on the balcony."

"No, it's not that. . . ." Fiona trailed off as tears rimmed her blue eyes.

"What is it, Fi?"

"I . . . I think I'm pregnant."

I stifled my initial shock and instead took Fiona's trembling hand from across the table. "Are you sure? Have you taken a test yet?"

"I missed my period, and I've been throwing up every day for the past three days. Marc's mother is onto me, and you know how strict and conservative that woman is."

I knew better than anyone—it had only been a few months since Madame Rousseau had thrown a royal fit at my *Bella Magazine* article and had taken away my chances for a prestigious teaching position in Paris.

"You know Marc will support you, though, Fiona. No matter what his mother thinks."

"That's the thing. For the entire time she's been staying with us, Marc has allowed her to get away with *everything*. She bosses him around like he's still a little boy, and he barely ever stands up to her, even when it involves me. Marc isn't like this with anyone else, but with her, he has absolutely no backbone."

"Well, if you're pregnant, he's going to have to get one real fast," I said. "Do you want me to come with you to the drugstore to pick up a test?"

She wiped at the tear rolling down her cheek, and it was then that I noticed she hadn't touched her wine. Fiona never turned down a glass of wine which meant she really did believe she was pregnant.

"No, that's okay, Char. You have to pick up Adeline and talk to Luc tonight about everything that happened today."

"I know it doesn't seem like it right now, but as soon as Madame Rousseau leaves your apartment, you and Marc can go back to normal. And you know what a wonderful guy he is. If you really are pregnant, he'll support you no matter what. And he'll make a wonderful father."

"I know he will. But what if I slept with Marcel that night? How can I look Marc in the eye and tell him I'm having his baby when I may have just had sex with another man?" she whispered.

"Fiona, you don't even know if you're pregnant yet. Let's not jump to that conclusion until we know more. Have you remembered anything else from that night?" I asked.

"No, I don't remember a sodding minute after that first glass of champagne in the limo." Fiona's gaze lifted to mine. "But I woke up naked in his bed, Char. That can only mean one thing."

"About that," I said. "There's something I've been meaning to ask you. This might seem like a weird question, but were you wearing a lacy black thong that night? With little pink jewels on it?"

"Char, I may have done something awful while I was drunk, but this is still me, the conservative British girl you're talking to. If I remember correctly, I was wearing full-coverage black cotton underwear that night. And in the morning, they were nowhere to be found."

"Really? Because that morning when Marcel asked me to come talk with him outside on the balcony, I saw that thong lying on the living room floor. After I found you in his bed, I just assumed it was yours."

"Well, you assumed wrong. I'm sure a guy like Marcel has a different girl in his bed every night—and clearly he doesn't bother to clean up after himself." Fiona's head dropped into her hands. "I feel disgusting, Charlotte. What have I done?"

"Maybe he really was with another girl that night," I said.

I noticed the slightest flicker of hope gracing Fiona's tired eyes. "You said you're meeting with Nicolas tomorrow?"

I nodded.

"I need you to ask him what happened at Marcel's apartment. And if he doesn't remember or he won't tell you, ask him for Marcel's number. I'll call him myself. I have to know."

I nodded, squeezing Fiona's hand. "Of course, Fiona. Whatever you need."

Half of my delectable tart remained untouched on my plate, but my appetite vanished as I thought about Luc's words to me. He'd called the Boucher family "toxic." He'd said they ruined his family.

I just hoped they wouldn't ruin Fiona's.

TWENTY-TWO

"Repeat after me: My name is Vincent Boucher, and I am the publisher of *Bella France*."

Vincent flashed me a bold smile as he straightened his chic violet tie. "My name iz Vincent Boucher, and I am zee publisher of *Bella France*. My teacher iz Charlotte Oliver, and today, she wears a dress red zat is stunning while she teach me zee English."

My new English student and boss apparently thought it would be fun to take some creative liberty with his language exercises. I chose not to comment, and instead went about correcting Vincent's grammatical errors.

"In English, adjectives are placed before the noun," I said slowly. "So instead of *une robe rouge,* or 'a dress red' as you said, you will want to say . . . ?"

"A red dress," Vincent finished, once again flicking his gaze down to my chest. This guy took sexual harassment in the workplace to a whole new level.

I thought of the dreamy look that had flashed through Mireille's eyes when she'd announced to me just the day before that she and Vincent were "in a relationship." Had she seen the way he looked at other women? Did she honestly believe this man was capable of being in an exclusive relationship?

And more to the point, did she have any idea what had gone down in this very office right after I'd spoken with her?

I'd thought Mireille seemed wiser than to fall for the King of Sleaze, but clearly Vincent's charms had won over yet another unsuspecting victim.

Or perhaps Mireille's version of a relationship was sharing Vincent with a million other women. Maybe that was one of the new *rules* I had yet to fully embrace in my new French life.

I cleared my throat and folded my hands in my lap, careful not to touch Vincent's desk where he'd just *been* with Brigitte the day before. *Disgusting.* Or as the French would say, *dégueulasse.*

"Also, instead of saying '*the* English,' you would simply say 'English.' Contrary to what you're used to in French, it's not necessary to always use an article in front of a noun in English," I said.

Just as I was about to work with my eager student on his typical French pronunciation of "the," which sounded more like "zee," a harsh rapping on the door interrupted us.

"I tell zee receptionist I am in lesson and not to disturb, but *c'est la vie,*" Vincent said with a shrug. "*Oui?*" he called out.

Although I'd told Mireille I had absolutely no interest in shacking up with Vincent, she'd still seemed hesitant to leave us alone together this morning for our lesson, and I fully expected to see her narrow eyes glaring down at me when the door opened.

But the perfectly sculpted, unshaven face, and the messy head of dark brown hair that appeared in the doorway proved me wrong.

"Marcel, what a nice surprise," Vincent said in French. "Brigitte and I were just talking about you yesterday."

But Vincent's youngest heartthrob son couldn't have been less interested in what his father was saying. Instead Marcel's piercing brown gaze was fixed on me.

"What is *she* doing here?" Marcel barked in French.

"Charlotte iz my new English teacher," Vincent said slowly in English as he leaned back in his cushy chair, not the least bit ruffled by his son's snappy attitude.

Dressed in a pair of slim dark jeans and a black T-shirt, Marcel stormed through the office, glaring at me all the while. "Tell her she needs to leave."

"I'm sitting right here, you know," I said. "You don't have to talk about me in the third person."

"I am appalled that any son of mine would have such rude manners when speaking to a beautiful woman," Vincent said.

"Did you forget that Charlotte is *Luc's wife*?" Marcel spat. "What are you doing?"

"Again . . . I'm sitting right here," I reiterated.

While the two of them continued to argue, I stealthily reached for my iPhone inside my purse, pressed the Record button on the new app I'd just downloaded this morning, and when I was positive neither of them was watching, I casually let the phone slip into the crevice of my armchair.

"I think the lady is capable of making her own decisions about where she works, regardless of who her husband may be," Vincent said. "And I made her an offer she couldn't refuse. Isn't that right, Charlotte?"

"An offer she couldn't refuse? If only I had a euro for every time I've heard you say that."

My hands trembled only slightly as I gathered the English texts I'd brought in for Vincent's lesson. "I'll leave you two alone. Looks like you have some quality father-son bonding to catch up on."

Marcel huffed as I let myself out of Vincent's office, closed the door behind me, and walked down the hall with a huge smile on my face.

I was becoming *quite* the spy.

Ten minutes later, both Vincent and Marcel stormed past the reception desk where I was chatting with my new friend and future model, Chantal.

Vincent stopped only briefly, and for once he couldn't have seemed less interested in my dress *or* my breasts. "I'm taking an early lunch with Marcel," he said. "We'll pick up where we left off tomorrow. In the meantime, I've left some correspondence with my assistant for you to translate."

"Of course," I answered.

Marcel shot me a silent warning with those heartthrob brown eyes of his, and I smiled curtly in return.

Oh, Marcel, you are severely underestimating me.

As soon as they were gone, I fished through my purse for a few seconds. "Oh, shoot. I think I left my cell phone in Vincent's office. Is it okay if I go back there and get it?"

Chantal smiled. "Of course. And you know where Monsieur Boucher's assistant's office is located, right?"

"Yes, I'll go check in with her about the translations. Thanks for the chat, Chantal," I said before doing my own stiletto sprint past a few flying clothing racks, past the art department, and down Vincent's secluded hallway to his corner office.

Once inside, I jetted over to the black armchair where I'd left my iPhone, and after a quick pillow removal, I found that little white beauty, still recording.

I almost kissed the screen, but instead I pressed the Stop button, tucked my phone safely inside my purse, then took another quick peek out into the hallway to make sure no one was coming.

With no sign of life in Vincent's private wing, I closed the door and dashed over to his desk. My heart raced as I scanned the area, but the sleek black laptop I'd seen him using this morning was nowhere to be found. That computer probably contained all sorts of incriminating evidence. No way would he leave that unattended. Vincent may have been the biggest womanizer I'd ever met, but he *wasn't* stupid.

I tried the three desk drawers, but they were all locked. Humph.

On the surface of Vincent's large desk, I only found a mug full of black pens, an unused notepad, and a black telephone. No clutter. No documents strewn about. No evidence to steal.

I realized I should've considered myself lucky simply to have scored that recording of Vincent and Marcel's conversation. I didn't have time to mess around in Vincent's immaculate office. I wasn't going to find anything here.

But just as I headed for the door, a bright pink dot caught my eye in this sea of black office furniture.

I crept over to the black leather couch on the other side of the office, and digging my hand in between the cushions, I discovered a long pink satin ribbon.

Before I could search the other cushions, the sound of heels pounding down the hallway outside sent a shot of adrenaline through my veins. I tucked the ribbon into my purse, and just as the door opened, I lifted up my cell phone.

"Found it!" I said as Mireille appeared. Her pale face looked even more washed out than it had this morning, and dark circles surrounded her fiery eyes.

She arched a suspicious brow at me as I walked past her. "My phone must've dropped out of my bag during our English lesson earlier. I'm off to finish up my translations. See you tomorrow, Mireille."

"Charlotte." Mireille's stern voice shot right through me. Of course she wasn't going to let me get away that easily.

I flipped around, flashing my best poker face. "Yes?"

"Yesterday, after we spoke, did you come back to Vincent's office before he canceled your lesson?"

"Why do you ask?" I stalled.

She placed her hands on her hips and glared at me, the kindness I'd found in her eyes the day before now only a brief memory. "Just answer the question."

I thought about lying to her, but the frantic look on her face reminded me of myself, only one year ago, when I'd discovered my fiancé's online dating profile and learned he'd been lying to me for months.

No matter how bitchy Mireille could be, she didn't deserve this. No woman did. It was bad enough that Vincent was leading her to believe he could actually be a one-woman kind of guy.

I refused to lie for him.

"Yes, I did walk down to Vincent's office after we spoke," I said.

The pained look in her eyes told me she already knew the answer to the question she was about to ask. "And did you see . . . or hear anything?"

I nodded. "Yes, I did. I'm sorry, Mireille."

Mireille's eyes darted past me to the floor, and as she lifted a hand to her face, I noticed her fingers trembling. "*Quel salaud*." *What a bastard*, she whispered.

"You're too good for him," I said, taking a step closer. "He's involved in things you don't want any part in. Trust me."

"You have no idea what you're talking about," she snapped, turning her face away from me. Just as she took off down the hallway, I was certain I spotted a tear streaking down her cheek.

Everything Luc had told me about Vincent was coming true. He left a trail of destruction everywhere he went.

I wouldn't let him destroy me though. Or my marriage.

I forced myself to wait until I'd left the offices of *Bella France* to listen to the recording. I didn't want to risk anyone at my new place of work finding out what I'd just done.

As I exited the Metro at Bellecour, I slipped on my headphones, turned the volume on my iPhone up to full blast, and pressed Play.

Marcel's voice boomed through my ears as I booked it down the lively rue Victor Hugo toward Isabelle's lingerie shop.

"*Mais qu'est-ce que tu fous?*" *What in the hell are you doing?* Marcel growled.

"The way I run my publishing business is of no concern to you," Vincent snapped back in French. "What are you doing here, anyway? I thought you were filming in Paris."

Gosh, what a warm and fuzzy father-son relationship they shared.

"I was, but there's something important I need to talk to you about," Marcel said.

"I thought we agreed to do all of our business through Jean-Michel. It's safer that way."

Who was Jean-Michel?

"This couldn't go through Jean-Michel, *or* through Brigitte. It had to come directly from me."

"Well, out with it then," Vincent said. "I don't have all day."

"You need to shut down the operation," Marcel said. "And you need to leave the country tonight."

Leave the country?

I passed by a *boulangerie* and a caught a heavenly whiff of butter and freshly baked bread, and although my stomach was growling, I kept on walking. This was just too good.

"I don't have time for your games or for your paranoia, *mon fils*," Vincent said. "If you're angry at me for stealing Brigitte's affections, then—"

"I couldn't give a shit about that little slut. She's using both of us to support her drug habit, and she's using *you* to get back at Luc. I don't want anything to do with her, and I told her as much today. It was a mistake for you to involve her in this business. She's not stable. The other girls, they're smarter than Brigitte. They know how to get the job done, and they want to become stars. They know their involvement in *Les Bijoux* will get them there."

"Lower your voice," Vincent snapped. "And get to the point."

"My point, *Father*, is that it's over. And you need to leave the country tonight if you don't want to spend the rest of your life in prison."

"What in God's name are you talking about, Marcel? Have you been compromised?"

A few seconds passed before Marcel spoke. "Of course not. But do you think it's a coincidence that Luc's new wife just happened to walk in here, asking for a job? She's clearly been placed here to dig up dirt on you, me, and Brigitte."

"And who exactly do you think placed her here?" Vincent asked.

"Isn't it obvious?" Marcel said.

"Luc Olivier is a college professor, and he's just as oblivious as his father was." Vincent let out an evil chuckle that made my blood boil. "It's not possible."

"Believe what you want, but I'm telling you it has to be over. And you must leave. I'm trying to help you, Dad. This is your last chance."

"And what about you? You're not exactly innocent," Vincent scoffed.

"You don't need to worry about me. I'll take care of myself. I always have," Marcel said.

"This is nonsense. I want you to leave."

"Please, I know you've always considered Nicolas the smarter one, and I'm just the pretty boy pawn who helps you reel in all of the beautiful, young, desperate actresses so you can make your millions, but just this once, take my advice. You won't regret it."

"Have you mentioned this to anyone else?" For the first time in their entire conversation, I noticed a hint of panic laced in Vincent's bossy tone.

"Like I said, I knew this couldn't go through Jean-Michel, and I didn't want to tell you over the phone. I wanted to see you before—"

"*Ça suffit!*" Vincent's powerful voice shot through my ear, making me jump. "Nothing is going to happen to me, Marcel. There is no way this can be traced back to me *or* to you. Brigitte was the only loose screw, and as of yesterday, I've got her under control. I've been in this business almost as long as I've been in the publishing business. You must have more faith in me than that."

"It's different this time, Dad. Listen, I shouldn't even be here right now. I have to go."

"Wait, I'll follow you out."

I reached the storefront of Chez Isabelle just as I heard the sound of Vincent's office door clicking shut in my recording. As I let myself into Isabelle's palace of gorgeous lingerie, I thought about the fact that I was only one week into my job at *Bella France,* and only eighteen days into my marriage, and things were spiraling out of control.

TWENTY-THREE

"Charlotte, it's so good to see you," Isabelle said in her perky British accent, kissing me lightly on each cheek. Her long, sandy-blond hair swished over her shoulders as she fit a slinky black slip onto one of the mannequins.

"You too, Isabelle. Really, I can't thank you enough for being there for me lately. It's been a total lifesaver. You have no idea." I'd stopped by Isabelle's shop for gossip and support more than a few times over the past two weeks, and she'd even called me the day before to see how I was doing. She was mostly up to date on everything that had happened with Luc, Brigitte, and the Bouchers—*except* for this most recent news, of course.

Isabelle placed a concerned hand on my arm. "Is everything okay, Charlotte? You look a little pale."

"You won't believe the intel I just got," I whispered, casting a glance around the store to make sure no one was listening.

"Intel? You're starting to sound like a secret agent," she said with a giggle. "What's going on?"

I waited until the only other customer left the store before continuing.

"You remember what I told you yesterday, about the discussion I heard between Brigitte and Vincent?"

"And their crazy office sex? How could I forget?"

"Well, I waited up for Luc last night and told him about all of it, but he acted really strange and told me I should stop eavesdropping. Then he spent at least two hours on his laptop before going to bed."

"That's weird."

"I know. And after what I found out today, I'm not sure if I should take this information directly to Luc. He's still not telling me what he knows, and he's just going to get angry that I've been spying again."

"You're probably right. I wouldn't say anything to Luc just yet," she said, straightening up a table of lacy panties in the center of the store. "So what did you find out? I'm dying to know!"

I plucked my phone out of my purse and pulled up the recording. I stared at it for a few seconds, thinking over what I'd heard on my walk to Isabelle's store. I was beginning to form a pretty solid theory on what was going on behind the scenes with Brigitte and the Bouchers, but I still couldn't be one hundred percent sure.

"Hello? Charlotte?" Isabelle's sweet voice called me back to the present. "You look like you're about to faint or break into a messy sob, or perhaps like you could use a glass of wine."

"Yes, wine would be good," I said with a flustered laugh.

"Well, the store has been rather quiet all day. Who am I kidding—it's been quiet for months now. But this afternoon, we can use that to our advantage." Isabelle smiled deviously as she bustled to the front door, flipped over the "Out to Lunch" sign, then locked the door behind her.

"Isabelle, you don't have to—"

"Nonsense," she quipped as she headed for the checkout counter, then bent down and rustled around for a few seconds. "These early afternoon hours are usually my slowest because most of Lyon are still eating their three-hour lunches or they've gone home to take a midday nap."

Isabelle popped up from behind the counter holding two wineglasses and two minibottles of Cabernet Sauvignon. "We may as well embrace the culture, no?" She didn't wait for me to answer as she unscrewed the tops and poured us each a glass.

"Lingerie *and* wine—I should've gotten a job here instead of at the magazine!" I said, accepting the glass without hesitation.

"All right, tell me what's going on," Isabelle said.

Isabelle's advice had been spot-on up to this point, so I was hoping she could help me figure out what to do next.

"The plot is thickening with the Boucher family drama," I began. "And I've continued to take matters into my own hands."

"As any smart woman would," Isabelle said. "So, what did you do?"

"I was giving Vincent his first English lesson today, and Marcel stormed into his office right when we were getting started. Before I left them alone, my phone may have *accidentally* slipped out of my bag, and the Record button just happened to turn on."

Isabelle's sapphire eyes widened, reveling in the drama. "You sneaky girl! I can't believe you recorded their conversation! Can I hear it?"

"Please don't think I'm awful, and please don't tell anyone about this." My finger hovered over the Play button.

Isabelle lifted up her wineglass and gestured to all of the racy lingerie filling the store around us. "Do you really think I'm in a position to judge you? I have three small daughters and I own a lingerie store. Can you even imagine what the other mothers say about me?"

"It's just that there's something really crazy going on with Vincent, Marcel, and Brigitte. And Luc knows more about it than he's telling me. I didn't want to be in the dark any longer, so—"

"Charlotte, you don't have to explain yourself to me. Trust me, I understand needing to do *whatever* you have to do to look out for yourself and for the people you love. Even if it may not be considered moral by others' standards." She focused back on my cell phone. "Maybe I can help. Let's hear it."

I pressed Play and watched Isabelle's confused expression as she listened intently to Vincent and Marcel's argument.

When the recording finished, Isabelle took an exceptionally long sip of wine. Finally, when she came up for air, she asked me, "What do you think it all means? Do you have any idea what this operation is they're talking about?"

"*Les Bijoux*? Well, I can't be one hundred percent certain, of course, but I think I'm starting to form a theory."

"And?"

"Okay, this might sound insane, but what if *Les Bijoux* are prostitutes and Vincent is their pimp? Well, maybe he's not a pimp in the normal sense of the word, but he could be the one cashing in on all the action and running it from behind the scenes—possibly with the help of this Jean-Michel character he mentioned." I emptied the rest of my minibottle of wine into the glass and took a sip before continuing. "Based on what Marcel said, it sounds like they target young, desperate actresses who are looking for a break. Then they pimp them out to God knows who—maybe rich film executives who can promise them their next role. And I think that Luc's ex-wife, Brigitte, is one Vincent's *jewels*—or prostitutes."

Isabelle took the last swig of her wine, then set the glass down on the counter.

"That's quite the theory," she said.

"I know it sounds absurd, but from the little I know of Vincent, and of his obsession with women, I can totally see him running an organized prostitution ring. After listening to this recording and after the conversation I told you about between Vincent and Brigitte yesterday, do you have any other ideas on what else could it be?"

Isabelle suddenly seemed lost in thought. "Who else have you told about this?"

"You're the first person. I'm not sure who to take the recording to."

Isabelle drummed her long fingernails against the countertop. "Hmm, let me think."

"Of course Luc would be the obvious answer . . . but his secrecy has me worried. Does he already know about all of this, and if he does, why hasn't he done anything about it?" I said. "And of course I'm still supposed to be meeting Nicolas Boucher at seven o'clock tonight at La Cour des Loges Hôtel. I don't get the impression that he's the type of guy to involve himself in whatever his dad and brother are working on behind the scenes, but who knows? I can't trust any of them at this point."

"Who will be watching Adeline while you're meeting with Nicolas? Doesn't Luc work late?" Isabelle ran her fingers down the stem of her wineglass, her eyes zeroing in on my cell phone.

"I've already arranged for Luc's sister Sandrine to pick Adeline up from the *crèche* at five o'clock and watch her back at our apartment until I get home. So I'm all set there. The real question is—what should I do with this information?"

She whipped her head up, and for the first time since I'd met her, I noticed a flash of fire in those sapphire eyes of hers. "You're involving yourself in something you don't know anything about, something that, quite honestly, sounds dangerous. I think you need to leave all of this alone."

"So you don't think I should mention this to Luc or to Nicolas? But what if—"

"Destroy the recording and see how it all plays out. This isn't something you want record of when the shit hits the fan. Trust me." Suddenly Isabelle's cell phone buzzed. "Would you excuse me for a minute?" she asked.

I nodded as she took her call into the back room, just as she'd done the week before . . . and several times since.

That was strange.

I left the counter to walk through the lush racks of lingerie while pondering my next course of action. A new collection featured toward the back of the store caught my eye. Not that I had any business buying more lingerie for myself right now, but it certainly didn't hurt to take a peek.

An intricately designed black lace slip fell effortlessly from a white satin hanger. The straps were thin and delicate, and they criss-crossed in the back. Three tiny jewels sparkled right where the two straps crossed, and more showy stones lined the hem of the slip. I placed the sexy piece back on the rack and thumbed through the rest of the collection. Mock emeralds, rubies, sapphires, and amethysts studded all of the bras, panties, thongs, and nighties.

I picked up a ruby-studded bra, then checked the tag to see if was my size.

But the word printed on the tiny label made me do a double take.

Les Bijoux.

As a chill slithered up my spine, I thought about the pink satin ribbon I'd removed from Vincent's couch. It was the same kind of ribbon that Isabelle used to tie up her lingerie gift packages.

I shoved the bra back onto the rack and turned with a start to find Isabelle watching me from the corner.

"Is everything okay?" she asked.

I swallowed, forcing a smile. "Yes, just checking out the latest collections. They're all gorgeous, as usual."

She smiled back at me, but it wasn't her usual, bright smile. She looked tense . . . and scared.

Walking back up to the counter, I found Isabelle eyeing my cell phone again. I snapped up the phone, then pulled up the recording once more. "You know, I think you're right," I said. "I had no business recording their private conversation, and whatever they're up to doesn't concern me. I'm going to delete the recording."

Aiming the screen totally out of Isabelle's line of sight, I hit the Save button and tucked the phone back into my purse. "There, it's gone. I'm just going to do what Luc asked me to do and trust him. He said I have nothing to worry about, and he's probably right. I'm sure it will all be fine."

Isabelle nodded. "Of course it will be. You're doing the right thing, Charlotte. You've had enough drama this week. No need to cloud up your new marriage with even more." Isabelle picked up her sleek black purse from behind the counter and smiled at me. "That was my daughter's school calling, and she's sick again. I'm so sorry to run, but I have to pick her up."

"I totally understand," I said. I sincerely hoped that the name of Isabelle's new *bijoux* collection was only a coincidence. She had three little daughters to look after, and she'd been so kind to me these past few weeks. There was no way she could've been involved with the Boucher family this entire time, was there?

"Is your daughter all right?" I asked as I followed her out of the store.

Isabelle waved her hand. "Oh, yes. Just a little stomach bug. All the kids are coming down with it this week."

After Isabelle closed up behind us, she gave me a quick kiss on each cheek before we both jetted off in opposite directions.

Even though I didn't want to acknowledge my gut feeling on this one, I had a sneaking suspicion that Isabelle's daughter was just fine.

I also had a feeling that she knew I wasn't as stupid as I was making myself out to be.

TWENTY-FOUR

After that bizarre encounter with Isabelle, I decided my meeting with Nicolas couldn't wait.

Standing in front of the fancy, five-star Cour des Loges Hôtel in Vieux Lyon, I dialed Nicolas' number.

"Charlotte?" he answered.

"*Bonjour,* Nicolas. I was wondering if you might be available to meet a little earlier than seven o'clock tonight?"

"Of course. What time were you thinking?"

"Um . . . would right now work? I'm outside your hotel."

A long pause traveled over the line before Nicolas responded. "You're here right now? Is everything okay?"

"I really need to talk to you, Nicolas. It's urgent."

"I'm in room 302. Come on up."

It was my first time inside La Cour des Loges Hôtel, and with its high ceilings and grand, stone archways, it looked more like the inside of a medieval castle than a modern-day hotel. I took the elevator up to Nicolas' floor and headed down a long, candlelit hallway before pausing outside his door.

If Luc found out I was meeting Nicolas alone in his private hotel room, things could only go from bad to worse. But until Luc spilled his secrets, he couldn't expect me not to have a few of my own.

Before I could change my mind about my next course of action, I knocked on Nicolas' hotel door.

When his rugged face appeared, for once I did *not* think about his outrageously hot piano sex scene immediately upon seeing him.

Instead, the concern I saw in those stone-gray eyes of his made me see him as a person, as a friend. He ushered me into his beautiful hotel suite, past a crackling fireplace and a king-size bed, its covers all rustled about.

"Please, have a seat," Nicolas offered as we reached a cushy tan couch lining the back wall.

I sank into the comfortable sofa and finally let out the breath I'd been holding since I left Isabelle's shop. I had no idea if talking to Nicolas could help anything right now, or if it would only serve to further sabotage my already desperate situation. But as he sat down beside me and gazed at me with those sad, sincere eyes of his, I realized I had nothing left to lose. And judging by the look on Nicolas' face, he didn't either.

"Why did you want to meet tonight?" I asked him.

"Like I said, I have something important to give you," Nicolas said. "Something I need you to pass along to Luc for me. I've tried several times this week to reach him, but he won't take my calls. I even tried to go to his work at the university when I arrived in Lyon yesterday, but . . ." Nicolas trailed off, seeming unsure if he wanted to continue.

"But what? I asked.

"Never mind, it's not important." Nicolas' jaw tightened as he stood from the couch and walked over to a sleek black suitcase next to the bed. He unzipped the top pouch and pulled out a large manila envelope.

Gripping the envelope tightly in his hands, he paced over to the window and gazed down at the cobblestone street below.

"What is it, Nicolas? What's inside that envelope?"

He turned back toward me, lowering his heavy gaze. "The contents prove without a doubt that Luc's father was innocent. But they also bring to light a different truth, a truth that I myself didn't want to believe, and a fact that I am certain Luc and certain members of his family will not be pleased to learn as well. I wanted Luc to see this before anyone else does. Even before you, Charlotte. Can you promise me you will give this to him?"

I eyed the envelope, wondering what this shocking truth was that Nicolas was talking about. And if I were to hand it over to Luc without first taking a peek inside, would Luc even share its contents with me?

Nicolas hesitated before handing me the envelope. "I've thought long and hard about whether or not I wanted to hand this information over to Luc, but after everything that's happened between our families—after what Luc believes I did to him many years ago—I think he deserves to hear the truth. And he deserves to hear it from me."

"Are you referring to Marion?" I asked. "Sandrine told me what happened. Or at least she told me Luc's version of the story."

Nicolas focused on the floor, regret tracing the lines around his eyes. "It was shortly after I'd landed my first big role in a movie. My picture was on the cover of every magazine, and women would literally throw themselves at me. I have to admit that, at first, it was fun. But I honestly never had any interest in Marion. She was Luc's girlfriend, and considering Luc and I had only just begun to talk again after our parents' divorce, I would never have crossed that line. One night, I invited them over for dinner, and Marion came a half an hour early—alone. She told me that she was in love with me and that she wanted to leave Luc."

Nicolas ran his hands through his dark brown hair before continuing. "The look in her eyes, though, wasn't sincere. She was in love with the idea of me, with the actor she'd seen on screen. I told her that wasn't the real me. That she was making the biggest mistake of her life leaving Luc. Just as I asked her to go, she got really emotional, and I made the mistake of hugging her. Right when Luc walked in the door, Marion kissed me. The timing couldn't have been worse. Luc loved Marion; he was planning to marry her. In his eyes, from that day forward, I was just like my father. Luc ended things with Marion, and that's when he met Brigitte. He was too hurt to notice what a mess Brigitte was, and I think he just couldn't handle being alone. He'd lost his family, his best friend, and the woman he loved, all within a five-year time span. So he married Brigitte without having a clue of the disaster he was getting himself into."

A sickening feeling seized my gut as the pieces of Luc's past began to come together. I only wished it had been Luc filling me in all along.

"Do you think that's why Luc married me?" I said. "Just another Band-Aid to cover up his troubled past?"

Nicolas' silence made me fear the worst. Had I been wrong about Luc's love for me? Were his romantic gestures all just a lie so he didn't have to be alone? Had his love been a lie too?

"Luc may have a troubled past, but he isn't a stupid man. He wouldn't make the same mistake twice. Marrying Brigitte was a mistake, but out of that error, he got Adeline. And if I know anything about Luc, I know that the last thing he would ever want is for his daughter to be the child of *two* divorces. He wouldn't have married you if he wasn't sure of his love for you. I'm certain about that, Charlotte."

"Then why won't he tell me *anything*?"

Nicolas shook his head. "I don't know. I really have no idea what Luc is up to, but I want to believe the best. I don't want to see you get hurt."

"You seem to be the only one."

After a few seconds of silence, Nicolas spoke. "Why did you come to see me early, Charlotte? Did something happen?"

I pondered telling Nicolas about the recording, about my *bijoux* theory, and about the new possibility of Isabelle's involvement in it all, but until I knew what he was hiding inside this envelope, I felt it was best to keep my mouth shut.

There *was* something I needed to ask him, though.

"Do you know who was photographed kissing on Marcel's balcony when we stayed at his apartment in Paris on Saturday night? None of us can remember a single thing past that first glass of champagne in the limo, and I really need to know what you remember about that night."

A curious gleam passed through Nicolas' gaze, and just as he opened his mouth to respond, the sound of a key in the door made him stop.

Right as I turned my head, I noticed a short red dress hanging in the closet.

And as the door opened, I realized that my hunch had been right all along.

Clad in a slinky black top, dark skinny jeans, and a pair of shimmering gray heels, Lexi strutted into Nicolas' hotel room like it was her second home.

"Lexi . . . I had a feeling it might be you," I said.

She set her purse down on the nightstand then walked hesitantly over to me. "We were going to wait to tell you until a little more time had passed, but I couldn't lie to you, Char."

Lexi shot Nicolas a sweet smile before taking his hand in hers. And for the first time since I'd walked into his hotel suite, the worry that had plagued Nicolas' expression was wiped clean by his rugged, movie-star grin.

"So, you're together now?" I asked.

Lexi's cheeks blushed the shade of a cherry tomato as she nodded, then batted her long eyelashes up at Nicolas.

Oh man, she had it *bad.*

"But what about Dylan? Have you told him yet?" I wasn't about to beat around the bush. I'd had enough secrets to last a lifetime.

"We broke up on Sunday," Lexi said. "I didn't want to tell you earlier because you were already so worried about what happened with the tabloids, and I was afraid you'd think it was your fault."

Lexi and Nicolas kept their hands tightly intertwined, and all the while the dreamy gaze in Nicolas' eyes told me that *he* had it bad too.

"The truth is that the minute Dylan and I moved in together, everything went to crap. You know that, Char. The tabloid debacle was just the icing on an already stale cake. Dylan is moving out this week, which is why I wanted to get out of Paris for a few days. And when Nicolas invited me down to Lyon, I could hardly refuse."

"I'm sorry I didn't say anything earlier, Charlotte," Nicolas said. "We were planning to tell you tonight when you came to the hotel, but you caught me off guard when you arrived early."

"So, on Saturday night, the picture of the couple kissing on Marcel's balcony—it was you two?" I asked.

Both of their heads shook violently. "No, that wasn't us," Nicolas said.

"Nothing like *that* happened between us Saturday night. As much as Dylan and I were having trouble, and I knew we were nearing the end, I wasn't going to cheat on him," Lexi said.

"I took Lexi for a late-night stroll around Paris, and we talked all night long. I brought her back to Marcel's apartment around three in the morning."

I remembered Lexi's excited face when she'd received that call on Sunday morning on the Paris Metro. She'd had that same secretive smile the day before when we'd shared dessert and wine.

It was all coming together now, except for one slight problem.

"You've been saying this entire time that you didn't remember anything that happened on Saturday night, Lexi. But you did remember," I said. "You remembered everything."

Lexi nodded. "Nicolas and I didn't have quite as much to drink as the rest of you. I'm sorry I lied, Char. I—"

"It's okay. I understand, and I'm glad the two of you have found each other. But I have to ask, do either of you know who was photographed kissing Marcel on the balcony that night?"

Judging from the topless mess Fiona had been when I'd awoken her in Marcel's bed, I was still certain she'd been the intoxicated culprit, but with her recent pregnancy scare, she needed to know for sure.

Lexi shook her head. "After Nicolas and I came back from our walk, the apartment was silent. We said good-bye, and I passed out on the bed beside you, Char. At least I thought it was you. The room was so dark—I can't remember why I thought it was you and not Fiona."

I turned to Nicolas. "Do you know who it was?"

Nicolas's hesitation told me he knew something—something he didn't want to spill.

"Please, Nicolas," I said. "It's important."

He sighed. "My brother was definitely with a woman on the balcony that night, but I'm certain it wasn't either of your friends," he said to me, a solemn look on his face.

"What do you mean?" I asked. "Are you saying . . . ?" I couldn't even finish my sentence, because what I thought he was implying was too sickening for me to acknowledge.

Had it been *me* on that balcony kissing Marcel Boucher?

"Was it Charlotte?" Lexi blurted.

"No, that's not what I meant," he said quickly.

My hand shot to my chest. "Oh, thank God. You just about gave me a heart attack."

"If it wasn't Charlotte or Fiona, then who was it?" Lexi asked, placing a hand on Nicolas' arm.

"It's a woman he's been seeing for a while now . . . in secret."

"Is it Brigitte?" I asked.

"Wait, isn't Brigitte dating your dad?" Lexi said to Nicolas.

A look of disgust passed through Nicolas' eyes. "Yes, Brigitte is dating my father, and while I do believe she has tried to lead my brother Marcel on, he's not buying it. He never was. It wasn't Brigitte on the balcony that night. It was a woman named Isabelle."

Holy shit.

"You're certain?" I asked Nicolas.

"Yes, I'm positive," he answered.

"Thank you, Nicolas. You have no idea how much you've helped," I said before taking off for the door.

"Charlotte, where are you going? Is everything okay?" Lexi asked.

Right before I jetted out, I nodded at her. "Not yet, but it will be."

TWENTY-FIVE

I charged through the gates of Université Jean Moulin Lyon 3 and headed toward the School of Management, which housed the finance courses. The last time I'd walked these halls was when I'd taken classes here as an undergraduate, back when my biggest concerns were deciding which Lyon bar my girlfriends and I would be partying at that night and making sure we woke up in time for class the next day.

My, how things had changed.

Pushing past a loud group of college students lingering in the hallway after class, I rounded the corner into Luc's department. The administrative assistant was just hanging up the phone as I stormed into her office out of breath.

"*Bonjour*, I'm looking for Luc Olivier, Professor of Finance," I said in French. "Do you happen to know if he's in class right now?"

She tilted her head and raised a confused brow. "I'm sorry, which professor did you say you were looking for?"

"Luc Olivier," I said more slowly this time. Then I remembered to smile. And breathe.

"You must have the wrong department," she said. "We don't have any professors here by that name."

My smiled wilted. "I'm certain this is the correct department. I'm his wife, Charlotte. He just started teaching finance courses here this semester. Perhaps you're not familiar with his name since he's new to the university teaching staff."

The woman rustled around on her messy desk, finally plucking up a sheet of paper underneath a stack of notebooks. "Here is a list of all of our finance course offerings this semester, and to the right you'll see the professors' names. I assure you, *madame*, you will not find the name Luc Olivier on this list."

I took the paper from her, scanning it frantically for my husband's name.

But it wasn't there. Professor Luc Olivier was nowhere to be found.

Nicolas' words came rushing back to me. He told me he'd tried to find Luc at the university . . . and then he'd trailed off, as if he didn't want to tell me the rest.

He didn't want to tell me the rest because it meant that Luc had been lying to me all along about his job.

With a shaky hand, I placed the course list back on the receptionist's desk. "*Merci, madame*," I managed to say before turning and walking slowly out of her office.

Students' light-hearted banter echoed through the hallway, but I barely noticed.

How could Luc have lied to me about something as basic as where he worked? Even if I could excuse all of the other secrets he'd been keeping—about Brigitte, his father, his relationship with the Boucher family—how could I overlook this one?

And if he hadn't been spending his long "teaching" days here, where in the hell was he?

Tears stung my eyes as I pushed through the double doors of the university wondering if, once again, I'd given my heart away too rashly, only to be left in the dust by another man who wasn't who he said he was.

I gazed down at the sparkling diamond on my left ring finger, wondering if our promise to love and stand by each other forever had really meant as much to Luc as it had to me. It certainly didn't seem that way.

My feet crunched over the newly fallen leaves as I walked numbly away from the university, saddened that my happy memories of this school would forever be replaced with Luc's lie, with his betrayal. How had I made such a colossal mistake to marry someone without finding out who he really was before I tied the knot?

Had I learned nothing from the cheating debacle with my ex-fiancé the year before?

Or from the disaster of my parents' marriage?

I'd been planning to take the envelope and the recording to Luc, and tell him about Isabelle's potential involvement in Vincent and Marcel's *bijoux* scheme. I was going to turn all of the evidence over to my husband, without asking him to explain to me what he already knew.

I was planning to trust him. To stop questioning him. To believe that he had some sort of plan to deal with Brigitte and the Bouchers. To trust that he would take whatever steps necessary to protect me and Adeline.

But how could I trust Luc, how could I help him, when I didn't even know where to find him?

I reached the *quai* of the Rhône River and watched as the late afternoon sun cast a yellow shimmer over the choppy waters. I pulled out my phone to call Lexi, but before I dialed, it buzzed in my hand.

It was Sandrine, Luc's sister.

"Hello, Sandrine?" I answered.

She spoke hastily, her voice all high-pitched and frantic. "I just went to pick up Adeline at the *crèche*, and they said she'd already been picked up by some other woman who was claiming to be me. What's going on, Charlotte? Do you know where Adeline is?"

Panic seized my chest. "That's impossible," I said.

"Could it have been one of your friends?" she asked.

"No, my friends don't know where Adeline's school is, and even if they did, they would never have lied and said they were you."

"Well, who would?" she snapped.

"I don't—" A startling realization silenced me.

Only one other person knew I'd arranged for Sandrine to pick up Adeline today.

"Isabelle," I whispered.

"Who's Isabelle?" Sandrine asked.

I scoured the tree-lined boulevard for the nearest cab. "Isabelle is the owner of this lingerie store I love, Chez Isabelle. Luc bought me something from her shop when we first got back together, and since then, she and I have become really good friends—or so I thought. She's the only other person who knew you were picking Adeline up for me today. And she's the only one with a reason to do this."

"What are you talking about, Charlotte? Are you in some kind of trouble? Tell me what's going on."

A sleek black cab with tinted windows swerved up to the curb. "Sandrine, if you talk to Luc, tell him I know he isn't a professor, and tell him Isabelle has Adeline. I have to go."

I hung up the phone and swung the cab door open.

But just as I stepped one foot into the car, a strong hand wrapped around my wrist. I tried to yank my arm back, but the man who pulled me into the backseat was much quicker. He slammed the door behind me as the car screeched down the street.

I only managed to steal a brief glance at the man's salt and pepper hair and severe hazel eyes before he pushed me down into the seat, growled at me in French to stop screaming, then dealt me a violent blow to the head.

A whiff of familiar, flowery perfume wafted past my nose, making me suddenly and acutely aware of the pain shooting through my head and drumming away at my temples.

I tried to bat open my eyelids, but the jarring ache behind my eyes stopped me.

Where am I?

A drop of something wet rolled down my cheek, and when I tried to lift my hand up to wipe it off, I realized my wrists were tied behind my back.

What the—?

"Putain!" shouted a familiar male voice. "What in God's name are you doing, Isabelle?" he continued in French.

At the mention of that name, my eyes popped open.

Isabelle's long, sandy-blond hair came into focus as she argued with a fuming Marcel amid the racks of silky lingerie in her store.

"You'll understand when you hear this," she snapped before messing with something in her hands.

I tried to move my legs, but realized my ankles were tied to a chair; I presumed that the liquid still rolling down my face was blood.

Before I could summon up the energy to speak, the tense argument I'd recorded earlier between Marcel and Vincent played loudly through the store, their voices only serving to intensify the pounding inside my head.

I cast a quick glance at my surroundings and noticed they'd placed me in the very back of the store. It also looked as if the blinds on the front window had been drawn shut.

As the recording finished, I remembered something.

Adeline.

"Where is she?" I called out, my voice scratchy and hoarse. "Where is Adeline?"

Isabelle swiveled around, revealing a wild, unhinged look in those gorgeous blue eyes of hers. "Don't worry, Charlotte. Adeline will be fine."

She walked toward me, her pace oddly calm despite the fact that she was clearly losing her mind.

"Then why did you take her? What do you want from me?" I asked.

"I need to know if you've let anyone else hear this recording. And I needed to find out what Nicolas was going to give to you." That's when I noticed the manila envelope in her hands.

"No one else has heard the recording, Isabelle. I promise. You can delete it right now, and it will never see the light of day. And I haven't even looked inside that envelope, so I have no idea what Nicolas is up to either."

"How can I trust you?" Isabelle asked, continuing her cool, slow pacing.

"Isabelle, we're friends. I would never want to do anything to hurt you." Judging by the fact that she'd had me followed, kidnapped, and tied up against my will, it was clear that Isabelle and I were not on the same page with where our friendship lies. "You have what you want, so let me go and take me to Adeline, please."

Isabelle placed a hand on her hip and thought for a moment, then lowered her deranged gaze back to me. "I think it's too late for that now, Charlotte. If only you would've stayed out of it all along."

Marcel stepped in front of Isabelle. "This is a mistake," he said sternly.

Isabelle waved my cell phone and the manila envelope in his face. "Were you planning on telling me about any of this, Marcel? Or were you just going to leave me high and dry while you left the country with your father?"

He grabbed her wrist, then wrenched the phone from her hands. "I was going to protect you, Isabelle. I love you. You know that. But now you've done this. . . ." He shook his head in my direction, clenching his jaw as anger soared through his eyes. "It has to be over. It's all over now."

She pulled her wrist from his grasp and stormed toward me. "Tell me who else has heard the recording!" she yelled. "If you were so quick to play it for me—someone you've only known for over a month—then I don't believe you would've kept it to yourself."

How could I have gotten so close to Isabelle this past month without noticing how crazy she was?

"No one else has heard it, Isabelle. I swear. I was going to give it to Luc, but I . . . I couldn't find him at work. I don't know where he is."

"What about Nicolas?" she snapped. "Did you play it for him?"

I shook my head. "No. I told you earlier that I didn't trust him either. Please just calm down. I'm sure we can figure this all out." I pulled at my wrists, but they wouldn't budge. If Isabelle had hurt Adeline, I would never forgive myself. How could I have been so stupid as to trust her?

"Is that what you want me to do, too, Marcel? Calm down?" Her shrill voice echoed through the store, rattling my frazzled, throbbing head.

I wouldn't let her win, though. I had to get the hell out of there and find Adeline. "Isabelle, think about your daughters," I said. "You don't want to do anything you'd regret. Just untie me and take me to Adeline, and we'll forget any of this ever happened."

"Think about my daughters?" she screeched. "That's what I've been doing all along. That's why I got involved in this business in the first place!" She charged back over to Marcel, squaring her gaze in front of his face. "I didn't want to support your father's fancy little prostitution ring, but with my store on the brink of closing, you knew I had no choice but to take your offer. The money from those orders has helped me keep my apartment and has kept food on the table for my girls. And you promised me, Marcel. You promised no one would ever find out. That's why we agreed to keep our relationship secret. But the secret is out, and now we need to fix it so everything can go back to the way it was *before* Miss Charlotte over here started playing detective."

"No one else besides Charlotte has any clue you're involved, Isabelle. You have to trust me on that," Marcel said, but the doubt in his movie-star eyes told me he knew more than he was letting on.

"Then why did you tell your father it's all over? And why did you tell him to leave the country?" she hissed. "You would only say those things if you knew we'd been busted."

Marcel lowered his voice. "*We* haven't been busted, but my father has. I felt it was only right to give him the chance to leave France before he gets arrested."

"I see where your loyalty lies," she huffed. "And what about *Les Bijoux*? What will happen?"

Marcel shook his head. "It's over, Isabelle. I'm sorry, but it's over."

Isabelle's face froze in panic. "My beautiful lingerie line *and* your father's precious girls—his so-called *jewels*? All of it?"

"*Oui*. The *prostituées*, the lingerie—everything," Marcel said, his shameful gaze meeting the floor. "It's finished."

Isabelle hurled the envelope across the room, then paced frantically through the aisles of lingerie. "I had the *bijoux* lingerie line tailored specifically for this dirty operation of your father's, and I just placed a massive order at *your* request. This is my livelihood, Marcel. You know that! What will I do now? How will I support my girls?"

"I'll help you, *mon amour,*" Marcel said, stopping her with a firm hand on the shoulder. "I won't let anything happen to you or to your girls. I love you, you know that."

She shrugged him off of her. "The last time I depended on a man, I was left with nothing. No way to take care of my children, no money, nothing! I'll never make that mistake again, let alone with someone who's romping around Paris with a different girl in his bed every week." Isabelle flicked her angry gaze over to me. "Charlotte's friend *Fiona* knows all about Marcel's skills in the bedroom, doesn't she?"

"What are you talking about?" Marcel asked her.

"In one of our daily gossip sessions, Charlotte so kindly informed me that she discovered her friend Fiona naked in your bed that morning. And it's funny, because when I showed up unannounced at your apartment that night, you insisted on keeping me in the living room and out on the balcony. You did *not* want me in your bedroom that night, and now I know why."

So Nicolas hadn't been lying. It *had* been Marcel and Isabelle kissing on the balcony the night of our champagne-induced memory loss. And the black-and-pink thong I'd spotted on Marcel's floor—it belonged to Isabelle.

But that still didn't explain what Fiona was doing naked in Marcel's bed the next morning.

"You really don't know how to keep your mouth shut, do you?" Marcel snapped at me.

"I'm sorry, I wasn't aware that Isabelle—my new *friend*—was dating you, because she never told me." I couldn't help but let out a little sarcasm. The mess that Isabelle and Marcel had made of their lives was not going to garner any sympathy from me.

"It wasn't what it looked like," Marcel said.

"Then what was it?" I asked. "It looked to me like you took advantage of how drunk my friend was to have another meaningless exploit."

Isabelle crossed her arms and leveled her fuming gaze at Marcel.

He opened his mouth to speak, but Isabelle cut him off. "The truth, Marcel. I want the truth."

"The truth is that Charlotte's friends were falling all over me all night. I wasn't planning to do anything with any of them. I was furious my brother was going to see you in the first place, Charlotte, and the only way I could keep an eye on the situation was to ask you all to stay at my apartment. Nicolas left with your friend Lexi, and I thought the rest of you went to bed in one of the guest rooms. But when I walked into my bedroom, I found Fiona asleep in my bed.

She'd already taken off all her clothes. I tried to wake her up and get her to put them back on, but she just mumbled something about how she likes to sleep in the nude and how she missed some guy named Marc. Only a few minutes later, you showed up at my door, Isabelle."

"What a convenient story," Isabelle remarked.

Considering Marcel's reputation, it did seem farfetched that he would have a naked girl in his bed and not try to sleep with her. And I wouldn't have pegged Fiona as the type to insist on sleeping in the nude, but for Fiona's sake, I honestly hoped Marcel was telling the truth. And I hoped I would make it out of there safely so I could tell her.

"What did you mean when you said you needed to 'keep an eye' on the situation that night?" I asked Marcel.

"I'm sure you'll find out soon enough," Marcel said before taking a step closer to Isabelle and running his thumb down her cheek. "I'm telling you the truth, *mon amour.* I'm in love with you, and I was finished with all of the other women. They are meaningless to me. It's you I want."

Oh, these Frenchmen! Do they ever turn off the romance?

Marcel pulled Isabelle into his arms then planted his lips on hers. I'd seen enough of Marcel's overly dramatic movie kisses. The last thing I felt like doing right now was watching another one from my vantage point as the tied-up, beaten-down hostage.

"Now that we've gotten that all worked out," I interjected, "can you please let me go?"

They held their kiss for another few seconds before Isabelle turned to me with a new fire in her eyes.

"I'm not going to ruin anything for you, Isabelle. I promise," I assured her. "Until this afternoon, I had no idea you were connected to Marcel or his father in any way. I would never want to hurt your ability to provide for your daughters."

She walked over to me, slowly shaking her head. "I'm so sorry, Charlotte. But I can't do that."

It was then that I noticed the shiny knife she'd pulled out of her pocket.

Oh, God.

"Isabelle, think about what you're doing here," I said. "If you hurt me, you'll lose your girls forever."

Marcel's eyes widened when he noticed the knife in her hand.

"Don't try to stop me, Marcel." Her voice crackled as she ran a finger over the sharp blade. "I'll handle this."

Just as Marcel lunged at her, the sound of shattering glass pierced my ears.

My muscles instinctively tensed, bracing for a blow.

But instead, a troop of black police boots stormed through the racks of lingerie, guns aimed at Isabelle and Marcel, who had tumbled to the floor as Marcel struggled to ply the knife from his crazy girlfriend's hands.

A deep, steady voice sounded from the lineup. "Drop the knife."

That couldn't be . . .

I lifted my gaze to the man who'd just spoken, but I couldn't believe it was true. I blinked a few times, thinking it must've been the blow to my head that was making me imagine the sight of the handsome, sexy man standing amid all of these armed officers.

But he was as real as the pounding of my heart.

"Luc?" I managed to spit out.

Still dressed in the dark jeans and white-collared shirt he'd left the house in this morning, Luc was the only one of the bunch *not* dressed in a police uniform.

But he did have a gun, and like the others, it was pointed at Isabelle and Marcel.

He nodded at me before repeating his warning. "Drop the knife, Isabelle."

Isabelle's hand went limp, the knife clattering to the ground as tears poured down her cheeks. She sobbed into Marcel's shoulder as he held her tightly. "It's over now, *chérie*," he whispered into her hair. "It's over."

I barely heard them going on like the pair of tormented lovers they were as I watched my husband scoop the knife off the ground and rush toward me.

As two of the policemen pried Isabelle off Marcel and cuffed them both, Luc cut the ropes off my wrists and feet.

I was too stunned to ask Luc all of the questions burning on the tip of my tongue, but I did manage to say one word: "Adeline."

"I have her," Luc said. "She's safe."

I released the breath that had been lodged in my lungs, and it was only once Luc had freed me from the chair that I noticed my entire body was trembling.

Luc wiped the blood from my cheek, then wiped a tear from my eye. "And you are too, *mon amour*. You're safe now."

"But . . . I don't understand. Are you some sort of undercover cop or something?"

"I'll explain everything once we get you out of here. I promise." He wrapped his strong arms around me and pulled me into his chest. And for the first time since this entire scandal had begun, I stopped questioning him, stopped doubting him, and instead placed my trust in my husband and let him hold me tight.

TWENTY-SIX

After a quick trip to the hospital to stitch up the gash on my forehead and to confirm that I did, in fact, have a concussion from the blow I'd been dealt earlier in the black "taxi cab," Luc drove me back to our apartment where his mother and sister were waiting with Adeline.

The minute we walked in the door, Sandrine wrapped me up in a tight hug while Luc's mom kissed him on the forehead, then promptly shook him by the shoulders.

"You had us all so scared," she said in French. "What were you thinking?"

Luc sighed. "*Oui*, I know, *maman*. I will explain everything."

"Have you known all along what's been going on, Charlotte?" Luc's mom asked.

I shook my head, but thought better of it the minute my temples started pounding again.

"*Maman*, I think Charlotte needs to rest," Sandrine said, ushering me toward the couch.

"I want to see Adeline first," I said. "Is she asleep already?"

Sandrine nodded. "Yes, we just put her down. She was exhausted, the poor little thing. But thankfully she was only exhausted from playing with Isabelle's daughters. She had no clue anything bad was going on, and she was only a little confused as to why this strange woman picked her up at the *crèche*. Thank God she's okay."

Luc followed me back to Adeline's room, and when we peeked inside, we found her all curled up under the covers, clutching Luc

Penguin, Charlotte Penguin, and Adeline Penguin tightly to her chest. Thankfully, Brigitte Penguin was nowhere to be found.

I took a careful seat on the edge of Adeline's bed, stroking her pretty auburn hair as she breathed lightly in and out. Luc sat on the other side of the bed and kissed Adeline on the forehead.

"Luc, what if something had happened to her?" I whispered. "I would never have been able to forgive myself."

Luc took my hand and smiled at me. "Nothing did happen to her, *mon amour,* and *none* of this was your fault. Now come with me. It's time for me to tell you the truth about everything."

I gave Adeline a kiss and silently thanked God that our little girl was okay. She wasn't only Luc's daughter anymore, she was mine too. And I would do everything in my power to protect and love her for the rest of my life.

Luc took my hand and led me back into the living room where Sandrine and Michèle were waiting for me with a pillow, an ice pack, two pain pills, and a glass of water. Once they got me all settled in on the couch, the three of us turned to Luc and waited for him to begin.

He sat down in the armchair facing us and, finally, he told all three of the women in his life the full, uncensored truth.

"I guess I'll have to start from the beginning," Luc began in French. "In high school, when Dad was convicted of embezzlement and sent to prison, I know you never believed me, *maman* and Sandrine, but I knew he was innocent."

Luc's mother crossed her arms and pursed her lips, but thankfully she stayed silent. It was all I could do to force this dazed, pounding head of mine to focus on Luc's words. If the two of them started arguing, I'd have to leave the room.

"There was just no way a man who had managed our family finances so poorly for so long would have the know-how to commit a financial crime of that magnitude. Plus, they never did trace where all of that money ended up. It looked as if it was transferred through several offshore accounts—but then, it never turned up."

Sandrine nodded. "Yes, but I figured Dad had managed *that* money just as poorly as he'd done with our family finances."

Luc shook his head. "No, that wasn't the case. I'll tell you exactly where that money did go, but first let me explain how I found out in the first place. I know you have all thought that I worked in finance for several years in Paris before making a career change to teaching."

"Clearly we know now that wasn't the case," Sandrine said. "So what *have* you been doing?"

I thought back to the image of Luc leading a pack of armed French policemen into the lingerie store before he'd busted both Isabelle and Marcel. I still could hardly wrap my throbbing head around it.

"It was a necessary lie," Luc conceded. "After college, I trained to be an undercover agent for the government, and my focus was on investigating financial crimes."

"Did you do all of this for Dad?" Sandrine asked. "Because you believed he was innocent?"

"Yes, I knew all along who was truly behind the embezzlement, and I wanted to bring the truth to light in the hope that it could fix our family, not to mention save our father's reputation and career."

"This family is broken for many more reasons than for what your father did," Michèle admitted. "I had a hand in it all too, you know. If I had never married Vincent—"

"*Maman*, please. I will get to Vincent in a moment," Luc said, flaring his nostrils as he said his ex-step-father's name.

"In order to obtain my position with the government," he continued, "I had to act as if I believed that Dad was guilty, and I had to cut off all contact with him—or at least pretend to. The idea of the government hiring the son of a man who'd been convicted of embezzlement was crazy enough, let alone if I was still talking to him. But you see, even my word that I'd cut off all ties with my father wasn't enough. I had to have a friend on the inside to help me get the job, and this is where my friend Guillaume Dubois came in."

"That name sounds familiar," Sandrine said. "Did you go to college with him?"

Funny, like many of the names I'd learned in the past three weeks, I'd never heard the name Guillaume Dubois out of Luc's mouth.

"Yes, he was one of my closest friends, and more than anyone I know, he understands what it's like to have a dramatic family. Both of his older brothers are ex-cons, and one of them is currently in prison." Luc turned to me before continuing. "In fact, Charlotte, do you remember the couple that crashed our cocktail cruise before our wedding reception in Annecy?"

"I may have been smacked in the head earlier, but I could never forget that." I thought back to the pretty girl with long auburn hair who'd accidentally boarded the boat we'd taken out on the Lake of Annecy. She'd told me she was a wedding planner and that she was absolutely mortified that she'd crashed our wedding. Later we'd found out they were wanted by the police.

"What do they have to do with your friend Guillaume?" I asked Luc.

"The guy who crashed our wedding cruise is one of Guillaume's brothers—the one who's *not* in prison. But I want to allow Guillaume to explain all of this to you. He has invited us to his family's vineyard, which isn't too far from Lyon. Once you're feeling better, of course."

"A trip to a French vineyard sounds amazing after the day I just had," I said with a tired smile.

"You won't have a day like this ever again, *chérie,* I can promise you that," Luc said as he reached over and squeezed my hand. "So to get back to the story, I worked on many high-profile cases, and because my cover was never blown—well, until now of course—I moved up quickly in the organization. In addition to investigating financial crimes, I moved on to investigate and bust organized crime rings."

"Wait a second," I spoke up. "When we first met last year at the Cité Universitaire, you said you were going to grad school—but you weren't going back to school, were you? You were living there undercover, and *you* were the one who busted that drug ring at the Cité that we read about in the paper on the last day of our honeymoon."

Luc raised a brow and grinned at me. "Yes, that was me."

"I thought it was weird that a thirty-year-old once-married man would live in a student dorm. I guess this explains why you kept disappearing for weeks and months at a time, and why you barely ever told me anything about your past."

He nodded. "Yes, *chérie*. Part of that was due to the divorce and custody battle, of course, but the other part was due to my job. I'm so sorry I couldn't tell you." He looked to his mom and sister, who were now staring at him with mouths agape. "I'm sorry I couldn't tell you two either. It was imperative that I keep my cover to do what I entered the organization to do."

"Which was to take down Vincent Boucher," I said.

"Even with a concussion, you are catching on quickly, *mon amour*," Luc said, flashing that sexy smile of his my way. Despite all of the drama, the secrets, and the lies, the fact that I now knew my husband was an undercover government agent had just raised his sexiness level to the max.

"You did all of this to get revenge on Vincent?" Sandrine asked.

"Not for revenge," Luc said. "I did it for justice. Justice for our father and for our family. I knew Vincent was behind the embezzlement, but because he is such a master at making sure none of his illegal activity is traced back to him, it has taken many years to build a solid case against him."

"What about the information Nicolas provided in that envelope?" I asked. "He said that whatever was inside proved without a doubt that your father was innocent."

"Nicolas must've found a way to break into his father's confidential files, and he did find some old financial documents that show proof of Vincent's involvement in the embezzlement case, but I'd found that same proof years ago."

"If you've had the proof all along, why did you take so long to arrest Vincent and to prove Dad's innocence?" Sandrine asked.

"Because I started to figure out that Vincent was involved in something much bigger than just embezzling company funds. And I wanted to bring him down for everything. Not just for what he did to our father."

A troubled look washed over Michèle's cold features. It must've been hard for her to hear that the father of her children really had been innocent all along, and that Vincent—the man she'd made the mistake of marrying next—had been the true culprit.

"So what is this big thing that Vincent has been involved in?" Michèle asked quietly. "And what does it have to do with that lingerie store?"

Luc nodded to me. "If Charlotte is up for it, I'd like for her to tell you. It seems I have finally met my match. She has become quite the spy this past week."

I pressed the ice pack harder to my temple and smiled at my husband. "Well, I had to take things into my own hands because you weren't telling me anything. At least now I understand *why* you couldn't tell me."

"So what did you find out?" Sandrine asked me.

I cleared my throat and launched into my story. "After overhearing and recording some of Vincent's private conversations at the offices of *Bella France* this week, I began to believe that Vincent was running an organized prostitution ring."

Michèle's face paled as she shot a hand to her heart. "A prostitution ring? Are you serious?"

I nodded. "Yes, I know. It's shocking . . . and appalling. From what I could figure out, it seemed Vincent had a team of people in the entertainment industry—Marcel and Brigitte included—who recruited young, beautiful, desperate actresses to sleep with wealthy film executives and other high-ups in the business. And—correct me if I'm wrong, Luc—but it sounded as if, in return, they were promised better roles and more money."

Luc nodded. "So far so good."

"And as I just found out—in a most unfortunate way, I might add—Isabelle, the owner of my favorite lingerie shop, was also involved. She was providing huge orders of her new collection—aptly titled *Les Bijoux,* because of the different colored jewels on the pieces—to the prostitution ring and was receiving a large sum of money in return for each order. She started dating Marcel Boucher some months ago, which was how she got involved in the first place."

"Is this all true?" Luc's mother asked him.

"Yes, I'm afraid it is," he said. "There's more, though."

"I'm not finished," I interjected. "Another player in this whole scheme is a man I had the misfortune of meeting for the first and *last* time today: Jean-Michel Boucher, Vincent's identical twin brother. He's the thug behind the scenes who takes care of anyone in the operation who's getting out of control, and he's also the main contact for everyone involved in the ring, so that nothing can be traced back to Vincent."

Michèle shook her head, making a loud *tsk* sound with her tongue. "I always hated Jean-Michel."

Sandrine turned to me. "You figured all of this out on your own?"

"Well, that last part I only figured out because earlier today, Jean-Michel pulled me into a car that I thought was a cab, knocked me out, and took me to Isabelle's. Luc filled me in on his identity while we were at the hospital. They had to put my statement in the police report, of course."

"So what happened to him after he left you at Isabelle's?" Sandrine asked.

"He was waiting outside the store in his car when my team arrived," Luc answered. "We arrested him on the spot. He'll be facing many years in prison, but not as many as Vincent."

"What's happened to Vincent?" Michèle asked.

"Other members of my team caught him just before he boarded a plane to Rio," Luc said. "He's finally in prison, right where he belongs. I'm sure you've figured this out by now, but the money that Dad was convicted for embezzling eventually found its way back to Vincent, of course. It was at this time that Vincent originally set up the prostitution ring. He used a good portion of that money to buy expensive diamonds and jewels for the women to wear on the job. In his messed-up head, the use of these lavish jewels differentiated his women, making them high-end escorts as opposed to lowly prostitutes. And this is obviously how the title *Les Bijoux* was born. More recently, Isabelle's line of jewel-studded lingerie was, of course, the perfect touch to Vincent's operation."

"So, you knew about Isabelle's involvement from the beginning, and this is why you bought me something from her store? Because you were investigating her?" I said, thinking back to Luc's first gorgeous gift for me from Chez Isabelle.

"Yes, *chérie*, but I didn't expect you to become best friends with the woman."

"I'm so sorry," I said, feeling another pang of guilt. "I can't believe I trusted her. I had no idea she could've been involved in any of this."

Luc reached over and placed his hand on mine. "Of course not. This isn't your fault."

"Are the women in *Les Bijoux* forced to be involved?" Sandrine asked.

"No, the women enter the operation voluntarily, and they are allowed to leave whenever they wish. Many of them do leave once they score their first big film role, but they are required to sign an agreement that they will never speak of *Les Bijoux* to anyone else, ever. Vincent's twin brother, Jean-Michel, acted as the main contact so that most of the women didn't even know Vincent was behind it all."

Michèle rubbed her head in her hands, looking as if she might be sick. "I can't believe Vincent would organize something so degrading to women," she said. "But then again, I can believe it. I'm ashamed I ever allowed someone with so little morals into my children's lives. I'm sorry, Luc and Sandrine. I'm so, so sorry."

"It was Papa too, you know," Sandrine said. "He trusted Vincent as his business partner. You can't take all the blame, *maman*."

"Sandrine is right," Luc said. "Vincent is a master manipulator. But he won't be able to ruin more lives now that he is behind bars."

"And what about Marcel?" I asked. "How did he know that his father was about to be caught?"

"A few months ago, when I learned of Marcel's involvement in *Les Bijoux,* we cut him a deal. If he would provide us with intel and help us bust his father once and for all, he would get off with a lighter sentence."

"That's why he warned me to stay out of all of this?" I said. "Because he was working with you all along?"

"Yes," Luc admitted. "I was the one who told him to give you that warning."

"Wait, it was you he was talking to on the phone that morning in his apartment? The same morning of the tabloid disaster?"

Luc nodded. "Yes, I'm sorry I couldn't tell you, *chérie*. I wanted to, but the only way to ensure your safety was to keep you away from the whole situation. As you found out today, unfortunately."

"So is Marcel still going to get a lighter sentence for helping you?" I asked.

"Because of the recording you took on your phone today, we found out he wasn't staying true to our agreement. He tipped off his father, which led to Vincent's attempt to flee the country. Because of that, Marcel is back where he started."

"*Humph,* so it was at least a little bit good that I stuck my nose where it didn't belong?" I said.

"Yes, in that way, it was good," Luc admitted. "But not at the cost of you being harmed."

"What will happen to Isabelle?" I asked.

"Marcel had told us she was supplying orders of lingerie to the operation in order to keep her business afloat and support her daughters. Having Adeline, I understood the desperation she must've felt to do such a thing, and we were hoping to let her off easy. But after what she did today—kidnapping both you and Adeline—I am not sure what will happen to her."

"I hope she gets the help she needs," I said, wishing it could've turned out differently. I really did like Isabelle—that is, until she tied me up and threatened me with a knife. "She was obviously at the end of her rope. What about her daughters?"

"From what I understand, Isabelle has a sister in Lyon who will care for the girls. They will be okay, Charlotte. You shouldn't feel guilty."

"And Brigitte? Was it really true that she was involved in all of this?" Sandrine asked.

I thought back to the disgusting show of *affection* Brigitte had shown Vincent in his office only yesterday, but decided to keep that nasty tidbit to myself.

Luc nodded, the stress of the day finally showing in the lines around his eyes. "Yes, she has been arrested too. It's never what I wanted for the mother of my child, but it was unavoidable. The minute Brigitte made the choice to involve herself with Vincent, she had to know it was going to end badly."

"And was she one of *Les Bijoux* too?" Michèle whispered, almost as if she could barely bring herself to say it.

Luc clenched his jaw as he squeezed his hands together. "Yes, she was. That's how she managed to land the starring role in her latest film."

Sandrine walked over and placed a hand on Luc's shoulder. "You did the right thing, Luc. Adeline can't grow up around that woman. It would only be destructive. You have to protect your daughter."

Michèle nodded in agreement. "You are very brave, my son. You've worked hard to expose the truth, and in doing so, you've saved our family. And you've saved yours." She looked over to me, and for the first time since I'd met her, kindness flooded into her eyes. "I know I was skeptical of your quick marriage, but I understand now. The two of you have a love that is very rare, a love most people only dream of having. Charlotte, you are going to be the best mother to our little Adeline, and I am honored to have you as my daughter-in-law."

A tear escape from my tired eyes, the emotion of what had happened today finally breaking down my defenses. "Thank you, Michèle. You have no idea how much that means to me."

Sandrine nodded. "I feel the same, Charlotte. You are part of our family now. And finally, this will be a family that isn't based on lies and secrets." She raised a brow at her brother before giving him a big hug.

"So what will happen to Dad?" Sandrine asked.

"The embezzlement case will be reopened, and we will provide the evidence that proves he was innocent all along. He'll probably win a very large settlement for being wrongly imprisoned. But he's already told me that he won't keep the money. He wants to give it to all of us."

A tear rolled down Michèle's cheek as she squeezed Sandrine's hand. "All these years, I've blamed him for everything. And all along . . ."

Sandrine hugged her mother. "*Maman*, you couldn't have known."

"Dad would like to have us all over for dinner soon," Luc said. "He wants to clear the air, start over. Would you give him that chance?"

Sandrine and Michèle both nodded. "Of course," Michèle said. "Do you have his phone number, Luc? I'd like to call him myself."

The smile that spread across Luc's face was bright enough to erase every last bit of pain still throbbing through my head. "He would love that," Luc said. "You have no idea how much he has wanted to make this right."

"Did Dad know about your job?" Sandrine asked.

"He suspected, but he didn't know for sure until today. I called him from the hospital to give him the news. I've never heard him sound happier."

"Thank you, Luc. Thank you for everything you've done to bring our family back together," Sandrine said quietly.

I gazed over at my strong, sweet, sexy husband and realized I'd never had as much love or admiration for anyone as I did for Luc in that moment.

Even though we'd gotten off to a rocky start, it was clear now that marrying Luc hadn't been a mistake. It had been the best decision of my life.

Later that night, after Sandrine and Michèle had left the apartment and Luc was helping me into bed, I remembered two final pieces of the puzzle that Luc hadn't yet explained.

"Nicolas said there was something else in that envelope, something besides the proof of your dad's innocence. What was it?" I asked.

Luc lay down beside me and placed his hand on mine. "I am so glad you waited until my family left to ask that question."

"Why?" I said, stifling a yawn. "What is it?"

"It is something I have suspected for many years now, but only Nicolas was able to find proof." Luc hesitated, the troubled look in his eyes making me fear whatever he was going to say next.

How could there be *more* after all we'd already learned?

"It turns out that in the early years of my parents' marriage, my mother had an affair with Vincent." Luc hesitated, then finally spit it out. "Soon after, she became pregnant with Sandrine."

"Are you saying Vincent is Sandrine's father?"

Luc nodded solemnly.

"Does she know?" I asked.

"No, and I'd like to keep it that way."

"Are you sure keeping more secrets from your sister is the right thing to do?"

"In this case, yes, I am certain. Sandrine has already watched one father—her true father—be wrongly imprisoned. She doesn't need to find out that her biological father is a womanizing criminal and that our mother has been lying to her all these years."

"Does Vincent know?" I asked.

"Yes, he does. That is why my mother married him. She was hoping to give him a chance to get to know his daughter, to create a real family with him."

"Clearly that didn't work out as she'd planned," I said.

"Obviously not."

"Will you keep just this one secret, *mon amour*?" Luc asked me. "After all the work I've done these past several years, it is important to me that my family has a chance to come back together. And this truth will only serve to tear us all apart again."

I thought about how I'd been turning to my girlfriends for advice from the minute Brigitte had stormed into our lives. And in the process, I'd been spilling all of the juicy gossip as it unfolded. Not that I wouldn't ever confide in my girlfriends anymore, but today, Luc and I had turned a new corner in our relationship, and from here on out, I wanted him to know that he could always trust me to keep our private lives *and* his secrets between us.

"Of course, Luc. The secret is safe with me," I promised as I cozied up to him underneath the covers. "You're quite the family man, you know that?"

He laughed as he wrapped his arms around me and kissed me on the forehead.

"You are my family, *ma belle.* You and Adeline. And now that this is all over, I hope you believe me now when I say I will always protect you both."

I smiled as I relaxed in Luc's warm arms. "Of course. You saved my life today, Luc. I can't thank you enough."

His lips brushed against mine—soft, warm, and sweet, the perfect ending to an absolutely insane day.

"Just another day's work for me," he said with a chuckle.

"Speaking of work, is *this* how you were able to pay for our wedding, for the guests' hotel bill, and for our lavish honeymoon? From your salary as an undercover agent?"

"It is so nice that I can finally be honest with you about this." A look of relief passed through Luc's eyes as he continued. "The truth is that I received a promotion and an *extremely* large bonus for the undercover work I did last year at the Cité Universitaire busting that drug ring, and I wanted to use some of it to make our wedding week special. Don't worry though, *chérie,* there is plenty more in savings, so you can take as much time as you need to find a new job."

"Wow, and all that time, I thought you were a poor graduate student. What are you going to do now that your cover has been blown?"

He laughed as he squeezed me tighter. "I am going to take some time off to spend with you and Adeline. And once you are feeling better, I have a few surprises for you. It is only day eighteen of our *lune de miel,* after all."

"Eleven more days of bliss," I whispered. "After what happened today, you better make it good." And with that, I drifted off to sleep, wrapped in the arms of my sexy undercover agent husband.

TWENTY-SEVEN

It was day twenty-six of our honeymoon period, and true to Luc's word, he'd made every single day since the lingerie store showdown nothing short of pure bliss. It had taken me a few days to recover from my concussion—not to mention from the stress of it all—but with the heavenly assortment of French pastries Luc served me in bed first thing each morning, and the endless supply of chocolate he kept by the bedside, I was feeling better in no time.

The only thing that was causing me worry these days was the fact that somehow, during the most insane twenty-four hours of my life, I'd lost the Paris journal where I'd been keeping all of my notes for *The Girl's Guide to Tying the French Knot.* I'd been carrying it around in my purse that day, so it could've been anywhere. I'd ransacked our apartment and asked Nicolas and Lexi to search their hotel room. I'd even told Luc about my book idea, and to my surprise, he thought it was exactly the right path for me to take. He'd even asked his men to search Isabelle's lingerie shop and Jean-Michel's car, but all to no avail.

I'd spent the past few days holed up in our tiny apartment, typing up everything I could remember, but I was beyond bummed that I'd lost the original notes. Today was my first day out and about, though, so I pushed aside my concerns and headed out to meet the girls at my favorite *crêperie* in Vieux Lyon: Le Banana's.

When I was only a block away, my cell phone buzzed.

"*Allô?*" I answered.

"*Bonjour,* Charlotte. It's Mireille Charbonneau from *Bella France.*"

I hadn't heard from anyone at *Bella France* since Vincent had been sent to prison, and I'd figured I would let the dust settle a little before getting back in touch. But Mireille had beaten me to it.

"Mireille, it's so good to hear from you." I was only hoping it really *would* be good to hear from her, but after everything that had gone down with Mireille's *lover,* Vincent, I wasn't entirely sure what to expect.

"You were right about Vincent," she said, cutting right to the chase. "I was stupid to get involved with a man like him in the first place. I don't know what I was thinking."

"I'm sorry about how things ended up, Mireille. I hope you're doing okay."

"I'll be fine," she snapped, but the disappointment lining her voice let me know she probably wasn't as strong as she was letting on. "The moral of the story is never to let a man get in the way of your career. On that note, I'd like to talk to you about *your* career here at *Bella France.*"

"Do I still have a career at *Bella France*?" I asked.

"Obviously with Vincent gone, we are restructuring, and it looks as if the new publisher is perfectly bilingual, so we won't have a need for your translating or teaching services. We will, of course, still honor the contract we made with you and your language school."

"Thank you," I said. "I know you weren't too keen on giving me a chance to write for the magazine, but—"

"You didn't let me finish," Mireille said. "I didn't call to talk about your translating contract."

"You didn't?"

"I called to talk to you about *The Girl's Guide to Tying the French Knot.*"

I stopped walking as a feeling of dread consumed me. "What? You . . . you found my journal?"

"That day when you were snooping around in Vincent's office, it must've fallen out of your purse. After you left, I decided to do my own little search into Vincent's affairs, and I found your journal on the floor next to his couch."

My cheeks blazed with heat as I thought of Mireille with her critical editorial eye reading through my first draft ideas. "I'm so sorry, Mireille. I'll come take it off your hands—"

"There's no need to apologize," she cut me off. "As much as I hate to admit it when I'm wrong, I have no choice but to do so in this instance. You have quite a voice, and I think *Bella France*'s new readership will think so too."

Was Mireille actually complimenting my writing? I walked over to the side of the old cobblestone street and listened to make sure I was hearing her right.

"We're just getting the online portion of our magazine up and running, and I'd like to offer you a weekly column, turning your chapter ideas into articles. You'll continue your theme—*The Girl's Guide to Tying the French Knot*—and you'll write the column in both English and French for *Bella Magazine* in the US and for *Bella France*. Yours will be the voice that connects our two magazines, so we'll need you to be quite serious about your commitment if you are to accept."

"Wow, I don't know what to say."

"You'll say yes, that's what you'll say. This is an opportunity that most girls would dream—"

"Yes, Mireille, I accept," I cut in. "Thank you so much."

"I expect the first column in my in-box by the first of October. My assistant will send you more details, and I'd like for you to stop by the office as soon as you can to sign your new contract, and of course to pick up your journal."

"Of course. That all sounds wonderful."

Just as I thought Mireille was about to hang up, she softened her voice. "And Charlotte, I'm happy you're okay. I'm sorry about what happened to you."

"Thank you, Mireille. I'm doing just fine now. I'm sorry for what happened to you too."

"As you'll soon learn, you have to have a thick skin in this business. It's no different with men. Remember, October first. Don't be late."

As I hung up the phone, I had to stop myself from skipping down the cobblestones like a giddy schoolgirl. Who would've thought the hard-ass editor-in-chief of *Bella France* would actually enjoy reading *my* ideas? And that she would offer me a job because of them?

Lexi had been right that day we'd had wine at Les Deux Magots Café in Paris: a woman should never give up her voice *or* her career dreams for a man.

When I arrived at the crêperie, Lexi and Fiona were already seated outside enjoying a bottle of Sauvignon Blanc.

I filled the girls in on my career news before we launched into our usual laughter-filled chatter.

"Lexi, I still cannot believe you are actually dating Nicolas Boucher," I said. "I hope you don't think I'm still imagining him naked on that piano."

Lexi laughed. "I actually told Nicolas to buy a piano so we can recreate the scene ourselves."

"Oh my God, I hate you," I joked.

Lexi smiled. "Bring on all the hate you want, ladies. I've never been happier in my life."

I placed a hand on Lexi's arm. "You know I'm only kidding. I'm so happy for you."

"Oh, don't lie, Char," Fiona cut in. "We all hate her a little bit. I mean, she's sleeping with Nicolas Boucher!"

"Shhh!" Lexi hissed. "Seriously Fiona, everyone within a ten-mile radius just heard you say that."

"I'd be shouting it from the rooftops if I were you," I said.

"The tabloids are already doing a fine job of that," Lexi said with a smirk. "You know we've already been featured on five magazine covers since we started dating."

"Oh, don't act like you don't love the attention," I teased.

Lexi grinned at me. "You know me so well. I *adore* it. And I adore Nicolas. I had no idea a relationship could be this fun or this easy. We haven't fought once!"

"The first six months are always the best," Fiona said. "Report back to me in five years."

The waiter arrived with four plates of steaming hot crêpes filled to the brim with cheese, ham, and veggies. After we'd all taken our first delicious bites, Lexi turned to Fiona.

"How are things going with you and Marc now that we know for sure it was Marcel and Isabelle kissing on the balcony?"

The smile on Fiona's face as Lexi spoke those words was priceless. I'd called Fiona from the hospital after the lingerie store incident to tell her what Marcel had said about her insistence on sleeping in the nude.

Fiona had confirmed that she did, in fact, always sleep in the nude, but that still hadn't been enough to convince her of her innocence. So, when Luc told me they were administering a polygraph test to everyone involved in Vincent's scheme, I'd asked him to throw in a question about what had happened that night, and he'd agreed. Thankfully, the polygraph results had proven that nothing had happened between Marcel and Fiona—not even a kiss.

"Things are *much* better," Fiona said, her grin widening. "And actually, I have some news."

"Oooh, do tell," Lexi said.

"The first bit is that last Saturday, Marc had a talk with his evil mother. He told her that if she didn't start making an effort to be kinder to me, she would never again be welcome in *our* home."

"I knew Marc had it in him," I said. "I bet that didn't go over so well with Madame Rousseau, though."

"Of course not. She left in a huff, but I'm sure the next piece of news will change her mind. . . ." Fiona trailed off, shooting me a wink.

"What is it?" Lexi asked. "Do you know already, Charlotte?"

I smiled. "If it's what I think it is, then yes, I might have an idea."

Lexi pinched Fiona's arm. "Well, tell us already! I'm dying here."

Fiona grinned, then patted her stomach. "I'm pregnant!"

Lexi's eyes widened to the size of quarters as she stared at Fiona's still flat tummy. "You're pregnant? Are you serious?"

Fiona's sweet smile widened. "I know it's a shock. Trust me, no one could've been more surprised than I was. And you should've seen Marc's face when I told him."

"I wondered why you haven't been drinking," Lexi said as she stood to hug Fiona. "That's fantastic. A mini Fiona or a mini Marc . . . You two are going to have the most adorable baby!"

"Will there be wedding bells anytime soon?" I asked.

"We're talking about it, of course, but first we're just getting used to the idea of having a baby. It's not what we expected to happen so soon after moving in together, but Marc is so excited that I can hardly not be. Motherhood, here I come!"

I squeezed Fiona's hand. "You're going to be the best mom, Fiona. I know it."

"As long as we don't have any more memory-erasing champagne nights that land us in the tabloids, I think I'll be just fine."

Giggles erupted from the table as we finished our crêpes. When the waiter returned to clear our plates, I was about to order dessert, but the girls stopped me.

"We're going to have dessert somewhere else today, Charlotte," Lexi said with a sneaky grin.

"What are you talking about?" I asked, but when Lexi avoided my gaze, I turned to Fiona. "Do you know what's going on here?"

"Maybe I do, maybe I don't," she said as she grabbed her purse and winked at me. "You'll just have to come with us."

Ten minutes later, after the girls had led me out of Vieux Lyon, across the Saône River, and onto the Presqu'île of Lyon, we arrived at the door of a beautiful apartment building near the Hôtel de Ville.

Lexi buzzed one of the apartments, and within seconds the large red door clicked open.

"Who lives here?" I asked the girls.

"You'll find out soon enough," Fiona said as she shot Lexi a knowing glance.

The girls ushered me through a long, dark hallway and into a mini elevator.

"What is going on?" I asked for the millionth time since we'd left the *crêperie*.

Lexi pressed the button to the top floor, then smiled over at me. "Don't you have any faith in us?"

When the elevator doors opened onto the sixth floor, we emerged to a beautiful balcony with a breathtaking view of the rooftops of Lyon and the majestic Fourvière Basilica up on the hillside.

"What is this?" I mumbled, but the girls only giggled as they led me along the balcony to the sole apartment door on this floor.

Before we even had a chance to knock, Luc opened the door, his chestnut eyes glinting in the sunlight as he grinned at me. "Welcome home, *chérie*."

"What—?" I started, but Luc had already taken my hand and kissed me on the cheek.

"You'll see. Just come in," he said.

As soon as I walked into the foyer, the divine aroma of melted dark chocolate wafted past me, but I didn't have time to figure out where it was coming from because a chorus of familiar voices shouted in French, "Surprise!"

Inside a beautiful living room stood Adeline, Luc's sister Sandrine, his mother Michèle, Fiona's boyfriend Marc, and Nicolas.

Fiona and Lexi joined their respective men while everyone smiled at me, and I stared back at them all in a state of confusion.

Adeline ran up to me and hugged my leg. "This is our new home, Charlotte!" she squealed in French. "Daddy got it for us. He said we'll fit better here. Isn't it pretty?"

I scooped Adeline up and kissed her on the forehead before looking over to Luc. "Are you serious? We're moving here?"

Luc shot me a devious grin. "Yes, *mon amour.* Now that we are a family, I thought we needed a home that was bigger than the size of a closet."

I laughed as I glanced around at the shiny hardwood floors and the glistening French windows which opened to the most stunning view of the city. "It's incredible, Luc. Thank you so much."

He gave both me and Adeline a kiss on the cheek. "Only the best for my two girls."

"Come on," Sandrine said. "You haven't even seen the rest. My brother really outdid himself this time."

"I'd say after what happened to Charlotte last week, she deserves a fresh start," Michèle said.

All of our friends and family trailed us through the new apartment as Adeline took my hand and led me from room to room, jumping up and down and giggling like the adorable little girl she was.

In addition to the large, sunlit living room, our new home had three bedrooms, two bathrooms, and the biggest closet I'd ever seen in France. When Adeline pulled me into the quaint kitchen, I quickly discovered where the scent of chocolate was coming from.

Luc removed two large cake pans from the oven. "What better way to start off our new life in our new home than to share a little *fondant au chocolat* with all of our friends?" Luc said before placing the pans on the stove and, once again, giving me one of his knee-weakening grins.

"Do you like, *mon amour*?"

I didn't care that everyone was watching. I wrapped my arms around Luc's neck and kissed him on the lips. "*J'adore,*" I said before kissing him once more.

Nicolas walked up to us and patted Luc on the back. "I told you this is an honest guy, Charlotte," he said in French.

Luc laughed, then patted Nicolas on the shoulder. "It's so good to be your friend again."

Lexi winked at me as the guys started talking and Fiona and Marc came in for a group hug.

Finally, after the excitement settled down a bit, Luc and his mother served us all a piece of *fondant au chocolat*, which apparently Luc had made all on his own while I'd been out to lunch with the girls.

As I savored my first bite of gooey, melted dark chocolate, I turned to my husband and squeezed his knee under the table.

"Will the surprises ever end with you?" I whispered in his ear.

Luc winked at me, flashing his sexy grin and his even sexier dimple. "I hope not, *ma belle*."

As he gave me a chocolaty kiss on the lips, I hoped the *good* surprises would never end either.

EPILOGUE

As it turned out, Luc's surprises had only just begun. The day after he'd gifted me and Adeline with a new, beautiful apartment for the three of us in the heart of Lyon, he'd woken me up by telling me to pack my bags for Paris so we could do our Paris honeymoon right: no secrets, no drama, and no ex-wife.

I'd insisted on taking Adeline with us because we were a family now . . . and to be honest, after what had happened with Isabelle, I couldn't stand the thought of leaving our little girl behind. Luc admitted he'd been hoping I'd want to bring her with us.

So, on day twenty-nine of our blissful *lune de miel,* after three magnificent days in Paris and a scrumptious family dinner of Nutella crêpes, we walked toward La Tour Eiffel at Adeline's insistence to get one last glimpse of the impressive monument before we headed back to Lyon in the morning.

"*Papa*, is it okay if I call Charlotte *'maman'?*" Adeline whispered in Luc's ear as he held her in his arms.

Luc grinned at me before whispering back to her, "I think Charlotte would like that very much."

Adeline handed Luc the stuffed penguin she'd been carrying around all night before lunging in my direction and throwing her tiny arms around my neck. "*Je t'aime, maman,*" she said sweetly.

I hugged her back and told her I loved her too.

Just then, the tower lit up in a show of brilliant, twinkling white lights. I pointed up to the sky. "Adeline, look. The tower is sparkling!"

She lifted her excited gaze to the beautiful Paris lights, then rested her head on my shoulder.

Luc wrapped his arm around my waist as the three of us strolled underneath the shimmering Tour Eiffel, one happy little French family with a lifetime of adventures yet to be had.

ACKNOWLEDGMENTS

I would like to send a warm thank you to my amazing Montlake editor, Kelli Martin. Your excitement is contagious, and I am so grateful to have the opportunity to work with you on my Paris books. To the entire dream team at Amazon Publishing and Montlake Romance, thank you for all of the hard work that goes on behind the scenes to bring my stories to readers.

To Andrea Hurst, editor extraordinaire. Thank you for helping me to make this novel shine. And to my fabulous agent, Kevan Lyon. I am truly grateful to have you on my side.

I would like to thank my husband, Sean, for being there for me through deadlines and the occasional (or frequent) writer's meltdown. Your love and support mean everything to me.

To Sophie Moss and Angie Tennis, for taking spur-of-the-moment trips to France with me, and for the memories we made there that inspired some of the scenes in this book. And to all of my friends in Paris and Lyon who have shown me around my favorite cities, shared a glass of wine with me at a sidewalk café, and given me story ideas. *Merci.*

Special thanks to Alana Albertson for reading early chapters of this novel, and for urging me to make it even juicier. And to all of my talented writing friends who've taught me so much, especially Karen Johnston, Sharon Wray, Mary Lenaburg, Sophie Moss, Marion Croslydon, and Tracy Hewitt Meyer. Words can't express my gratitude.

To all of my fabulous girlfriends from Ohio to DC, New York to Paris, San Diego to Seattle, and everywhere in between. You never cease to uplift and inspire me, and I am so blessed to have each of you in my life.

To my mom, for saving every story and poem I've ever written, and for encouraging me to follow my dreams even when no one else did. Thank you so much. And to my dad, for always making me laugh.

Finally, I would like to thank my loyal readers for taking another trip to Paris with me in the pages of this book. I hope you enjoy reading about Charlotte's adventures as much as I enjoyed writing them! Thank you for making this journey so rewarding.

ABOUT THE AUTHOR

Photograph © Kevyn Major Howard 2006

Juliette Sobanet is a former French professor who writes sassy, romantic women's fiction with a French twist. She is the author of *Sleeping with Paris, Kissed in Paris, Dancing with Paris, Midnight Train to Paris*, and *Honeymoon in Paris.* Juliette holds a B.A. from Georgetown University and an M.A. from New York University in France, and she has lived and studied in both Paris and Lyon. She recently relocated to sunny San Diego, California, where she lives with her husband and their two massive cats. When she's not writing, she's eating chocolate, practicing yoga, or scheming on when she can travel back to France. Visit Juliette's website at www.juliettesobanet.com.